MW01135949

RESTORED

OTHER BOOKS BY
KIMBERLY RAE

STOLEN WOMAN
STOLEN CHILD
STOLEN FUTURE
THE SHADOW
SHREDDED
SHATTERED

PLAIN & STUBBORN
COMING HOME TO HUDSON

CAPTURING JASMINA
BUYING SAMIR
SEEKING MOTHER
DIGITALS
PROJECT FOUR
ABNORMAL RESULTS
SOMEDAY DREAMS

NON-FICTION TITLES:
CAPTIVE NO MORE
SICK & TIRED
YOU'RE SICK, THEY'RE NOT
WHY DOESN'T GOD FIX IT?
LAUGHTER FOR THE SICK & TIRED
HELP FOR THE SICK & TIRED

PRAISE FOR STOLEN WOMAN
BOOK ONE IN *THE STOLEN* SERIES

...a combination of expert journalistic research and page-turning story-telling....I highly recommend this book!
-Kathi Macias, Award-Winning Author of *Deliver Me From Evil*

...exceedingly well written.
-Jeannie Lockerbie Stephenson, Author/Editor of 37+ books including *On Duty in Bangladesh* and *Write the Vision*

I'm on pins and needles to see how this story - with all its plots, tensions, and layers - will end!
-Shawne Ebersole, Association of Baptists, Bangladesh

This is a book you can't afford not *to read. God can use one person—each reader—to make a difference. And the place to start is right here...inside these pages.*
-Susie Shellenberger, Creator *SUSIE* Magazine, Author of 40+ books

Stolen Woman contains many twists and turns that totally kept me guessing. Right when I thought I had it figured out, I was wrong. This book which is full of mystery and suspense also contains a great message of hope and redemption for those who seem like they are in hopeless situations. I could also personally identify with the message that no matter how bad we mess things up, God can turn our mistakes into something good. The book also contains a surprise element, which I thought was very sweet.
-Cari Jean, HubPages, Faith's Mom's blog

... beautifully written voice in the fight for freedom.
-Chad Salstrom, Co-founder Origin Coffee & Tea

...as well written as Karen Kingsbury and others I have read! Wow! What a message. I couldn't put it down.
-Kim Olachea, Educator & Seminar Speaker

I was intrigued from the beginning. Excitement, adventure, suspense and romance awaited on every page and chapter. Exactly the kind of book I like.
-Laura, Blue Ladybug Mamas

In Kimberly Rae's novel Stolen Woman, she juxtaposes the natural beauty of Kolkata, India, with the insidious evil slithering under darkness on street corners where women are sold to the highest bidder. Rae's message of hope and the education the novel provides should open our eyes to an issue which can no longer be ignored and needs everyone's efforts to eradicate.
-Truckers Against Trafficking

You will want to read this!
-Joe Olachea II, Pastor Lakes Community Chapel, Board Member at America's Keswick

I read it in a total of 6 hours! It was SO hard to put down! I was sucked into the culture of India, Asha's romance, and her riskiness of rescuing a friend!...I highly recommend this book to anyone!
-Mary Beth, Blue Ladybug Mamas

You'll undoubtedly get caught up in the suspense, romance and battle between good and evil in a red light district. And, you'll likely come away with a deeper understanding of Christ's call to the Church to be His heart and hands to offer hope to the broken-hearted and freedom to the those sitting in darkness.
-Dawn Herzog Jewell, Author of *Escaping the Devil's Bedroom*

RESTORED

FREEDOM IS WITHIN REACH

Kimberly Rae

RESTORED

www.kimberlyrae.com

Cover Design: Narrow Way Design
Original Cover Photo: Photographer/Model Janna Prosvirina, Austria
www.kuoma-stock.deviantart.com
Photo Adaptation for Cover: Narrow Way Design

Library of Congress Cataloging-in-Publication Data
Rae, Kimberly
Restored/Kimberly Rae - First edition.
Pages 341
Summary: "While Jean and Grant struggle with the reality of Grant's paralysis, Slash is due for release from prison, and those on his list of targets need to find enough evidence to convict him before he can exact his revenge." -Provided by publisher.
Library of Congress Control Number: 2017903492
ISBN-13: 978-1544071541
ISBN-10: 154407154X
[1. Romantic Suspense-Fiction. 2. Human Trafficking in Small-Town USA-Fiction. 3. Overcoming-Fiction. 4. Restoration-Fiction. 5. Forgiveness-Fiction. 6. Facing Fears-Fiction. 7. Power of Gospel-Fiction.] I. Title. II. Title: NEVER GIVE UP HOPE.

Printed in South Carolina, the United States of America

DEDICATION

To every woman
using her own story of
freedom to offer
restoration and hope
to others in pain.

CHARACTERS IN RESTORED

Stewart Henderson - Pastor at Brookside Baptist Church

Brenda Henderson - Stewart Henderson's wife

Grant Henderson - Stewart Henderson's brother, shot during Slash's plan for revenge

Jean Louise Jameson - Recovering victim, Grant Henderson's fiancé

Candy - Oakview's former town prostitute, new believer, started an outreach in strip clubs

Champagne - Candy's former roommate, on the run, wanted for her part in Slash's plan for revenge

Slash - Candy and Champagne's trafficker, in jail

Rod Carson - Former head deacon at Brookside Baptist Church, Jean Jameson's abuser, in jail awaiting trial

Alice Carson - Rod Carson's wife

Gladys Simmons - Oldest member at Brookside Baptist Church

Florence Simmons - Gladys Simmons' sister and Jean Jameson's former teacher

Susan Meeks - Church pianist, killed by Slash

Ian Craig – Sheriff in Edison, a nearby town, killed by Slash

Jose Ramirez – Law enforcement in Edison

Melanie and Star – Two trafficked women who want to escape the strip club *Hot Town*

Billy Bradon – owner of *Hot Town*, trafficker

A prostitute once stood
at a window,
a red rope in her hands.

The cord, a symbol,
carried the chance of freedom,
redemption,
a future and a hope,

if she had the courage
to believe...

Would he
go insane
before they let
him out?

Prologue

Late Saturday Night, January 10

Slash

Lockdown. The word stood proud and defiant between its two guardian synonyms of torment and despair. Prison, Slash was used to, but the silence of lockdown was unendurable. The air fogged thick with memories. He was eight years old again, locked in the basement for waking his mother to tell her he was hungry. He waited alone, terrified, nourished only by the certainty that when she sobered, she would be filled with regret and love him again. She would feed him and hug him, and say she was so very sorry. The booze made her mean. It wasn't really her.

They would go to the park and play. She would laugh. That night, she would sing him to sleep. He would store every crumb of joy, because once the headaches began, or one of her boyfriends came by, she would give in again and he would be discarded.

Slash paced the borders of his small cell, touching the cold block walls but seeing only the past.

"Mommy, I didn't mean to." His little boy voice was a plea. "The bottle slipped out of my hands."

She had pulled a knife from the kitchen drawer, and he knew that this time when she sobered, if she sobered, he would not open his arms to her. This person, this creature with bloodshot, wild eyes, was no longer his mother. She was darkness and silence and pain: everything he feared and everything he hated.

He had begged, backed away, turned to run. She raged toward him. Her feet slipped on the cheap wine spreading like blood across the floor. The knife slashed through the air...

Slash slammed his forehead against the wall and cried out his rage. The echo of his own voice mocked him. How many days had gone by? How many more were left? Would he go insane before they let him out?

The sound of his cell door opening had to be a delusion of his fragmented mind. A man stepped in, the officer who had assigned him to sixty days in solitary. Slash did not have the mental stamina to imagine killing him.

"I can't believe I'm doing this," the officer grumbled. He held out a book. "But Sheriff Craig liked her, so I couldn't say no."

Slash took the book in hand and glanced down. By the time he read the title and looked up again, the man was gone. Slash's cell door was locked tight again, shutting him away from life and sound and humanity.

Humanity he hated, but he hated the silence even more.

The book in his hand was a mystery. Why would anyone send him a Bible? He opened the cover and read scribbled words. Candy's handwriting. After all their years together, he would recognize her sloppy technique anywhere. Sloppiness had always disgusted him. He had to squint to make out the words.

"The truth will set you free."

His heart pounded. Had she put some kind of code into the Bible, a way to get him out? But why? Surely she despised him and wanted him dead. Was it a trap? A plan for escape so she could kill him, or one that would never materialize, to plague him with false hope?

He rubbed the back of his neck, under his hairline. He had nothing but time. He would read the whole book. Every word.

He sat on the miserable imitation of a bed and flipped through the first few pages. Truth, Candy had written. There was no such thing. No real freedom either. Only release from one prison cell to another until death, then a face-to-face meeting with the devil.

Slash had given over his soul long ago. That was a truth, but not one that would ever set him free.

"Who are you hiding from?"

Chapter One
Sunday Afternoon, January 11

Brenda

"I need your help. It's an emergency!"

Brenda had a fingernail between her teeth before she realized she'd lifted her hand. She spoke into the phone. "Candy, what happened? Should I call the police?"

"No, just get down here."

"Where are you?"

"I'm hiding in the bathroom downstairs."

Brenda sent a pleading look down the aisle where Stewart reviewed the wedding ceremony with Florence and Doug. Florence giggled at something Doug said and her cheeks jiggled. Her sixty-six-year-old fiancé grinned as if she was the most adorable thing he had ever seen.

Stewart saw her at the back of the aisle near the stairs and sent her a wink. She motioned frantically to herself and then down the stairs. Whatever was down there putting such panic in Candy's voice, Brenda did not want to face it, or him, or them, alone.

"Are you coming?" Candy said through the phone. "Hurry!"

Brenda rushed down the stairs and flattened herself against the wall leading to the basement hallway. She peered around the corner. No one was in sight. "Who are you hiding from?" she whispered.

"Everybody," came the baffling reply.

"Are you sure I shouldn't call for help?" Brenda knew Slash wasn't scheduled to get out of jail for another two weeks, but maybe he escaped somehow.

"I don't need any police."

Brenda heard the creek of a door opening and once again peeked around the corner to look down the hallway. Candy leaned her head out of the bathroom doorway and waved Brenda toward her.

Brenda scanned the hallway one more time before hurrying down it, past the green room with Bible verses nailed to the walls, then the Sunday school rooms, office, and nursery. She arrived at the bathroom gasping for air. "Candy, what is it? What do I need to do?"

Candy swung the door wide and Brenda gulped down another gasp. She put a hand to her mouth and mumbled behind it, "What in the world?"

"Florence actually paid someone to make this." Candy ran her hands down the bridesmaid dress of bright yellow polyester, nearly every inch covered in dyed yellow tulle. Her sleeves puffed at the shoulders, a large bow covered the front of the high waistline, and the A-line skirt draped down to her calves. Yellow shoes brought the matching color all the way to her toes, and atop her head sat a massive yellow hat lined with a tulle bow and silk sunflowers.

"What am I going to do?" Candy asked miserably.

"This is the emergency?" Brenda put her hand against the wall and caught her breath. "You scared me half to death!"

"Brenda, are you okay?" Stewart came running down the hallway. "Is it the baby?"

She instinctively put a hand to her rounded belly. "No, we're both fine. I thought Candy was in danger." She darted a reproving glance Candy's way. "But she's just having a fashion emergency."

"A fashion what?" Stewart pushed his glasses up his nose. When Candy stepped out of the bathroom, his eyebrows shot up. "Oh, I see."

The look on his face was laughable. Brenda put a hand on Candy's shoulder but pulled it back away. "Oops, I just squished your sleeve."

Candy flattened the other one. "Please, squish something. Tell me I can skip the wedding. Or let me wear a big yellow veil so no one will know it's me."

Brenda worked at fixing the sleeves. "Florence was so happy when she told me about this dress. She said she'd saved the pattern for over forty years, from way back when she first dreamed of marrying Doug."

Candy moaned. "Don't tell me that. Now I can't beg her to let me wear something else." She pulled her skirt out to the sides. "If I were the nostalgic type, I'd say wearing an antique-looking, billowing tent of yellow was sweet, but I itch too much to feel sentimental about it. I'm a pale white woman with blond hair. Just look at me. I look hideous."

"Not hideous," Brenda said, searching for words. "Just really...yellow."

"And frothy," Stewart added.

"I'm a huge, walking doily."

A laugh escaped before Stewart could clamp his lips shut. "Well, just think, after the wedding this Saturday, you can take out the seams and make enough doilies and table runners for a whole house."

"You're scaring me, Preacher," Candy said, but she smiled. She turned to Brenda. "Do you think I could at least conveniently lose the hat? Or accidentally drop it down a garbage chute?"

Now that her heart had calmed down, Brenda was able to smile as she tugged Candy down the hallway toward the stairs, Stewart leading the way. "Let's at least show Florence and see what she says."

"She made an identical one for Jean," Candy commented, "but I don't know if Jean will leave the hospital long enough to come to the wedding. She's practically lived there the last month and a half."

Brenda forgot Candy's outfit and Florence's upcoming wedding for a moment, picturing instead a casket with Susan Meeks in it, Jean's dress covered in Grant's blood, and Grant now in a wheelchair, struggling to regain his body and his mind.

"I know." She put her hand to her stomach again. "I worry about her." They were almost to the top of the stairs. Brenda spoke with hesitation. "Candy, are you scared about Slash getting released soon?"

Candy stopped in the stairwell. "His last plan got botched, so he'll be more determined than ever to get revenge. He'll have had sixty days to make a bigger and more destructive plan than last time. I keep giving my fear to the Lord, but yes, I'm scared."

A bigger and more destructive plan? Brenda shivered.

"I've got verses about not fearing written all over the wall behind the coffee shop counter and upstairs where I live. I read them as loudly as I can at night when the dark thoughts attack." She continued up the stairs and into the auditorium. "God's Word is the only thing strong enough to battle evil. And He says His Word doesn't go forth void. That's why I—"

Florence noticed their arrival and squealed like a little girl getting a new doll. She came down the aisle, arms out toward Candy, her face beaming delight. "Oh, Candy, you look exactly as I always imagined my bridesmaids would look." She pulled her into a hug, smashing both sleeves flat. When she backed away, she commented, "You probably feel silly wearing something so old-fashioned, but it means so much to me to see this dress that I dreamed of for years, here at my wedding when I finally get to marry the love of my life. And it's the perfect shade, like a dress made of sunshine." She patted Candy's cheek with an age-spotted hand. "Thank you, Candy. You're a dear."

She meandered back down the aisle to Doug, who took her hand and kissed it. Brenda sighed. "They're so cute. I hope Stewart and I will be like that in fifty years."

Candy's shoulders dropped. "Is there something in the Bible that says you get extra rewards in heaven if you make a fool out of yourself for someone else?" she asked.

Brenda laughed again. How about, "Let all you do be done in love?"

"No. Got anything else?"

Stewart had kept out of the conversation, standing to the side. He smiled and put in, "Yes, the love chapter, first Corinthians thirteen."

"It doesn't say that love wears polyester."

"I think it does." He was grinning. "It says 'love suffers long, and is kind.'"

"You got me there." Candy scratched under one arm. "Wearing this through an entire wedding is going to be suffering long alright."

"I've got an idea." Brenda poofed a sleeve out, just for fun. "I dare you to come with me to the hospital in that dress. Bring Jean's with you. That'll get her mind off things for sure."

Candy scowled at her for a full ten seconds, then finally smiled. "Okay, but only if she has to wear the hat, too."

Late Sunday Afternoon, January 11

Jean

Jean aimed a bleary-eyed glance at the doorway when Stewart and Grant returned to the hospital room. Stewart kept up a steady rhythm of conversation, but Jean could see from Grant's shuttered facial features it had not been a good therapy session. Grant was good at hiding the pain from visitors and even family, but Jean had been beside him countless hours those first weeks of agony and learned the signs—on his face, in his gestures, through his tones—that communicated pain.

In the beginning, confused and drugged, he had cried, sometimes screamed, and Jean had shared his suffering, though there were days he did not know her name or even his own. The suffering continued, but now she agonized over how hard he tried to portray that everything was fine. That he was fine.

"Let's have a look at today's x-rays." Stewart sounded like a doctor, using the same purposefully neutral tone meant to put a patient at ease. He held two black-and-white films up to the light. "Hmm. This first one, from before your surgery, looks like somebody put your lower spine through a shredder." He held both x-rays out to the side so Jean could see. She already had them memorized, along with every other x-ray, CT scan and MRI taken in between. Stewart tossed a grin over at Grant. "This one from today looks like you got attacked by a hardware store."

Grant, absorbed with the task of transferring his body from the wheelchair to his hospital bed, did not look up at the films. "Either is a good description of how therapy felt today."

"It's a shame you can't switch the numbness from your legs to your back on command."

"And my head."

"Your head was plenty out of it for a while there." Stewart tossed the films onto the cut-in windowsill ledge and lifted Grant's legs onto the bed and arranged them, right ankle over his left, so when Grant rolled onto his stomach in two hours to avoid bed sores, his lower body would follow. "I'd rather not go back to you asking me every five minutes if I'm related to your great-uncle Herbert, and what happened to your cat named Jasper." He pushed Grant's chair back against the wall out of the way, but still within Grant's reach. "We don't even have an Uncle Herbert, and what was up with the cat? We never had a pet bigger than a goldfish." He turned to Jean. "Which Grant prophetically named Flushy."

Jean uncurled her legs from her chair and stood, automatically drawing the thin sheet on Grant's bed up to cover his legs. People reacted so differently to crisis and pain. Women visitors, including Grant's mother those first days, tended to avoid any mention of the shooting or anything that hinted of violence. The men, including Grant's father and Stewart, much to the cringing concern of their wives whenever they were present, seemed to deal with it by joking about it. How a bullet going through Grant's skull and another partially severing his spinal cord could be the catalyst for any kind of humor was a mystery to Jean, but perhaps it was a coping mechanism. Maybe it helped them the same way her useless fussing over Grant's blankets and pillows comforted her.

She checked his forehead.

"No temp today," he said. "The nurse at rehab already checked."

She tucked the sheet up to his chest. "What can I get you?"

He captured her hand and set those dark chocolate eyes on her face. "A doctor who'll release me from this place."

She touched his cheek, running her fingers up over his ear and behind it. The large section of dark, wavy hair they had shaved to get the bullet out had grown back to almost its original length. She could no longer see the staple scars lined like a constellation from his upper neck in a half-moon shape to his temple, but she knew they were still there. "I wish I could." When they did release him, they'd have the challenge of finding a new apartment that was handicap accessible. Had he thought of that? She pulled his thin, pea-green blanket from the floor where it had fallen and draped it over his feet. "Any other wishes?"

He caught both her hands and pulled her to sit on the small bit of mattress his body did not cover. "Stop fidgeting." He rubbed the backs of her hands with his thumbs. "Makes me antsy."

She overcame her inhibition over Stewart still being in the room and leaned forward to kiss his lips. They were warm. She checked his forehead again.

"Jean..." He pulled her hand down. "Do me a favor and for two minutes straight, let me pretend I'm not in a hospital waiting for the next IV change, humiliating catheter procedure, or therapy session."

Tears pricked behind her eyes but she pasted a bright smile on her face. "You got it. What shall we talk about instead for two whole minutes?"

"Let me think." His brow furrowed. Silence overtook the first minute. She was unable to bear the depression gathering in his eyes. Wasn't there anything else to talk about?

"Oh, I know!" She manufactured that smile-on-demand again. How long had it been since they'd really smiled, really laughed? Slash had destroyed so much more than the nerves that sent commands to Grant's legs. "Did you hear that Melanie and Star came to visit Florence and Gladys last week on their day off?"

He settled his gaze on her, but she knew she had lost his mind to a dark place. "Who are Melanie and Star?"

She responded as if his question held genuine interest. "They're the two women at the *Hot Town* strip club who want to get out. Remember? Candy was trying to help them and that's why Billy—the owner—won't let any of us go back anymore."

"If he works for Slash, you shouldn't be getting within a mile of the place, whether Billy lets you or not."

A beeping sound came from Stewart's direction. He pulled his phone from his side pocket and checked the screen. "It's from Brenda. She and Candy are here. I'll go meet them."

He left the room and Grant sighed. "So what was interesting about these girls visiting Florence and Gladys? Did they dance and Gladys faint dead away?"

She would have laughed at the thought had his tone not been so cynical. "Actually, Melanie brought her little girl, Sapphire. She's three, and according to Florence, Gladys turned into a complete pushover with her. She gave her candy and juice and let her touch everything. Then she sat her on her lap and told her stories about back when she had to walk to school, and she didn't have money for a pencil sharpener so she had to chew the edges of her pencils when the points got dull."

Grant shifted and winced. "Can't see Gladys as the grandmotherly type."

Jean wanted to ask if he needed pain medication but refrained.

"Now your mother—" Grant cracked a smile. "—I can see doing that. The minute Grace gets a grandchild, she's going to..."

He trailed off. Jean desperately wanted to reroute his thoughts from the unsaid words filling the space between them. Grace Jameson might never get grandchildren. Jean was an only child and Grant's doctors hedged around questions about Grant having children one day the same way they did when anyone asked if he would ever walk again.

Grant released her hands and leaned his head back. He closed his eyes, his way of shutting her out, of closing in on himself without being rude and asking her to leave.

Her sigh came from deep down, farther even than her heart which, though it still beat as it should, lately felt increasingly numb.

They had
turned the
TV off
too soon.

Chapter Two

Late Sunday Afternoon, January 11

Candy

Despite the exhaustion lining her face, Jean laughed at her appearance, but Candy kept her eyes on Grant, waiting for a smile. When it failed to come, Candy swiped her hat from her head and swooshed it down as she curtsied. "Sir," she said to Grant, "be aware that your future bride will be wearing an exact replica of this...creation." She grinned mischievously. "And I brought it for her to try on for you today."

"Surely not," Jean protested.

At that Grant did smile. It was short-lived, but real.

Candy jerked her thumb back to the door. "I left Stewart and Brenda out talking in the hallway. Pastor sure has gotten all mushy since she got pregnant. If they decide to have a bunch of kids, I may have to change churches."

No smile. Candy dropped her bag onto an end table and pulled out Jean's bridesmaid ensemble. "Go try it on, Jean," Candy whispered. "It might bring out those dimples you love."

Jean looked at her fiancé in doubt, but accepted the mass of yellow polyester and tulle Candy piled into her arms. Candy topped the stack with heeled shoes. One caught the tulle and hung by its heel, but the second dropped to the floor with a clunk. Jean left it in the center of the floor and made her way to the small bathroom, glancing back once with wary hesitation.

The moment the door shut, Candy moved to stand at the foot of Grant's bed. "How are you doing, really?"

He did not avoid her direct gaze. "You want the truth?"

She nodded.

A muscle worked in his jaw. "I'm fighting the reality that Slash is in prison, and—" He gestured to his wheelchair. "—so am I. But he will get out of his soon. I might be in mine forever."

"Not forever." Candy curled her fingers around the edge of his footboard. "Just possibly for this lifetime."

"Which will probably be long. Slash would likely enjoy seeing me live like this." He sat up, grimaced, and used his hands to adjust the position of his legs. "Have you heard anything from Champagne?"

"No."

He stared her down, looking for a lie. She told the truth, as much as she knew. "Champagne isn't under Slash any longer."

"According to her. Not the most trustworthy source."

"Grant, I'm worried about Jean."

He smashed a fist against the raised bedrail. His shoulders stretched across the width of his mattress, his large body as out of place in the small hospital bed as she was in her dress from the sixties. It had to be hard, to have so much strength yet be so confined. "So am I," he said. "I've worked like a dog to get out of here before Slash is released. They keep reassuring me I'm improving, but no one will promise to let me out of here. She comes and goes every day. Alone. Anyone could know that, could follow her."

Candy wiped her face. Her hand caught her hat and it fell to join the yellow shoe on the floor. "I've thought that, too. When we—"

Stewart popped his head into view, phone against his ear. "Jose called. Turn on your TV. Channel eight."

Candy found the remote control, pointed it to the television screen hanging above a small set of cabinets against the wall, and clicked on the local news channel.

"It's pretty crowded in here with you and that hat taking up floor space," Stewart said. "Brenda and I will watch at the nurses' station down the hall."

Candy tilted her head to better see the TV. "Oh no." In a row on the screen appeared photos of Susan, Ian, and Grant. The newscaster told the story of Susan and Ian's death, but spent the bulk of the time on Jean's heroic deed. "She saved her fiancé's life and, according to an anonymous source, stopped the criminal mastermind's plan to kill at least three more people that night," the female of the pair of newscasters said. "What a heroine."

Candy looked at Grant. His face and body were rigid. "They called me a week ago asking for an interview."

"I'm assuming you didn't give one."

"No, and I threatened them with a lawsuit if they showed a picture of Jean."

Candy turned back to the TV when her name was mentioned. Her face and Champagne's were posted side-by-side, while the reporter on site at the prison talked of Slash's history of human trafficking in Oakview, Charlotte, and Edison. The two newscasters debated the effectiveness of the system if a man like Slash could get out of prison after just two months. "They must have found somebody to talk," Candy said. "This is the first time in a long time Slash has been named in the news as part of a crime. Probably one of his connections who would love to get him out of the picture. He's not going to like that."

"Where is justice?" the woman asked the camera. "And if this criminal does get released soon, who might he target next?"

Picking up her hat and dumping it onto the bed next to Grant's feet, Candy commented wryly, "Why do I get the feeling we all just got sacrificed for three minutes of drama?" She clicked the TV off and crossed her arms. "Anybody wanting brownie points with Slash would love to be able to tell him they got to you and finished the job, or got Jean for him."

"You sound as ominous as that lady on the news."

"Maybe, but she was going for ratings. I'm trying to keep my friends alive." She scratched under her sleeve on one arm, then the other. "One advantage is that the TV never mentioned which hospital you are in. The other is that Slash doesn't know what Jean looks like. That can buy us some time if we can convince her to lay low."

"If he doesn't have someone looking for her already." Grant leaned forward, his eyes full of fire. "Candy, promise me something. Start keeping Jean away from here. If he gets out and I'm still here, I don't want her in this room. It will be the first, easiest place for Slash to look. You know that."

"Know what?"

Jean emerged, encased in yellow, chagrin on her face. "Well?" She pirouetted to give Grant full view.

Candy retrieved the second shoe from the floor. She flopped her hat on Jean's head but handed the shoe to Grant. "Putting the slipper on the princess is a job for the prince."

Jean surprised Candy by hefting her leg up and planting her foot on the bed next to Grant's arm. He sent her a soft smile and obligingly slipped the dyed-yellow shoe onto her small foot.

"There. Now I'm a daisy in full bloom." She sat on the bed facing him and leaned in to whisper, "You be the stem, Grant, and hold me up."

He cupped her face in his hands and she did the same with his. "I miss your dimples," she whispered.

"I miss my legs."

She leaned in to touch her forehead to his. "I can live with a Grant who is paralyzed, and I can even survive without your dimples, but please, don't ever hide away your heart from me."

"Um, you guys aren't alone," Candy inserted. "I'm over here in this big yellow circus tent, in case you forgot."

"Sorry, Candy." Jean stood and turned. She removed her hat and handed it back.

Candy looked her over. "Life at the hospital isn't doing you any good, Jean. You've got mega dark circles under your eyes."

Jean sank into the chair beside Grant's bed. "You're always so tactful, Candy."

"You need to get out of here. Come with me to lunch."

"Do I have to?"

Grant took her hand. "You should get away, Jean."

She looked at him and frowned. "If I had to go, I'd pick a place with a bed where I could sleep for a few hours."

"I'll take you home after lunch." Candy motioned toward the door. "Say, you did get that security system put in at your house, didn't you?"

Jean collected her non-yellow clothing and bypassed Candy on the way back to the bathroom. "Stewart installed it just after..."

"Good." Candy shared a look with Grant. "Let's get you some extra time at home over the next few days. You're starting to look like a zombie." Jean escaped into the bathroom but Candy said loudly through the door, "You're doing everything in the world to help Grant get better, but it can't be helpful for him to see you looking so worn out."

"I'll go with you, okay? You can stop shouting." Jean opened the door and Candy took two steps back.

"No fair! I didn't bring any clothes to change into."

It was Jean's turn to look her over. "Well, think of it this way: with you wearing that, no one will notice my dark circles, or that I look like a zombie."

Grant actually grinned. "You could turn into a zombie and I don't think people would notice."

Jean teared up and went over to Grant's bed. She kissed the dimple that had appeared on his right cheek, then the left one. "You sure you're okay with my being gone all afternoon?"

"Go and rest, Jean. It will make me feel better if you do. And wear your coat. Stewart said the temperature is dropping outside."

She hugged him goodbye. He glanced at Candy over Jean's head and gave a slight nod. Candy returned the same, understanding what he did not say. They would work together to keep Jean safe, whatever it took.

Late Monday Afternoon, January 12

Candy

Candy was ready with a question when Jose Ramirez met her at Sheriff Ian Craig's gravesite. "Is Grant settled at the new hospital?"

"He is," the police officer said, rubbing his hands together and blowing on them. "The name of which we will not say out loud just in case a reporter is hiding behind one of the bigger gravestones."

Brenda had called Sunday afternoon after Candy left the hospital with Jean and told her they had turned the TV off too soon. Following a commercial break, the newscaster had ended their program with their weekly *Positive Project*—this week's project encouraging viewers to send in early Valentine's cards to Grant Henderson, who might not ever walk again and could probably use some cheering. They named the hospital and exact room number where Grant stayed. Jose had arranged for his transfer to another hospital around two that morning. "Do you think the staff will take the situation seriously?"

Jose nodded. "I had planned to share minimal details, but several of the nurses had seen the show and told the others everything. So I went back this afternoon with a flyer with Slash's photo and a few of his thugs' photos on it, with instructions to call me or 911 if any of them are spotted. They made copies and now he's plastered all over the hospital."

"Thank you, sir."

"Jose is fine."

"Thank you, Jose." They stood at Ian's grave in silence for several minutes, then Candy asked, "Have you read the whole Bible?"

He gave her a half-smile that said he wondered what she was getting at. "I have."

"Did you ever find anything in there that said we aren't supposed to talk to people who are in heaven now?"

The half-smile extended to a full one. "No, I haven't."

"Good." She gestured to the marker with Ian Craig's name carved into it. "Before you got here, I'd been talking to Ian about Slash."

"He's getting out on the twenty-seventh. That's two weeks from today."

Candy shivered and pulled her coat tighter around her, flipping the collar up to shield her neck. She pulled her hair out of the collar and her hand brushed across the scar Slash had given her so long ago. His brand. A forever reminder that she once belonged to him, body and soul. "You haven't found anything to convict him."

It was a not a question. Jose responded only with a shake of his head.

"I gave him a Bible, you know."

"Really?" She heard the surprise in his voice. "Why?'

"I don't have any hope right now in the justice system as far as Slash goes." She put a hand on his uniformed arm. It was solid muscle. "Not that you aren't doing a great job. I just know Slash. He'll find a way through it and out. He always does. I've been fighting worry and fear every day and night, thinking of him and what he'll plan to do, but then it hit me."

"What?"

"Slash is evil. It owns him, just like he used to own me. If I want to fight that, of course the law can't be strong enough. The only possibility is God's Word." For a moment, sunlight slipped through a break in the clouds. Candy tipped her head back to soak it in. "So I took a Bible a couple days ago to the prison and begged the guy there to sneak it in to him. He finally said he would when he heard who I was. I'm pretty sure he thinks I'm crazy." She smiled at Jose. "But that's okay. I've had people think a lot worse."

"I admire you, Candy. You've got guts."

"Not really." Clouds overtook the sun again and she hunkered down as a gust of wind came through the trees, singing a song of woe through the exposed limbs. "I've just got Jesus, and His good stuff comes out every once in a while."

"If we could get the case to go to trial, would you testify?"

Just the thought had her trembling. In the life, speaking out in public was the easiest path to getting killed. "I would, but only if I knew we had enough to really put him away. My testimony would be worthless unless we had some firm evidence."

"You said once you had access to some of his internet activity. Would you be able to find something there?"

Candy picked up the potted poinsettia she had set at her feet and positioned it onto Ian's grave. The cemetery was a dreary place in winter. Ian didn't need the flowers; he was in heaven with more beauty and color than she could imagine, but she thought it might cheer his family and friends if they came by. "It's possible. He hasn't been able to cover his tracks in lockdown like he normally would. We've looked before, but I'd be willing to try one more time."

"It's all we've got."

She nodded but could not get herself to smile. Jose did not know what he was asking. Exposing Slash's internet activity also meant revealing his connections in Charlotte, Edison, and Oakview, all men who would lie and kill to keep their kingdoms intact. If Candy testified, whether it convicted Slash or not, she would be putting herself and all those she loved at risk all over again.

"God, is this what You're asking of us?" she asked in her car as she followed Jose to the precinct. "Susan and Ian are dead. Grant is in a wheelchair. Champagne is missing. Do you really want me to put big red target signs over all our heads again?"

She parked beside Jose and let out a sigh. "I guess it's going to start the moment Slash gets free, no matter what I do. I want to run away like Champagne and go someplace he'll never find me, God. But I can't take everyone with me, so we're all stuck. You're the only One who can get us unstuck."

In Jose's office, Candy sat at his computer and typed in Slash's main website. "He changed the password." She tried another. "This one, too. Since he's locked up, Slash would have had to tell someone the password to get it changed, and he's super paranoid about giving his password out." She tried a third. "Same thing. This is so weird. The only people who know his passwords are Slash, me, and..."

Jose motioned for her to continue. "And?"

She felt her eyes widen. "Champagne." She clicked on one last site. "She must have gone in and changed all of them. She said she was going to kill him. Maybe she decided taking everything away was a safer option. When he gets out, he won't have access to anything." Candy stood, then sat again. Her legs felt rubbery. "He is going to be insanely furious. He won't be able to do anything, to get to any of his girls or his funds or his connections until he gets those passwords." She gripped Jose's arm hard. "And he's going to think I did it. Jose, he'll be coming after me."

"I don't want
the sordid
details."

Chapter Three
Wednesday Afternoon, January 14

Florence

Florence said goodbye to Doug and placed the phone receiver back into its cradle against the wall. Candy had labeled it "old-timer cool" when she visited. "Did you get it at an antique store?" she had asked. Florence shook her head with a smile. They had bought it brand new. At sixty-five and seventy-eight years old respectively, it was she and Gladys who were the antiques.

"Land sakes," Gladys said from her spot on their one worn, rust-colored recliner. "You talk to that man like a lovesick teenager. Don't you have any dignity?"

Florence giggled, joy filling her that Gladys' tirades didn't bother her anymore.

"And you giggle like a ten-year-old."

Florence thought of her ten-year-old students, so long ago, who suffered at the hands of Rod Carson. She sighed. How she longed to be free from their haunting faces, but how could she, knowing they were still out there somewhere, victims without justice? "Gladys, what will we do if Rod gets set free?" she asked.

"He won't. They got too much evidence off his computer."

She pulled the living room curtain aside to look out onto the street. "But Rod switched all his money to a different bank right after the police came to their house. He had so much. What if he's able to buy his way out somehow?"

Gladys huffed. "What I want to know is how he knew they were on to him. I'd bet my last dollar Alice warned him."

"Never."

"How else would he have known? She might be bribing someone to help him escape as we speak. You know she never could say no to the man. I for one—"

Florence was spared further opinions by the doorbell ringing. She glanced out the window again. "It's Melanie and Star."

"They didn't come without Sapphire, did they?"

She opened the front door with a relieved sigh at the chill outside—Gladys always kept the heat on high and the house felt like eighty degrees, though she insisted that was just Florence hot-flashing. Florence greeted their three guests and welcomed them inside.

Little Sapphire, clad in pink from her winter hat with a furry ball on top down to her pink suede-like boots, rushed in first. "I'm here, Granny!" she called out, throwing herself at Gladys' ample middle. She squished herself into the pillow that was Gladys' stomach and Florence laughed out loud.

"Sorry about the Granny term," Melanie said, untying the belt of her long black jacket and removing it. Florence winced at the outfit underneath. Did that Billy Bradon never let them wear more than a yard of cloth at one time? "Neither of her biological grandmothers are in the picture and she's dreamed of having a Granny to talk about like her little friend at day care." Melanie summoned Sapphire to her and they sat together on the right side of the burnt orange couch. Star found a place on the left.

Melanie and Star were a strange pair. Both had to be in their early twenties, if that, but Melanie's long, luxurious chestnut hair, high cheekbones, and elegant aura made her seem much older than Star, whose half-shaved head and off-shoulder sweater made her look like a teen runaway. Had she run away? Was that how Billy had found her and lured her into that den of iniquity where she worked?

"I'll be happy to be Sapphire's Granny," Gladys said. She opened her arms and the little girl ran to spring into her lap. Gladys let out an "oomph" of sound and air, but kept her in the circle of her arms. "And I want you to stop sending her to that horrible excuse for a day care."

"A mean man works there," Sapphire declared. She dropped her voice low in what Florence presumed was a mimic of the director. "Stop that! Next time I'll beat you!" She snuggled up against Gladys. "I don't like him."

"See?" Gladys rocked the girl while her eyes shot daggers at Melanie.

"I can't afford any place better," Melanie said. "Billy has a deal with this guy. They watch our kids for free in exchange for—"

"I don't want the sordid details." Gladys took a fluffy bunny toy from the end table and gave it to Sapphire, who cooed over it and named it Bunny. Since their last visit, Gladys had bought three stuffed animals, one frilly church dress, and had baked two dozen cupcakes which she decorated with pink frosting and tiny plastic tiaras. "Nothing with that man's stamp on it is good."

Florence checked her watch. Where was Doug? Sometimes that man moved slower than a mule with arthritis. "Jean once asked me to see if Alice would let us use her house for a day care center. She said women might be more willing to leave *Hot Town* and places like it if they had an affordable, trustworthy place to leave their children while they looked for other work."

"She's right."

"I wish I could get in touch with Alice somehow to ask, but she's disappeared."

Melanie crossed one long leg over the other and shrugged. "It's not just a question of being willing, though, but being able."

"Able as in financially?" Florence had planned to stand until Doug arrived to save herself the trouble of getting back up, but her knees were complaining. She filled the spot on the couch between Melanie and Star.

"That's one reason." Star spoke for the first time. "There are plenty of others." At Florence's quizzical look, she added her shrug to Melanie's. "Billy likes to keep his employees dependent, let's just leave it at that."

Gladys' frown was a rainbow shape of unhappiness. "So even if we offered free childcare, you still wouldn't make the switch?"

"It's not that I wouldn't want to." Melanie avoided Gladys' gaze. "It's just that Billy...well, our club isn't like other clubs. He's..."

"Spit it out, girl," Gladys ordered. "What hold does this man have over you?"

Star ran a hand over the side of her head that still had hair. Florence wondered how often she had to shave the other side to keep it smooth, and if she ever nicked herself. "It would take all day to tell you," Star said, speaking for Melanie, who seemed to have retreated within herself for the moment. "And Billy wouldn't be happy to know we had squealed."

"He won't be happy that we're here at all." Melanie stood and held out her hand to her daughter. "Come one, baby. We'd better go."

Sapphire clung to Gladys. "I want to stay with Granny."

The roar of a large engine filled the air and Florence hefted her body up with a smile. "That's Doug. He told me he bought a new vehicle for our honeymoon trip and wanted to show it to me." She gestured them all to the door. "Let's go see!"

They filed to the front entrance like ducks in a row, Gladys at the rear muttering about Billy Bradon, "the low-down, no-good ingrate. He should be locked away with Rod Carson in a prison where it's impossible to escape, like Poltergeist."

"You mean Alcatraz." Florence stepped outside and stopped in her tacks. Her line of ducks crashed into her from behind. One by one they stopped and stared.

Star spoke first. "For your honeymoon trip?"

"He can't be serious." Right there in the driveway, a massive truck on extra huge tires bounced as it idled like it waited for permission to drive right over the house.

"A monster truck?" Gladys stomped her cane against the driveway cement. "Florence, you can't marry that man. He is out of his mind. Someone should put him under supervised care at once."

Doug Jennings opened the driver's door and hopped to the ground as spry as a fifty-year-old. "How's my beautiful bride-to-be?"

Florence blushed and waved away his ridiculous comment. Before she could speak, Gladys had her cane pointed at his truck and her words pointed at him. "What in tarnation are you thinking, Doug Jennings? You can't take Flo on a honeymoon in that monstrosity. It's downright sacrilegious."

Florence wasn't sure sacrilegious could be applied to things outside church, but now was not the time to clarify Gladys' vocabulary choices. "Doug, really, it's so high up. I'd never get in it without falling and breaking a hip or a leg or something important."

Her fiancé threw back his head and laughed. "You think I bought this for our honeymoon trip?"

"Well, you said—"

He took her hands and kissed her right there in front of God and everyone. Gladys harrumphed beside her but Melanie and Star smiled. Little Sapphire covered her face and said, "Eww, gross!"

"My sentiments exactly," Gladys agreed.

Doug ignored her. "This big truck here is a friend's. He brought it to the shop today and I drove it over to make sure the new ball bearings didn't click." He chuckled. "I thought it'd be fun to take it for a spin together back to the shop."

"But you said you bought a vehicle for our honeymoon."

"A camper, woman!" He put his arm around her shoulder and squeezed, walking her to the truck. "I bought us a camper. We're going on a road trip."

"Truly?" Florence felt possibilities bubble up inside her. This could be the answer she'd been praying for. They could go on a road trip and find the four girls Rod abused and help them. Not on their honeymoon, of course, but afterward, if Doug was willing. Her excitement burst free in a laugh. "Star, would you go into the living room and get the stepladder out of the closet? I'm getting in that truck to go see our new camper."

"You're going to kill yourself," Gladys warned.

"Can I come, too?" Sapphire jumped up and down and clapped. "Please, Mommy? Please?"

"Not now," Melanie said, taking firm hold of her daughter's hand.

Gladys whispered, "I have cupcakes in the kitchen."

Sapphire overheard. "Yippee!" She pulled free and raced inside. "I want a cupcake!"

Star made her way outside with the stepladder and Sapphire followed not long after. "Mommy, I need you to reach the cupcakes," she said. "I tried getting one, but it fell on the floor."

Florence called over, "If we had a dog, it could lick up the mess."

Gladys made a face at her, but Doug said, "We can get a dog if it would make you happy," and Florence felt herself beaming. She was climbing into the truck with the aid of Star, Doug, and the stepladder when she heard Gladys say, "That sister of mine has clearly lost her marbles and doesn't even know it."

At that, Sapphire urged her mother to the door. "We have to hurry!"

"What's the rush?" Melanie asked.

Sapphire pointed at the truck. "Miss Flo is about to go. We have to find her marbles before she leaves!"

Wednesday Night, January 14

Grant

Grant woke drenched in sweat, upright in his bed, his right hand extended holding an imaginary gun toward an enemy who wasn't there.

He dropped back onto the bed, the exertion draining his muscles. Flashbacks. Nightmares. Hallucinations. Did it matter what to call them? Sleep had become a thing to dread, a dark place where he saw Susan and Ian die, where he faced down the gunner whose bullets pierced his skull and then his spine. His memory could not produce that night, but his subconscious, in sleep, created it in vivid detail. Jean's screams. His blood. The man laughing. Slash gloating in prison.

Grant's legs were on fire. His brain couldn't send messages to his muscles to move, but the nerves in his legs still sent burning lightning bolts to his brain. Nerve pain, they called it. He grimaced and shifted, wanting the relief of medication, not wanting the side effects that would come with it.

Would it ever end? In the beginning, he had fought hard mentally and physically. He had learned to speak clearly again, had plowed through the days when he couldn't remember the names of colors or what year it was. He had endured the surgeries and invasive tests, and as soon as they let him, had pushed his upper body to the maximum level of fitness possible, rejoicing in every small victory, every inch down his torso that regained feeling.

Then the victories came less frequently, the days became more about enduring than overcoming, and he found his mind and will atrophying along with the muscles in his legs.

It didn't matter how he felt or that his body wanted to plateau. He had to keep going, to get better and get out of there. Slash's time in prison would be over soon. Did he still have his list of names? Did he read over it, planning more ways to make sure he succeeded this time in his revenge?

Susan and Ian were on that list. Now they were dead.

Grant and Jean had been next. Grant had offered his life for Jean's. Her quick thinking had saved him. Would Slash plan to finish him off, or go after Jean because she shot his paid assassins and stopped them from completed the plan?

Grant leaned to the side and beat his head against the bed rail, a failed attempt to distract his mind from the pain. His grip on the rail was hard. Had it been made of plastic, it would be flattened and distorted by now from all the hours he spent hanging on.

A nurse entered and rushed to his bedside, concern on her face. So she had seen him pound his head against the rail. Was she worried he would hurt himself? His laugh was without humor. "It's ironic," he told her as she checked his vitals and pushed buttons on machines that bordered his bed like turrets around a castle, or creepy lab equipment in Frankenstein's basement. "The ones who weren't affected at all were Candy and Champagne. Candy I'm glad about, but Champagne was the one he used to carry out the whole thing. She lived with Jean, you know." The nurse didn't know and probably didn't care. She checked his temperature and left the room. Grant kept talking. "Champagne took all our kindness and fed Slash with everything he needed. But nobody shot her."

The nurse returned with two white round pills in one of those tiny cups fast food restaurants used for ketchup. She handed him a plastic cup of water with a kiddie straw bent over so he could drink without dumping liquid all down himself. It wouldn't matter if he did; his hospital gown was soaked already with perspiration. In his dream, Jean had been the one to face the gun. She had been the one lying on the ground in a pool of blood.

He downed the pills and handed the little cup back. The nurse made a few notations on a paper secured by a clipboard, then turned to go. "Want me to turn out the light?"

He shrugged. If he slept, he was miserable. If he stayed awake, he'd be miserable. Who cared if the light was on or off?

She hesitated, then flipped the switch. Her silhouette went black in the doorway with the hall light behind her. "I hope you can get some rest," she said. Jean had said the same thing, in the same kind tone, before she'd left for the night. He had finally convinced her to go home to sleep. He could not have her there, not at night when it would be so easy for Slash to get to her.

Of all his nightmares, the one that would not let him go was the fear Slash would come after Jean, and he with his useless legs would not be able to protect her.

He felt the pills take the edge off the pain, or at least numb his mind into noticing it less. He needed to sleep. Tomorrow he would work harder, push more. He had to get his legs back. He would not feel Jean was safe until he was able to stand face-to-face with Slash when he came.

And he would come.

Grant fought the dark thoughts through the night. Dawn found him exhausted and feverish. Another infection. Another setback. More medicine that diluted his reason and made it hard to focus. Jean arrived fifteen minutes after her work shift at the bank ended, as dependable as the clock beside his bed. "Go away, Jean," he tried to say, his lips cracked and beginning to bleed. She wet a washcloth and held it against his mouth, then his forehead. The cool water was comforting, but her presence was not. "It's not safe for you here."

"Rest, Grant. You're sick."

She hadn't heard him, or maybe he was delirious and not talking clearly. He tried, again and again, to get her to understand, but she would not leave. Her concern for him was palpable, a blanket that suffocated rather than warmed. He fought to claw his way back to consciousness, but had to give up, drifting through a swamp of dreams and memories and visions of visitors he was not sure were really there. Eventually the antibiotics would win and he would wake up wondering how many days had passed this time.

"Rest, Grant," a soft voice said. "It's okay. Just rest." Then with concern, "God, help him, please."

God? Where was God? Grant needed to ask Him something, but could not remember what.

God did not seem to want to help him anyway, so what did it matter?

The darkness, the fatigue, the medicine all crowded in like vultures around a dying animal. He could see them, the vultures, their beaks open in bird grins, their faces somehow human. One looked like Slash. Another like Rod Carson. The third was Billy Bradon. A short kid came with a huge floppy hat in her hand and shooed the vultures away. He looked at the girl to thank her and she had an old lady face—was that Gladys? He was going crazy.

"We've got to get this fever down," he heard someone say. That wasn't Gladys. Or Jean. Must be a nurse.

He felt his bed shifting, heard the rails go up, and then was aware on some level that he was moving. Cold air surrounded him. They must have wheeled him into the hallway. That meant another trip back to ICU. Jean would be worried.

"Don't worry," he tried to say, but his mouth felt far away from his brain. The words floated in the air, but his arms were too weak to reach out and catch them.

"We're almost to the elevator," someone said. "Hang on, buddy."

Were they talking to him, or did someone else need to hang on? He tried to open his eyes to see, but the rocking of the bed, the creaking of the wheels on linoleum, and the sound of footsteps running all around him finally lulled him into a blissful, dreamless sleep.

"Your husband
with his
fat piles
of money
left you
stranded."

Chapter Four
Late Friday Night, January 16

Florence

The call came at 11:01 p.m. Gladys' loud snore in the adjoining room stuttered, stopped, then resumed before the shrill beckon of the telephone reached Florence's ears the second time.

With a moan, Florence rolled to her side and leaned her weight onto her left elbow, sliding her legs off the mattress and pushing herself to a sitting position in what the physical therapist said was the non-strenuous way to rise. "My old joints don't agree with you," she muttered as the telephone blared again. "Less strenuous, maybe, but there's no such thing as non-strenuous for me anymore."

Who would be calling in the middle of the night? Florence took the time to prod her swollen feet into the pair of fleece slippers set near the bedside table. It was probably Candy. She never seemed to know what time it was, and Florence was not risking pneumonia by walking across the hallway in bare feet just to hear Candy remind her about some church activity she likely already had marked on the calendar.

Gladys' snores coincided with the rings almost enough to drown them out. Florence shuffled toward the phone attached to the wall. "Hello?" she said, the word coming out raspy. She should have taken a drink of water before answering. On second thought, let Candy hear her gravely voice and maybe next time she would call at a decent time.

"Flo? Is that you?"

Florence felt the shudder run clear across her shoulders. It couldn't be. "Are you—are you—?"

"It's Alice."

"Alice!" The cord twined around itself and pulled Florence's arm toward the phone jack on the wall. "Where are you? Are you alright? What did you—"

"Is Gladys awake?"

Florence stopped her questions and peeked into the wood-paneled room off the hallway. "She's asleep. Snoring like Goliath as usual."

"Then whisper, please," Alice said. "I need your help, but I don't want anyone to know. Not even her."

"What's going on?" Florence not only whispered, but moved to stand close to the wall and put her hand between the phone mouthpiece and her lips, feeling like a teenager about to sneak out of the house.

"I need you to sneak out of the house," Alice said, and Florence coughed out her surprise. "Come to my house right now and I'll explain everything. We have to work fast."

"Right now?"

"Immediately."

"Alice, I'm getting married tomorrow! I can't just—"

"It's an emergency, Flo." Alice's voice was strained. "He called me."

Blood pumped fast through Florence's ears and made it hard to hear. "H-he?"

"Rod."

Florence put her free hand against the wall to hold herself upright. She breathed into the phone, unable to put the questions running through her mind into words.

"Florence, please come over. I—" The voice on the other line rose and held near panic. "I promised him something I never should have. Oh, Flo, I promised him—and we don't have much time to make it right."

The phone went dead. Florence shook the receiver. "Alice?" she whispered. "Alice?" she asked louder.

Gladys snorted and Florence heard sounds of her shifting in bed. After a wipe of each sweaty palm on her nightgown, Florence replaced the receiver and watched the cord corkscrew around itself. She had not sneaked out of the house since she was sixteen years old.

What on earth had Alice promised Rod? Was it something illegal?

Florence quickly replaced her nightgown with a house dress, grabbed her purse and keys, and slipped outside, forgetting about her slippers until the concrete walkway to the car sent pain messages through her feet and legs.

She started back toward the house, but then turned and continued to the car. Alice said it was an emergency and there wasn't much time.

If she ended up in jail tomorrow, she'd rather have her slippers anyway.

She started the car and sped the three miles to town, across Main Street, and out in the opposite direction toward Alice's house. She got stuck at the town's only four-way stoplight, no other cars in sight, and wished she had the nerve for once in her life to run the red light. Alice must have been terrified when Rod called. "That lying, cheating, thieving, child-abusing monster," Florence said, slamming the base of her palm against the steering wheel. "You're still bullying your wife even from jail." She sighed and put her head down onto her clenched hands. "And she's still afraid of you, like always."

Florence prayed for wisdom, and for the self-control to not ask Alice how much she had known all those years. When she lifted her head, the light was still red. Had she missed her turn? "This is no time for dallying," she said aloud. Turning on her blinker, she made a right-hand turn, then maneuvered clumsily around to face the light and make a right on red again, hoping God would appreciate her adherence to the letter of the law. Two more miles and she pulled into Alice Carson's driveway. She had never wanted to come back here. Ever.

Why hadn't Alice called the police, or Pastor Stewart?

The moment Florence's headlights brightened the Carson kitchen window, the front door swung wide and Alice emerged, squinting against the light. She rushed to the side of the car. Florence lowered the window a crack to hear Alice whisper frantically, "Turn off your lights!" Before Florence had them off, Alice was inside again, the door shut, no lights on in the house.

Florence resisted the temptation to call 911. She had nothing to report, just a case of the willies and an old friend who happened to have talked recently with her criminal husband. The fact that she needed help in the middle of the night did not bode well, but Florence could not refuse Alice's obvious desperation. Where had she been all these weeks? Had she gone to stay with that friend farther south?

"Did you drive all the way back here?" Florence asked the moment she stood inside. There seemed no need for the usual pleasantries, not with Alice shining a flashlight into her face and locking the door behind her.

"We don't have time for questions," Alice whispered.

"Why are we whispering?"

The flashlight swung toward the door leading from the kitchen to the rest of the house. "Follow me," Alice commanded.

She must be truly in the panic. Alice never commanded. She rarely even asked. Then again, maybe realizing her husband had a secret life changed her. It had certainly changed the rest of them.

"I don't know this house as well as you do," Florence said moments later, having bumped into two walls and one doorframe as she tried to follow the narrow flashlight beam ahead. "Why can't we turn on the lights? Why are you being so secretive?"

She received no answer. Alice led her into Rod's personal office, the room Florence had vowed to never get near again. "Alice, I'm tired, and I hate this room. Tell me what's going on." She backed against the wall closest to the door. "It's not like we're kids and having secret codes and made-up mysteries is exciting."

Alice crossed the room and pulled the curtains closed, removing what little moonlight had made its way inside. She walked back until she stood next to Florence, closed the office door, then flipped on the light. Florence covered her eyes until they could adjust while Alice talked.

"I didn't know what else to do. I didn't know who else to call. You already know what is on his computer. I couldn't bear to have any more people..."

Did she think people didn't know? "What did you promise him?"

"Oh, Flo." The white-haired women fell into a narrow recliner set opposite the desk and put her head in her hands. "I never should have said it. I should have shouted at him. Said no."

Florence felt her heart pumping hard. "What did you promise him?" she repeated.

Her friend, so much stronger in body than Florence, but so much weaker in spirit, looked up with tears in her eyes. "Rod kept track of internet activity on this computer, so he knew when the police looked at his bank account and found the funds he'd embezzled from the church. I hadn't touched the computer, so I'm sure it stood out."

"I'm sure it did." Alice had not even entered the office. Rod had forbidden it, and it was no surprise now why he had. Florence swallowed the names coming to mind to assign to the man.

"He put all the money into a different bank before the police could—what's the word when they take it all because it's evidence? Abscond with it?"

"Confiscate."

"Yes." Alice turned the computer on but Florence moved away. If Rod had a photo on his screen background, she did not want to see it. "I did not know where any of the money was until today."

"So you've been living on nothing?"

"There was enough cash in the house for me to manage."

"You mean you squirreled some away and it's fed you while your husband with his fat piles of money left you stranded."

Alice focused on the computer screen, her silence answer enough. Florence thought of a few more adjectives for Rod Carson. After several minutes and numerous clicks by Alice on the mouse, she pointed. "There. It's all there. Look."

Florence looked and choked down her shock at the number on the screen. "He stole that much?"

"Back when we first found out, I asked Pastor Stewart to check the church records, and he did some digging for me. About half of this money belongs to the church. The other half, well, it seems he was a bit of a gambler."

"A bit?" Florence needed to sit down. "So are you going to call the police and tell them where it is?"

"I can't." Alice wiped tears from her eyes. "I promised I wouldn't. Oh, Flo, I'm so ashamed."

"But—but that's evidence!" Florence sputtered.

"He said he'd come after me if I did. He said—"

"The man is in prison!"

Alice seemed to shrink into the chair. "He won't always be, not with the expensive lawyer he has. He told me he found a defendant who specializes in cases like his and never loses. He'll find a loophole or some technicality, and when he gets Rod out, he'll find me. It doesn't matter where I go or how far. He'll find me."

"And what if he does?" Florence wanted to throw open the curtains and turn on every light in the house.

"He'll...he'll punish me."

The words were whisper soft and full of terror. Florence leaned closer to where Alice actually shivered, her arms wrapped around herself. "Punish you? How?"

Alice lifted her eyes and Florence took a step back. "You have no idea," she rasped.

For a full minute, Florence held a hand to her heart and tried to think of what to say or do. Finally, Alice gripped the arms of the chair, stood, and said, "I know it makes me weak and helpless and pathetic, but I can't go against him, Flo. I can't." She set her jaw. "But you can." Her gaze filled with determination and she smacked her palms together. "Florence, you're going to steal every last dollar he has."

He would lock her inside the back room and use the many means at his disposal to get her to talk.

Chapter Five
Early Saturday Morning, January 17

Champagne

Daylight, the great revealer, showed just how dingy *Hot Town* had become. Billy didn't care about upkeep. He only spent enough money to maintain the illusion, and he only needed the illusion to work when the outside was dark and the inside's strobing blue lights hid the stains on the velour-covered floors and walls, the sagging wooden beams on the ceiling, and the knife gouges in the cushions of the few booths that remained usable.

Champagne found him sitting at one of the booths, his lack of personal temperance evident in the fat spilling over his belt and onto the table. His huge arms, displaying tattoos stretched to their limits along with his skin, were bare, his muscle shirt forcing her notice. He was what he himself would call washed-up goods, little better than damaged goods, which is what he would call her. People like them were passed over in this business by the new and the young, unless they could find and keep what had even more value than beauty or youth: power.

Billy wore his power like cheap cologne, strong and overpowering. She watched him count bills at the table, stopping to lick his thumb every few stacks, and reveled in his complete lack of awareness that his arrogance now had a price tag.

She slipped into the bench opposite him, smiling inwardly when he made her wait while he finished counting his money. Let him think he was intimidating her, or making her drool with envy over his riches. When he did finally glance her way, his permission to make her pitch, she remained silent until he was the one to ask, "Well, what do you want?"

"I have an offer you won't want to refuse."

He snorted. "I've heard that a million times."

"I have access to some of Slash's websites, including yours."

She had his attention now. He tried to sit up straighter, but his belly remained stuck against the table. "There's no way Slash would let you get to his sites. That's a stupid bluff."

She shrugged, stood, and walked away, stopping but not turning when he called after her. She waited until he asked her to come back, then smoothed her smirk into a calm and confident smile as she made her way back to the booth.

"Tell me what you know and what you want."

She told him only what she wanted him to know. If she revealed she had all of Slash's sites, and she was the only one who knew the password, he would lock her inside the back room and use the many means at his disposal to get her to talk. Then he would kill her. She told him just enough to whet his appetite, to make him think that if he could work her over, he could have just a little more of Slash's domain, and thus his power. It was an addiction with Billy and Slash both. Like pigs, no matter how deep they dug into the mire of this business, they still wanted more. She did not tell Billy she had been recording his internet activity for the past two weeks, his and other connections Slash had in the surrounding areas. Already she had enough evidence to land at least twenty traffickers, pimps, and drug pushers in jail for years, longer if she could get solid activity to prove they worked with Slash.

"If you work with me," she said sweetly, crossing her legs and kicking one foot outward in a slow rhythm designed to draw attention. Old habits died hard. "I'll give you access to the two clubs closest to *Hot Town*. You can take them over or shut them down, whatever you want."

He eyed the lines on her face, scars that disqualified her for any future in the life. She had stared at them herself in the mirror the day earlier, when she left Emily and her mother at a safe house in Virginia with the promise to her little sister that she would return soon, a promise she never intended to keep. The scars were her reminders, each time she saw them, of why she had to do this. If she succeeded, Emily would be free from the danger of such scars, of the worse ones deep inside her that could not be seen. Slash had threatened to force Emily into the business. Twelve years old wasn't too young for him.

That was why he had to die.

Billy slid his money until the stacks bunched together like a crowd in an elevator. "What's in it for you?"

"Revenge," she said simply. "Glorious revenge."

"You could have gotten that without coming here in person."

She tapped a long, red fingernail on the table. "I'm going to meet Slash in person and could use a little courage."

"The kind that comes in a bottle or a bag?"

"A bag." Billy was too cheap to have a personal set of surveillance cameras in addition to the two set up by Slash, but she glanced at the corners of the room just in case. "And I want a smaller bag for Slash, not enough to last, just enough to get him relaxed and talking." Let him think it was for Slash rather than an additional amount for herself if she was still too terrified to attack him. "And I'll be staying with someone who might need a little 'convincing' to let me go visit him."

He chuckled. "Would you want to convince this person to take a little nap, or get them to leave you alone permanently?"

"A little nap is fine. But they don't do drugs or drink, so the usual won't work." She wasn't telling Billy she needed to knock someone out without leaving any evidence that might show up in a drug test later.

"A real upstanding citizen, huh?"

"Yeah. Got anything?"

"How about that stuff Slash used to order when you had a client to snake over and didn't want them to know they'd been drugged? You still got one of those vaporizer things?"

Slash never let them keep anything, but Champagne could steal one. The trick would be setting it up, putting it where it needed to be, then getting out before it knocked her out, too. The men's bathroom in the hotel lobby might work.

He wrote a notation on a scrap of paper he'd extracted with effort from a pant pocket. "Why don't you just give Slash something that would take care of him for good?"

Her fingernail stopped tapping. He noticed and she covered by using that hand to toss her hair over her shoulder. She smiled. "Revenge wouldn't be as fun if he wasn't alive to suffer when I take his little world away, piece by piece." She reached across and ran a nail across the back of his hand. He pulled away and she laughed. "You'll help me, won't you?"

"No." He pushed himself off the bench and stood. "I don't believe you, Champagne. Slash wouldn't trust anybody but Candy with his website information. I don't know what game you're playing, but I'm not buying."

Champagne felt her nostrils flare with her quickened breathing. She recognized the familiar rush of fight or flight, but knew she needed to think instead. She faced him and said, "She's in on it."

He shook his head. "Not Candy. She's all religious now. Was trying to get my girls to leave and start coming to church with her."

She put a hand to her sternum and hoped the pounding of her heart wasn't showing through her thin top. "She thinks I'm using the passwords to get evidence against him, so they can put him away for good." Her tale was spinning wide, like a spider's web. She had to make sure she didn't get caught in it.

"And will you?" Billy asked. "Put him away for good?"

"Depends." She sauntered two steps in his direction. "I might, if I had the right motivation, the right person who was willing to be partners."

His eyes narrowed. "She give you all the passwords?"

Champagne felt the danger in his gaze as much as if he had pulled a knife from his belt. "No, she still has some. Said she wouldn't give the rest to me until she was sure of me."

He came near. She wanted to back away, but stayed still as he lifted her chin with his big hand and turned her head to one side and then the other. "I need to be sure of you, too. Come back with Candy and I'll give you what you want."

She had slipped into her own web after all. While she scrambled for a new lie to untangle herself, he added, "I told her she couldn't come back here, but I'll call her and tell her I changed my mind. If she really believes you're going after Slash together, she won't have any problem bringing you along with her little churchy friends next time they come. I'll have the bags waiting for you."

Champagne kept it short after that, knowing she had defeated herself. She could not face Candy again, could not let her know she was back in town. If Candy contacted the police, Champagne would find herself in jail with no chance of getting to Slash.

She left *Hot Town* and headed for Charlotte. She'd find a cheap hotel and continue collecting evidence. Two days before Slash's release, she would mail everything to Jose Ramirez. Then on Tuesday the twenty-seventh, with or without Billy's bags of heroin, she would visit Slash. After that, she would be marked for death, but Emily would be given life. Her sister would have a future without the fear Champagne had lived with every day for so long.

Champagne could not imagine such freedom, but she would buy it with her life for Emily.

Saturday Morning, January 17

Florence

"Of all the days," Florence muttered, pulling the creaking screen door open and shuffling into Alice's home. At least she had her shoes on this time. "You had to pick this one."

Had Doug not needed to spend the morning checking the engine and fluid whatnot on the camper, she would have asked him to come with her. She still had trouble passing Rod's office without wanting to take a baseball bat to the whole room. Hopefully she could get in and out quickly, before the fright that overtook her every time she entered Alice's home seeped in enough to mar the day.

A quick search showed the house was in order, the only oddities one large black duffel bag on the kitchen floor near the counter, and an unfolded sheet of stationary on the counter itself. Florence picked up the paper and read aloud.

Dear Florence,
Take a look out the front kitchen window.

Florence carried the letter over to the sink and edged Alice's lace curtains aside. After a cursory glance, she checked the letter again.

If you don't see a moving van parked across the street, call me. If you do, they are men I hired. After you leave, they will come in and ransack the house. Rod's lawyer is coming at one p.m. so don't dawdle. Take the bag with you on your honeymoon. I don't want there to be any chance of him finding it at your house while you're gone. When you get back, please use it, every bit of it, for good. Pay back what was stolen. Replace evil for good. Most of all, please use the bulk of it to help Rod's five victims, especially Jean. Money can't ever replace what was taken from them, but it might provide ways to help them heal or move forward. I'd go to them myself, but you know why I can't.
Thank you, dear Flo. Your friendship is worth more to me than every bit of that money. After today I'm throwing my phone into a storm drain on the side of the road. Maybe I'll be in touch someday.
Love, Alice

Florence set the letter down. Grunting with the effort, she hefted the large bag from the floor onto the counter. Her hands did not start shaking until they had unzipped the bag and her mind registered what she saw: stacks of hundred dollar bills, secured by rubber bands, filling every inch of the bag. She checked the one side pouch and gasped to find the deed to the house. Quickly, she stuffed the letter from Alice inside with the deed and zippered the bag shut.

"I feel like a drug runner," she whispered into the empty room. She tried to carry the bag by hanging the handle over one shoulder, but her joints failed her and the bag dropped to the floor. Huffing, she used both hands to heave it up again and carried it like she would an overfilled brown bag of groceries. It took some maneuvering to get out the front door and down the porch steps without tripping, but she reached her car without mishap and was pleased to note she was only slightly out of breath. Carrying all the groceries since Gladys injured her hip was paying off. She locked the bag securely in the trunk, hobbled to the driver's seat, started up the Oldsmobile, and pulled onto the small neighborhood street.

A glance in the rearview mirror showed the two men in the moving van watching her departure. Florence drove away but on impulse circled the block, returning as the van parked in Alice's driveway. The driver bumped the edge of her carport roof. He rolled down the window, looked out at the damage, then backed up several yards straight toward Florence's vehicle. She honked. The van jerked and its brake lights flashed. The driver got out. "Sorry," he yelled back at her car. "I didn't see you there."

Florence could tell the moment he recognized her. His jaw slackened. He glanced toward the house and stammered, "We're just, uh, just turning around. We, uh—"

"It's okay." Florence locked her car and started toward the porch, motioning them to follow. "I know why you're here." When all three were inside, she said conspiratorially, "I was wondering if I could help you destroy things."

At their blank stares, she added, "Not through the whole house, mind you. I'm getting married this afternoon and have to go have my hair done." She checked the time. "But before I go, there's something I have wanted to do for a long time. Do you by chance have a baseball bat?"

The first man shook his head. "No, ma'am. We've just got an empty truck. And this letter." He pulled a sheet of stationary, a match to the letter Alice had left for Florence, from his back pocket. "We're supposed to leave it when we're done."

"But how are you going to wreak havoc if you didn't bring any bats or pipes with you?"

He seemed to be fighting a smile. "We aren't supposed to break anything, just mess things up."

Florence thought of Rod's lawyer, of the smirk she imagined on his face. "No, that won't do. It has to be believable. I don't want that man showing up at all of Alice's friends' homes, mine included, asking nosey questions."

The other man offered, "We have a big wrench in the back with the spare tire. And one of those poles to unscrew lug nuts."

"Perfect." Florence smiled. Her hair appointment could wait just a bit. "You can have the wrench. I'll take the pole thingy." She started toward the office. "I sure wish I was allowed to tell Gladys about this. I haven't had this much excitement since Doug and I smashed his neighbor's pumpkins back in 1972!"

"Where could
she be?
The wedding
is supposed
to start in
five minutes."

Chapter Six
Saturday Afternoon, January 17

Jean

Jean considered her reflection in the mirror hanging near the bathroom of the church foyer. "I feel badly leaving Grant in the hospital alone." Tiredness lined her face and the makeup she had applied that morning could not hide the dark circles under her eyes, but it was likely no one would notice her face much, not when they had a two-foot-wide yellow hat to look at instead.

"Stop worrying." Brenda, shorter than Jean, was able to stand beside her without getting pegged by Jean's hat brim. "He's out of ICU. The doctor said the danger has passed." She adjusted the sea foam green scarf around her neck and patted Jean's arm. "Oh good grief," she murmured. "Stupid sleeves." She pulled Jean's sleeve back into its original rounded shape. "He could use a couple hours of sleep, and you could use a break." She started to pat her arm again but moved her hand to the spot between her shoulder blades. "Let yourself enjoy this, Jean."

Jean told her facial muscles to pull out and up into a smile. "I'll try." She shifted her arms, then her smile came easily. "Though it will be hard with this dress itching like I'm wearing burlap."

Florence entered the foyer from the outside, her white gown covered in lace and beads, a white version of Jean's hat resting over her silver hair. She beamed at Jean. "Isn't it a gorgeous day? When the wind isn't blowing, it almost feels like spring." She hugged Jean and Brenda, and held out her bouquet of daisies and sunflowers. "Aren't they beautiful?"

"They are." Brenda fixed Florence's hat, gone atilt when she hugged Jean. "As are you, Florence."

Jean nodded. "I'm so very happy for you."

"I'm pretty happy for myself." Florence touched the flowers to her cheek and sighed. "I've waited for this day for so many years, and now here I am. The music is playing, everyone is waiting for me to walk down the aisle, and my two lovely bridesmaids are—wait, where's Candy?"

"I thought she was with you."

"No, I called and asked her to help with...something. Oh dear." Florence peeked into the auditorium, then checked the door to the outside. "Where could she be? The wedding is supposed to start in five minutes."

Brenda's face filled with mischief as she whispered to Jean, "Maybe she lost her dress and won't find it until the wedding is over."

Gladys slipped through the double doors from the auditorium into the foyer. "Are you ready, Flo? That piano player you hired is getting fidgety. I just know he'll start playing the wedding march any second now unless you tell him to hold off." She adjusted her own beige hat, a match to her beige dress and purse, and glanced at Brenda. "He says he's a professional, but the boy doesn't look a day over eighteen."

"Candy isn't here," Florence said, worry tinging her voice. "I don't know what to do."

Gladys handed Florence her flip phone. "Call the whippersnapper and tell her to get her bleached blond head over here right now." She opened one of the double doors and Jean looked through to see people turn and stare. Her palms began to sweat. She would have to walk down that aisle with everyone looking at her, not just today, but at her own wedding. Who thought of that tradition anyway? Why couldn't the man walk down the aisle and everyone stare at him?

Nudging her body through the opening, Gladys said, "I'll tell him to play something long, just in case. Preferably Chopin or Bach. None of that sappy elevator music. You give the signal when she shows up and you're ready." She looked back at her sister. "You look pretty, Flo. And you deserve to be happy."

Gladys closed the door behind her and Florence searched for a tissue to dab her eyes. "Oh, I can't cry now. What would Doug think, me walking down the aisle all puffy-eyed and red in the face?"

Brenda held out her hand. "Want me to call Candy for you?"

"Yes, please." Florence handed over the phone. "Ask her if—"

The side entrance door opened and a gust of wind whirled inside with Candy. "I almost didn't make it!" she huffed.

Florence took one look at the duffel bag in Candy's hands and gasped. "What are you doing, Candy? You were supposed to put the bag into the camper where it would be safe, not bring it inside!"

"I know, but the camper's locked. I can pick a regular lock, but that thing has a big brass padlock on it."

Florence put a hand to her head, knocking her hat askew. "I didn't even think of that. Doug has the key."

Candy dropped the bag at Florence's feet and went to the double doors leading to the auditorium. She pulled one open a crack and peeked through. "The place is packed. There's no way I'm running down that aisle to ask Doug for the key. That would cause even more of a stir than the first time I came down that aisle."

Jean recalled the day Candy arrived, scandalizing the church and starting a chain of events that would transform them all. "I'm not so sure about that."

Candy grinned back at her. "None of them have seen our dresses yet. Or our hats."

Jean touched her own wide-brim creation. "Where is your hat, Candy?"

Candy's hands flew upward. "Oh, drat! I took it off in the car. It kept knocking the rearview mirror and I thought I was going to wreck. Be right back!"

She disappeared and Florence wrung her hands together. "What are we going to do? This bag is of utmost importance, but it's my wedding. I don't want to stop it just to—oh, why did I ask Candy to help instead of someone else? Well, I know why. She didn't have a hissy fit over me smashing that computer with a pipe. But still..."

Brenda's eyebrows went as high as they could go. "You smashed a computer?"

"It's too long a story to tell you now," Florence said. "Right now I have to figure out what to do with this bag."

"If it needs safeguarding, you could put it in the little bathroom here in the foyer," Jean suggested.

"But it's, um, full of, well, it needs to be locked away someplace safe. Very safe."

Brenda started digging through her purse. "I have a master key that works on that bathroom door. No one should need to use it during the wedding, so we could lock the bag inside until you can get the key from Doug."

"That would be perfect!" Florence hugged her. "Brenda, you're a gem. Now I can get married without fretting." She nudged the bag with her foot. "I was starting to think Candy would have to carry this thing down the aisle with her."

Candy rushed in, hat mostly in place. "I heard the music and thought I might have missed the grand entrance."

Jean shook her head. "I'm not going down the aisle without you."

Candy caught her reflection in a mirror hung near the bathroom door. "Can't say I blame you there." She pulled Florence into a long hug, then crossed to the doors. "Miss Flo, let's get you married!"

Saturday Afternoon, January 17

Brenda

As sweet and loving as the wedding was, Brenda's bladder was no match for the long ceremony. During the final song, she sneaked out the back, glad to still have her master key, and opened the door to the small foyer bathroom.

Florence's duffel bag sat on the toilet. Brenda tried to lift it off. "This thing is heavy." She slid it forward until it fell to the floor. It landed on its side and she strained to roll it, telling herself not to give in to curiosity and take a quick peek inside. What could be so important that Florence would care more about keeping it safe than walking down the aisle at her own wedding?

She heard the familiar strains of music that signaled the bride and groom were being announced and would be making their way through the crowd. She had better hurry.

After washing her hands, Brenda debated trying to pick the bag up and place it back on the toilet but decided against it. Stewart had been very clear she was not to do any heavy lifting. Whatever was in the bag would be just as safe on the floor.

She slipped out of the bathroom, double checking to make sure she had locked it, then stood guard as the attendees who were not staying for the reception filed through the foyer and into the windy sunshine. A few tried the door, but finding it locked moved on. After about ten minutes, Stewart found her there.

"I wondered where you had gone off to." He put his arm around her waist. "You okay?"

"Fine." She smiled and nudged his glasses up on his nose. "I'm helping Florence with something. You go on ahead downstairs to the reception. I'll be there shortly."

"Okay." He grinned. "I'd be chivalrous and wait with you, but I want a piece of the groom's cake before it's all gone. None of that white fluffy kind for me. Doug got an ice-cream cake."

Candy was the next to find her. "I told you this dress was going to itch like crazy. I had a hard time not doing a jig up there." She yanked on her huge sleeve. "I got the key from Doug for the camper. Let's get that bag out there. Florence won't be able to enjoy her own reception until she's sure it's taken care of."

"Must be some important stuff in there," Brenda said when she let Candy into the bathroom and Candy swung the bag up and onto her back.

Candy grunted and angled so Brenda could reach the bag. "Take a look and see."

Brenda slid the zipper a few inches, let out a squeak, and pulled it closed again. "What in the world?"

"Can you come with me? I can't open doors and hold this thing with both hands at the same time."

Brenda followed Candy. "Did Florence come into some inheritance or something? That's a lot of—" She dropped her voice to a whisper, even though the foyer had cleared. "That's a lot of money for a honeymoon."

"It's not for the honeymoon, but I'll let her tell you about it. Come to think of it, I probably wasn't supposed to say anything to anybody." Candy let out a breath. "How did she carry this thing out to her car?"

Brenda moved to walk beside her and Candy added, "I'm trying to not draw attention to us, but it's kind of hard to do wearing this dress."

"Let me help." Brenda removed Candy's hat and held it over the bag.

Candy laughed. "That sombrero came in handy after all. I could have used that on some of my shadier dealings back in the day."

They arrived at the camper and had settled the bag safely inside when Florence appeared in the doorway, holding her hat against the wind.

"Is everything okay? Is the bag safe?"

"You're good to go, Miss Flo," Candy said. "Or I should say, Mrs. Doug now."

Florence beamed. Brenda helped keep her dress and train from getting caught in the camper door as she came inside. She dropped onto a padded bench under the largest side window and fanned her face. "What a glorious day. All of it was just as I hoped it would be." She giggled. "Except for going to Alice's and hatcheting her computer."

Brenda itched with curiosity, even more than her belly itched from her skin stretching. "What is this all about?"

Florence reached across to where Candy had dropped the duffel bag and opened a side pouch. She handed Brenda a letter, which when read, brought tears to Brenda's eyes.

Candy found a box of tissues and handed it over. "You're really hormonal these days."

Florence swatted Candy's leg. "It's a wonderful thing Alice is doing. That letter will make a huge difference in a lot of people's lives."

"Sure will," Candy said. "But you didn't see me blubbering all over myself when I read it. Then again, I was too busy helping those guys trash Alice's place."

Brenda looked at them both, her shock compounded when Florence giggled again. "I sure did enjoy whacking that computer into smithereens. I would have stayed for the whole party if it hadn't been for my hair appointment." She patted her silver curls. "Some things should not be compromised on one's wedding day, even if it means missing out on mayhem and destruction for a good cause."

"Well, don't you worry." Candy propped her feet up on the table next to the bag. "We mangled it good."

"And you left the letter?"

"Front and center on the kitchen counter."

Brenda returned Alice's letter to the bag and zipped the side pouch closed. "Another letter?"

"For Rod's fancy-pants lawyer. It said Alice was leaving the bag of money on the floor next to the counter, and then she was leaving town and disappearing for good." Candy leaned her head back, but her hat got in the way. She flicked it off. "It was a stroke of genius on her part. The lawyer will come in, find the note, but see the house is ransacked and the money is gone. He'll assume somebody took it, and—"

Florence grinned. "Which is true."

Candy smiled with her. "And he won't be able to trace Alice or have any leads to what happened. That will end any possibility of him getting paid the big bucks to get Rod out of jail, so he's going to quit just like that. Rod will be out of luck."

Brenda sat, her legs feeling like rubber beneath her. "What a wonderful thought."

Florence patted the bag. "And we'll be using some of this money to buy the best prosecuting lawyer out there. We're going to make sure justice is served, and none of Rod Carson's victims ever have to fear him again."

Brenda touched the bag, full of such promise. "Where do you think Alice will go?"

Florence took one of the tissues from the box Brenda held and wiped her forehead. "Wherever it is, I hope she'll be happy."

Candy stood. "And now we should go find that new husband of yours and tell him where you are. I'm sure he's wondering what happened to his bride."

Florence used the tissue to fan her face, much like her sister Gladys did when she was mortified about something. "I hope we leave soon. I've been looking forward to this honeymoon trip for quite some time."

Candy elbowed Brenda and grinned, until Florence added, "I really need to catch up on my sleep."

Brenda hid her smile behind her hand, but Candy howled with laughter. Florence looked at Brenda, her face puzzled. "What'd I say?"

Saturday Afternoon, January 17

Grant

Grant pushed all his anger into his arms and bench-pressed the eighth rep of three hundred pounds. Before the shooting, he had been able to do ten reps of three-hundred and fifty without a sweat. "You shouldn't have told my brother."

Sarah, his physical therapist, stood behind his bench as spotter. She remained unfazed. "It's been a week since the doctor gave you permission to leave the hospital during the day. You need some fresh air. You need to get out of here, get back to your life."

He could feel the veins in his neck straining. His strength gave way before his anger. He set the bar onto its stand and waited for his breathing to calm enough to speak. "I want to *walk* back into my life." He sat up. "Help me do that."

"It's my job to help you."

By habit, he tried to stand, and the fire pulsed fresh when his legs remained stagnant where they were. "You're helping me build my upper body. I want to walk again. Now."

She brought his wheelchair over beside the bench and locked it in place. "Don't bother using that tough-guy tone with me. Every male I've worked with has hit me with it during the anger stage. I've had guys cuss me out, and one even threw a dumbbell at me." She gestured for Grant to get back in the chair and smiled. "But he missed."

Grant glared at the chair, hating it, hating his need of it. "Why do you do it?"

She leaned over him, her eyes full of purpose. "Because after the anger comes acceptance. If I can get you through to that point, you can heal. And I don't mean your legs."

His heart still raced from lifting and his chest rose and fell with his heavy breathing. How could so much power surge above his waist and so little below it? Only half of him felt alive. Did that make him half a man? Way back at the beginning, the doctor had told him that had he completely severed his spinal cord, he would be paralyzed for life. With his being only partially severed, there was hope. "Once the spinal shock wears off," the doctor had said, his words crisp like his lab coat, "we'll check for sacral sparing. The severity of the neurological deficit is what will make all the difference."

Grant had not understood what the terms meant then. He did now, but no one had ever gotten around to telling him how long it would take for his spinal shock to wear off, or if it already had, what they had found. "What if I don't want to accept?"

"Come with me," she said, and walked away. He had gotten used to her abrupt demands. She never pushed his chair when he was in it, and never waited for him, expecting him to make do, catch up, get it done. He did the awkward contortion necessary to get his body from the bench to the chair, unlocked the wheels, and made his burning arm muscles push him across the room and down a hallway to another section of the hospital gym.

She spoke as soon as he was at her side. "Take a look at that guy over there, on the rope." A man of average height and build, in his mid-to-late thirties, pulled himself hand over hand up a rope connected to the ceiling. His legs, dangling below, were small compared to the conditioned bulk of his upper body. "Simon has accepted his paralysis. He lives a full life, just without walking. He flies planes, goes hang-gliding on weekends, and has a wife and kids who have all adapted to his chair."

"So you brought me here to convince me to just live with the idea of never walking again?"

"Not necessarily." She pointed across the room to another man in the far corner, probably in his early twenties, leaner than Grant, his face so focused on a walker set in front of the high bench where he sat, the rest of the gym occupants did not seem to exist to him. He had his hands on the walker and his entire body strained. Grant felt his own body pushing forward, upward, willing him to succeed. *Get up. Do it. Stand.*

The man's face turned red. His cheeks rounded with his hard breathing. Grant's hands pressed against his armrests. His lower body lifted off the chair when the man's did off the bench. Grant could not go higher than an inch or two in his chair, but the man lifted higher. Five inches from the looks of it. Ten. He raised to a standing position, the weight clearly mostly on his arms, but still, he was standing. Grant's breathing quickened. He leaned forward. The man maintained for three seconds, then his leg spasmed and he fell back onto the bench, clearly spent. He lifted his t-shirt from his stomach and wiped his face with it.

"That's Norman," Sarah said. "He refuses to accept life in his chair. He's gone off all pain meds or anything that will numb his legs, and works out hours every day for the sole purpose of walking again. It's been a year, but as you can see, he's not stopping."

"He stood up." Grant looked at her. "Help me stand up."

She leaned over and put her hands over his forearms on the armrests. "Listen, Grant. My job is to help you learn to live well with the paralysis you have. Eight out of ten guys with your level of injury never walk again."

His jaw worked. "If you wanted me to accept that, why did you show me the guy standing up?"

"Because he's given up a year of his life for it." She kept her gaze locked on his. "If you want to work toward walking, fine. But you have to be willing to learn to live well in the meantime, too. Learn how to function out there. Get back to the people who care about you."

"Not in this chair."

She pushed away from him. "Yes, in that chair. At some point, you're going to get discharged from this hospital. Are you going to be a hermit until you can walk again? That's selfish, Grant. Pure and simple."

He focused on the guy in the corner. His head fell back against the wall and sweat streamed down the sides of his face. His arms dangled limp at his sides. "What is it that makes the two out of ten walk?"

Sarah had her arms crossed where she stood. "What?"

"You said eight out of ten of us never walk again. What's the difference for the two who do?"

She uncrossed her arms. "Nobody knows. Might be physical. Might be mental. Likely both."

He looked back at Norman. "I'm getting married. I want to start a sports ministry. I need my legs."

"You don't need legs to have a ministry, or a marriage, or a happy life if you choose it."

He ground his teeth. However valid her argument, it still didn't fit what he wanted. "Are you going to help me walk or not?"

"No, Grant. My job is to help you learn to live with what you've got now, and what you've got now is an incredibly strong upper body that can function in the real world just fine if you'd learn to use it properly."

He turned his chair. "I'm going back to my room."

"You're pouting, Grant."

His jaw hurt from clenching it so hard. "Call it what you want. I'm done here."

He had
ordered it for her
months ago,
the day he asked
her to marry him,
out on the lake
on a cold
autumn day.

Chapter Seven
Saturday Evening, January 17

Jean

Jean should have brought a change of clothes. She thought of going home, but wanted to have all the time with Grant she could before the nurses shooed her away for the night. At the hospital, she carried her plate of cake, peanuts and wedding mints into Grant's room with a smile. "You should have come," she said brightly. "Florence was so happy, and the ceremony was perfect."

Grant sat in his wheelchair facing the window. Jean wished they would give him a room with a view other than the parking lot. He did not look at her. "Perfect, huh?"

"Well, except for my itchy dress." He glanced back at her and she twirled. "I left my hat in the car. I can only handle so much staring in one day."

He turned his face back to the window.

"I brought you some cake."

"Did anyone mention Susan?"

Her grip on the plate tightened. "What do you mean?"

"Florence had asked her to play at the wedding."

She chose her words carefully. "She was missed today, of course."

"But everybody wants to move on, not let it get them down that she's dead."

"Grant..."

"It must be tough, having to stick it out with me." His voice was devoid of feeling. "If I'd died, you could have stayed later at the reception, enjoyed the food and the friends all moving on with their lives."

She closed her eyes. "Grant, don't."

"Go back to the wedding, Jean. Enjoy the company of the people still living."

The Styrofoam plate cracked in her hands. "I want to stay here with you."

"Why?" He turned and his gaze on her was cold. "Out of pity? You want to rescue me like you used to take in all the helpless wounded birds or squirrels you found in the woods as a kid? I'm another broken creature you feel sorry for?"

She moved near. "I love you, Grant.

I did before and I do now. What happened hasn't changed that."

"What happened," he said caustically, as if angry that she kept the words vague, "changed everything. It's a deal-breaker, Jean. You need to call your mother and tell her to stop the wedding plans."

She sat in the hospital chair beside him so she could look him in the face. "That's the last thing I want to do."

"Look at me, Jean." He gestured to his legs. "How will I provide for us? For a family? What if we can't even have a family? If I knew I would be able to walk again, things would be different. But we don't know that. I'm not sitting beside you at my wedding while you stand."

"Grant, please." She set the plate in her lap and reached for his hand. "Doug says your job is waiting for you as soon as you're well enough to work. You can be a mechanic in a wheelchair. And we could adopt if we can't have our own children. There are so many who need loving homes. I won't—"

He turned his head away. "You don't understand."

"I don't understand?" Her temper flared. "No, *you* don't understand." She pressed a finger against his sternum. "You have no idea what it was like kneeling next to your body while you were bleeding out. You don't know what it was like to wait through Ian's funeral, and sit through Susan's funeral, all the while terrified—" She started to cry and pulled her hand from his. "—wondering if I would have to go to your funeral next. I begged God to spare your life, and didn't give Him any stipulations on the condition you had to be in." Her voice had gone high and tinny with emotion but she did not care. "Do you think I spent those days and nights in the hospital praying that God would let you live only if you would have full use of your legs?"

He remained silent but was at least looking at her now. She swiped the back of her hand across her cheeks. "Paralysis may be a deal-breaker for some women, but it's not for me. I don't ever want to hear you insult the depth of my love for you by suggesting it, ever again. Do you hear me, Grant Henderson?"

His stunned gaze remained on her face and she waited for a response, but whatever he might have said was curbed when a nurse entered, plastic gloves on, the familiar tray of vials used for collecting blood hanging from one hand. "The vampire is back," the nurse said cheerfully.

"No more blood today," Grant said. "You've taken enough."

"The doctor wants more tests run." She set the tray onto his bed while Jean stood with her plate and stepped out of the way. After sorting vials, the nurse took the chair Jean vacated, scooted closer to Grant's wheelchair and tied a plastic blue band around his upper arm. "It doesn't bother him to order more; he's not the one getting stuck."

Grant untied the band and threw it on the bed. "Then give me the needle and tell him to come in here." He pushed one wheel and pulled the other, turning his back on them both.

The nurse looked back at Jean rather helplessly, but Jean had no help to give. Unable to speak without tears, she set the wedding fare on the small, wheeled table on the other side of his bed, and slowly, silently, left the room.

In her car, she turned off the radio and drove home in silence. Once there, her thoughts were so focused on the all-encompassing hurt, she nearly tripped over the small package resting on her doorstep.

She picked it up. Probably the Tens Unit she'd ordered to try to help with Grant's pain. She carried it inside, checking the return address. "China?" She found a pair of scissors and cut the packing tape from the side and middle seam, and opened the box.

Whatever it was must be fragile. She peeled layer after layer of protective wrapping away to reveal a porcelain bowl, turquoise in color, with ribbed edges. It had been broken and the cracks repaired with gold.

"Oh, Grant." Jean closed her eyes and clutched the bowl to her chest. Kintsugi, he'd said the method was called. Fixing something broken with gold, making it a masterpiece. He had ordered it for her months ago, the day he asked her to marry him, out on the lake on a cold autumn day when they still had hope for the future.

When she still had him. He had told her the bowl was her, broken by her past but now a precious treasure. His treasure.

Jean let out a primal cry of rage and threw the bowl across the room. It crashed against the wall, cracking along all the original break seams and at least as many more.

Her heart shattered with it. "No. Oh no. No. No…" She dropped to her knees. "I'm sorry. I didn't mean it." Her tears cascaded onto the shards she collected in her hands. They cut into her palms but she grasped them tighter. The pieces were her. Her and Grant. Both broken now.

She collapsed to the floor amid the pieces and sobbed. "God, help us."

Monday Morning, January 19

Candy

Candy dropped her handful of jagged clay shards on the coffee counter. "Oh, Brenda, I'm a wreck."

"Not you." Brenda leaned onto the counter and smiled. "Just your mugs."

"Jamaica's mugs." Candy rubbed her hands over her weary face, forgetting until she pulled her hands away that they were covered in gold glitter. "I'm going to owe her half my salary just to pay for all the stuff I've broken while I lived here."

"You're trying to fix them with that Japanese method Jean told us about, aren't you?"

"Yeah, but I can't afford the real gold stuff, so I was using paste and gold glitter. I guess trying a cheap substitute doesn't work." Her eyelid itched. She used her sleeve-covered arm to wipe it. "There's a heap of object-lesson meaning in that statement, but I'm too tired to delve into it." She picked up a mug handle. "What am I going to do with all these pieces?"

Brenda rounded the coffee counter where specialty brews competed with pastries and scones for prominence. One hand held in her rounded belly while she reached down under the counter and pulled out an empty cardboard box, the top edges cut off. "Put everything in here and leave it for a while. You don't need added stress right now."

"I thought this might get my mind of Billy and Melanie and Champagne, but all it's doing is reminding me how totally out of control I am, and how I can't fix anything."

Brenda stiffened. "Champagne? You heard from her?"

"No, but Melanie sneaked in the back this morning before I opened and told me Champagne came to *Hot Town* to talk to Billy. Why would she be back and not come see me?"

"Maybe because she's an accessory to murder and you'd put her in jail?"

"Hadn't thought of that."

She could tell Brenda wanted to say more. Instead, Brenda reached for a cherry-filled European bit of fluff with a name Candy could not pronounce and stuffed a huge bite into her mouth. Too polite to talk while chewing, Brenda's silence gave Candy time to find a paper towel and swipe her face free of some of the glitter. She had to look like a kindergartener on craft day. A messy one.

Brenda finished her bite, opened her mouth to speak, then must have changed her mind because she shoved another bite in. Candy gave up waiting to hear her words of caution or her recommendation to go find Champagne and purge her of any information that might help convict Slash. What they really needed was her witness testimony, but even that might not be enough, and no one was going to testify against Slash anyway if they valued their life. "The weird thing is, Billy called me about an hour ago. Said he'd changed his mind and I could bring the church ladies back to visit his girls again." She slid the mug pieces into the box. They clattered loudly and several customers in the shop turned to see the source of the commotion, their eyebrows going up when they saw Candy's face. She must not have gotten much of the glitter off after all. "Something really strange is going on over there. I don't trust Billy any more than I can throw him, and you've seen him so you know I wouldn't be able to throw much more than his kneecap. But I can't pass up an opportunity to get back into *Hot Town*, especially if Champagne has something to do with this and I might get the chance to talk to her."

Brenda's smile was tinged with sadness. "If Susan were still here, she'd want to go as an undercover cop again and see what evidence she could find."

"An undercover cop. Great idea." Candy pushed the box of mug shards onto the shelf under the counter, out of sight for now. "I need to call Jose. Watch the counter for me for a minute, will you? You can eat another one of those fluffy cherry things."

Candy did not wait to see if Brenda took another pastry. She ran to the phone and the moment Jose answered, said with conviction, "Billy is setting some kind of trap, but I think we can turn it into an opportunity. Are you in?"

"Hello, Candy." Jose's voice was wry through the phone. "How do I always know when it's you?"

"Sorry. We've got a lot to talk about. You might as well come over here. The coffee at the precinct is lousy."

"You think all coffee is lousy."

"And you don't have any whipped cream."

"Fine. I'll be there in twenty."

She hung up and ran back to the counter. "Did I miss any customers?"

"No." Brenda licked a cherry-covered finger. "Unless you count me."

"Thanks for your help. Jose's coming over. He'll be here soon."

Brenda smiled. "You might want to wash your face before he gets here."

Candy turned one of the copper sauce pans to the backside to see her reflection. She looked like she had a case of golden measles. "Right."

Late Monday Night, January 19

Champagne

Champagne flipped channels, then turned off the TV and threw the remote across the room. She got up from the bed and paced. Slash was getting released one week from today. Seven nights from now she would return to Oackview, to his hotel room, with a knife. She pictured his face and started shaking.

She had needed those bags from Billy, the two to keep her calm and give her the courage she knew she didn't have, and the one she had told Billy was to knock out a non-existent roommate.

Champagne was staying alone at a hotel, but Billy didn't need to know that. There was no way she was telling him she was blacklisted by Slash and if Whip, his current main fist, saw her and could get to her, she was dead. If Whip was anywhere in the hotel the night Slash got released, she would have to put him out long enough to get the job done and get away. He needed to stay alive, though. Slash dying on his watch would fall on him, so he'd make sure to cover it up if he could. Make it look like an accident. It might not even end up in the news and she wouldn't have the police to reckon with at least.

But Billy had messed everything up with his condition of bringing Candy to *Hot Town* with her. She couldn't meet Candy, not before the job was done. Candy and those friends of hers were too good, and something about them was contagious. Whatever it was had changed Candy from the inside out, and Champagne couldn't let it get to her, not before she did what she had to do. Talking to Candy or being near her before next Tuesday was out of the question. She had considered contacting another of Slash's connections for the drugs she needed, but if Billy got wind of it, she'd have more problems to fix. No, she would just have to go without, come up with some other way to get past Whip, or get him out of the hotel that night.

The glass she had picked up from the end table near the bed slipped from her hand and dropped to the stained Berber carpet beneath her bare feet. It fell to the side and the golden liquid inside spilled out. She imagined Slash's blood spilling when her knife plunged into his heart and the shaking in her hands overtook her entire body so violently she had to lie down on the bed and curl into a ball until it stopped.

The closer the days came to Slash's release, the more sleep, or any kind of relief from the fear, eluded her.

"Sleep-deprivation causes all kinds of problems," Candy had once told her. They had been arrested and were killing time before some no-name from Slash's lower-rung contacts came to bail them out. "Once I got arrested and Slash was mad at me so he didn't send anyone for a week. I slept the entire seven days. It was the meth—had kept me awake for, I don't know, a month it felt like." Candy had chuckled at that. What else was there to do but laugh? "You should have seen my mug shot. People think it's side effects from meth, the shakes and paranoia and hallucinations, but it's really exhaustion." She had pulled her knees up on the bench where they sat waiting their turn to be processed, and put her head on Champagne's leg. "Speaking of sleep, maybe Slash will forget about us tonight, or longer. I wouldn't mind a couple days without anybody knocking on the door."

Sleep might do Champagne more good than drugs at this point, but every time she opened the box of sleeping pills she'd bought on her way out of Oakview after seeing Billy, she could not get herself to take them. If she slept too hard, she might not hear if one of Slash's men came after her. Going to see Billy had been a risk. If he had a way to contact Slash in prison—which he shouldn't be able to with him in lockdown but nothing seemed impossible for Slash—Champagne could already have someone targeting her. She had to stay alive for seven more days.

She kicked the fallen glass aside and went to sit in front of the laptop she'd bought with Slash's money. She hadn't taken much out of his account, not enough to raise red flags if Slash was able to check his funds before she got to him. Not nearly as much as he owed her for all the years she was his property. That would come in time. She'd get everything, money from every drug pusher and pimp and trafficker who wanted the password to his site back, enough to provide for Emily's future away from all of this.

Working to distract her thoughts, she typed up the e-mail she would send to Slash's connections once he was dead. It was short and direct. She had all the passwords. Their site information would be sent to the police unless they paid her to buy them back, and to buy her silence. If they resisted, she had flash drives containing hours of digital content, recorded surveillance of drug and human trafficking—plenty of blackmail to encourage their cooperation, and raise the price for her partnership. After they had paid, and she had downloaded and saved the transaction, with digital trails linking each e-mail to its source, all the flash drives and files would go to Jose Ramirez. She would have given them to Ian Craig, but he was dead.

She shook her head. "You can't do anything about that now," she said out loud. They didn't help, the words, but she said them again, then turned her attention back to the internet. She wrote and recorded and filed incriminating data, filling one more sleepless night, with only six more to go until the night she waited for, and dreaded, the most.

"I am
prepared
to slap
you."

Chapter Eight
Tuesday Afternoon, January 20

Jean

Jean positioned Grant's chair at the table farthest from the counter in *Jamaica's Place*. Brenda served customers, who seemed to enjoy the change of being waited on by someone who actually liked coffee. Jean surveyed the table where they'd been told to meet Candy. On it were two mugs filled with whipped cream, but a spoon in only one, meaning both cups were for her. "She must be planning a long talk."

"What?" Grant asked.

His tone said he was being polite but did not really care. She was weary to her bones of that tone. "Nothing."

"I don't want to be here, Jean."

She sighed, but kept her voice light. "I know, but Candy never takes no for an answer, and besides, the doctor said to go somewhere two hours a day from now on. He wants you out of the hospital."

"I want out of this chair."

Jean had long since given up responding to comments like that. She wandered over to Candy's table. Next to the mugs sat a stack of what Jean originally thought were papers, but a closer inspection revealed they were eight-by-ten photographs. A woman's face filled the top photo, bruises across her jaw and blood dripping from a cut over her eye. Jean wanted to look away, but was drawn by the woman's eyes. Such hopelessness. Such horrible acceptance. Who was she? What did she have to do with what Candy wanted to talk to Grant about?

Had something happened with Slash? Did she know something new?

"You've gone pale as a sheet," Grant said. "Are you okay?"

"Fine," Jean murmured. "It's nice of you to notice."

"What?"

"Nothing." She walked to Candy's table and picked up the photo. Underneath it, another woman's face stared up at her, this one so beaten and bloodied Jean could only tell she was female by the stringy blond locks running over her shoulders and the nametag that said Sharon. The third photo and fourth in the pile were more of the same. Jean wondered if over time, people like Candy and Champagne got used to seeing images like this. Did they become numb to them, forcing themselves to decide this was normal to endure, to survive?

"Hey."

Jean had not heard Candy approach. She jerked and dropped the photos. "Sorry." She kneeled and scurried to press them into a stack on the floor, then returned them to the table. "What are these for?"

"We'll get to them in a minute." She seemed distracted, or perhaps it was Candy's look when she was focused. Jean was still not good at reading people, but Candy usually carried her feelings out front on her face. Today was unusual, or perhaps Jean was just seeing everyone as closed and shut away these days.

She sat with another sigh. When had she started thinking such dark thoughts? Was she giving up hope, too?

"I've got something to say to you, Grant Henderson." Candy turned to Jean. "You can stay or you can go. Your choice."

Jean hid her curiosity behind a shrug. "I'll stay."

"Okay." Candy pulled in a deep breath, then let it out. "Grant, you're being a jerk."

"Thanks," Grant said without feeling. "I knew talking to you would be encouraging." He angled his wheels to the left. "Are we done?"

"No."

He turned back to face her. "Want to pray over me while I'm here?"

She stared him down. Jean swung her gaze from one to the other, animosity radiating from Grant, frustration from Candy. Maybe they weren't so hard to read after all.

"This dark, Eeyore cloud you've been under lately has got to go. You think it's just you living in the anger and bitterness, but it's not. You're making everyone who loves you suffer, but especially Jean."

Jean felt herself drawing inward, trying to shrink. "Candy, you don't need to—"

"Yes, I do. Somebody needs to stand up for you." Candy sat stiff as a board and pointed a finger at Jean. "This woman gave up five years of accumulated sick days to be with you day and night those first weeks in the hospital. When those were gone, she came every day after work and stayed after everyone else had gone home to sleep. She spent Christmas in the hospital! She's hovered over you like a mother and worked for you like a maid. And you've gotten used to it and don't even notice. Worse than that, you dump all your lousy feeling-sorry-for-yourself comments on her. You're wallowing in this yucky black sludge and making her sit in it with you."

Jean watched Grant's face. It was blank, unrevealing. "You said it was an Eeyore cloud," he said blandly.

"Shut up." Candy picked up the photo on the top of her stack and held it inches from Grant's face. "Look at this woman."

"How can I not? You've got her close enough to kiss."

"Then kiss her if you want to." Candy's sarcasm matched his. Her words were hard as rocks. "See her face? She got all that, plus a couple of bruised ribs and a broken wrist, because she smiled at the pizza delivery guy and her boyfriend didn't like it." She handed the photo to Jean and picked up the next one, shoving it in front of his eyes. "This is one of Billy Bradon's girls. She asked for help from a policeman, but turned out he was just one of Billy's guys in a costume sent to test her." Candy pushed the photo closer. "She's dead."

She tossed the photo to Jean. It flew to the side like a Frisbee and Jean went chasing after it. She returned to find three more pictures on her chair. Candy was flipping through them quickly, shooting story after story at Grant, carving into his cynicism. Jean held her growing pile of photographs, trying not to look at the faces being handed to her.

"You think your life is over," Candy said when the table was empty except for her untouched mugs and spoon. "You think something so terrible was done to you, and yes, it was a bad thing. It's a bad thing that you are paralyzed and in a wheelchair." She leaned forward and pointed at his knees. "But I know a hundred women—and I'm not exaggerating; I can give you their names—who would trade places with you in a heartbeat." She stood and waved her arms. "They would take your life, wheelchair and all, and you know why? It would mean they were safe. Nobody was going to beat them up tonight. Nobody was going to force them to sell themselves twenty times before midnight to guys who won't even bother to ask their names. They'd get to take a real shower. Sleep for more than fifteen minutes between customers." She flung her hands toward Jean and her eyes welled with tears. "They'd have someone who wanted to give to them instead of just take." The tears fell. "They'd be loved. Do you have any idea how precious a gift that is?"

She sat down, dragged her chair forward until her legs hit the foot pedals of Grant's wheelchair, and then surprised Jean by putting her hands on his legs. "You've lost something, I know." Her voice was choked, full of emotion. "But look around you, Grant, at what you have." She swiped at her nose with the back of her hand. "And most of all, look up." She grabbed for Jean's stack of photos. Most of them dropped to the floor, but the few she caught she dropped onto his lap. "These women are living in Satan's playground. As awful as their lives are now, it's going to be even worse after death if they don't learn about Jesus and turn to Him. You might never get to use your legs again in this life, but you'll get a new body in heaven and be perfect for eternity." She pushed against his legs as she stood, sending his chair back half a foot, and circled the table, throwing her arms in the air. "What is wrong with you, man? You've got Jesus!"

By now, everyone in the shop was staring. Brenda sent a sympathetic glance Jean's way. Jean checked Grant's face. It might as well have been made of mortar. Whatever might be going on inside, nothing revealed his feelings, except that the knuckles of his hands where he gripped his armrests had gone white.

Candy kept going. "You've got the God who died for you promising to be with you and help you and turn even the worst things into something good. You've got the options of peace and joy and hope right in front of you and all around you, but you can't see any of that because you won't stop staring at your legs." She crossed her arms and stood over him.

Grant did not look up. "That was—"

"Beware what you say." Candy took the photos Jean had retrieved from the floor and set them back on the table with the rest. "If you let out one sarcastic or negative comment, I am prepared to slap you."

He did look at her then, and closed his mouth.

"Good choice."

Without a word, without even a glance at Jean, Grant turned his chair and wheeled through the tables to the large glass door leading to the sidewalk and the car. Jean and Candy watched him go, along with every customer present. "Well, I said it, and it needed to be said." Candy put a hand on Jean's shoulder. "I just hope I didn't make things worse."

Jean closed her eyes and stood, wishing for the courage to ask for a hug. "I don't think you could make things worse at this point."

When Candy pulled her into an embrace, and then Brenda joined them and added her arms around them both, Jean fought to keep from breaking down. Candy whispered, "Then we'll pray God will make them better."

She prayed right then, out loud. If there were any new visitors to *Jamaica's*, they were surely surprised, but the locals would not be. Candy prayed with customers nearly as often as she served them whipped cream. Jean did not catch many of Candy's words, but rested in the love that carried them, and in the comfort of the God who loved them all.

"Guess you'd better go," Candy said when they parted. "That man in a sludge puddle under an Eeyore cloud is waiting for you."

Candy could always make her smile, even through tears. "Thank you, Candy."

"Oh sure." Candy picked up one of her mugs of whipped cream and held it up in a toast. "I'm not good at a lot of things, but anytime you need someone threatened with a good slap, you let me know!"

Wednesday Afternoon, January 21

Stewart

Stewart tried to cover his uncertainty with humor. "I thought today's physical therapy lesson would be learning to get in and out of a car, but it sounds like you got to do that yesterday."

Grant wheeled beside him through the hospital parking lot. "Yeah, I got to have a little field trip to *Jamaica's Place*."

A lifetime with his brother had taught Stewart that Grant's don't-care demeanor meant he was bruised on the inside but didn't want anyone to know it. "Want me to take you back there today? Get a donut or something?"

They had reached the car, but Stewart did not know what to do next. He wished Grant's therapist had come with them. Should he open the passenger door for Grant? Was Grant allowed to sit in the front seat? If Stewart asked either question, would Grant feel like a toddler?

Stewart stood battling indecision until Grant thankfully moved past him and opened the front passenger door himself. He pulled a small padded plank from behind his back and set it half-on, half-off the seat in the car. "No, thanks. I can't handle the well-wishes and the I'm-sorrys today." He lifted his body from the chair onto the plank and slid over into the car. "And I really can't deal with all the questions."

Stewart noticed Grant's chair today had no armrests. Was that a new permanent chair for him or just to use when traveling, so he could move in and out of it easier? Stewart wanted to ask—there were a lot of things he wanted to ask—but Grant was tired of being a living documentary. Stewart moved to shut Grant's door before depositing his chair in the trunk. "From what I heard about yesterday, sounds like Candy didn't ask all that many questions."

Grant scowled. "Candy hits below the belt."

"That shouldn't be a problem, since you can't feel anything below the belt."

Stewart had let the words out without thinking, and cringed. He hid his surprise when Grant let out a chuckle. Grant shut the door but lowered the window to say, "Actually, I feel a lot more than people think."

Stewart looked him in the eye. "I know."

Grant nodded and Stewart turned away with the chair. It was all they needed to say for now. Stewart drove them through town, detouring a block away from *Jamaica's Place*, then on past the park with the basketball court. School was still in session so the court sat empty, one lone, half-flattened ball sitting on the free-throw line like a kid without friends. Grant stared out his window, quiet, as they passed. Stewart kept silent with him, praying his idea would be helpful. Had he known Candy was going to meet Grant yesterday and let him have it, he would have given Grant some time before this trip, but it couldn't be helped now. Besides, the team only had one game this month in Charlotte. Next week their game was in Raleigh, three hours away. Slash would be getting out of jail by then, so none of them were going to want to be out in the open more than necessary.

Thoughts of Slash, of how he and Brenda had both been on his list of targets, cluttered Stewart's thinking until they reached the outskirts of the city.

"Charlotte?" Grant asked. "What are we doing here?"

"I thought I'd take you someplace where nobody knew you."

Grant's glance held appreciation. "Tell me we're going to the Cheesecake Factory. I want a steak, and the biggest piece of red velvet cake they've got."

"You're supposed to get cheesecake."

"Okay, I'll get a piece of that, too."

Stewart turned his blinker on to pass a grandma in a big black Lincoln. He smiled. "I'm all for going there, just so long as I bring a piece back. Cheesecake is on Brenda's list of major cravings right now." He grimaced. "Along with fried eggs made with garlic. Our house reeks like an Italian restaurant."

"That's not so bad."

"It is at six in the morning."

Grant half-smiled. Stewart pulled onto Westminster Avenue and into the parking lot near the First Presbyterian church gym. He turned off the ignition. "Before food, though, this is our main stop. They're expecting us."

"Are you preaching here or something?" Grant opened his door. "At four in the afternoon?"

"Nope."

"Then what are we doing here?"

Curiosity was good. Stewart gestured to the church. "Come inside and find out."

Grant followed him through the main entrance door into a gymnasium. What looked like a game of scrimmage was in process, but though noise filled the court, it was not the usual squeaking of tennis shoes on the waxy wooden floor. Fans cheered as a shot was blocked and the ball stolen. The players rushed to the opposite side of the court.

Stewart watched his brother. Grant's eyes had not left the players since the moment they entered. He did not notice the bleachers, fans, or the man wearing a whistle walking their way.

"What is this?" Grant asked.

"Wheelchair basketball. They're called the Rolling Hornets. They play teams from all over North Carolina and even other states."

Grant stared. When the man with the whistle introduced himself as Jim, one of the assistant coaches, Grant absently put a hand out to shake his, but his eyes did not leave the court. One player's chair butted up against another, hard, and the other player tipped and almost fell to the side, chair and all. People yelled encouragement. The game went on. They crashed against each other, threw the ball, reached high, shot and scored.

Grant gestured forward. "Their chairs..."

The wheelchairs were different. Stewart had never seen any like them. The wheels were positioned so they tilted outward at the bottom and inward at the top, as if a huge hand had pinched the upper half.

"Basketball wheelchairs are specially made to maneuver without getting caught against each other," the assistant informed them. He grinned. "As you can see, it's important to have equipment that fits the sport. These guys aren't going to make it no contact to keep from getting stuck together."

"Where do they all...who..."

Grant did not seem to know what to ask. Jim sat on a bleacher level with Grant's chair, balancing his legs comfortably on the floor beside the bleachers so he could face Grant. "Our players come from all over the area. Most of the adults are paralyzed or amputees due to accidents." He pointed at passing players. "That guy's motorcycle got hit by a drunk driver. The player behind him was in an equipment explosion on his construction site." He leaned around a shouting fan and gestured to a man with broad shoulders sending a three-pointer toward the net. "Jake's battalion hit a land mine in Iraq. They never found enough of his legs to even try to put him back together."

Stewart hated talking over Grant's head, but there was no room left on the bleachers. He moved to stand behind Grant's chair and told Jim, "As I mentioned on the phone, Grant wanted to start an after-school sports ministry in our town. A lot of the kids are in broken homes and below the poverty line. We've got problems with drugs."

"It's a great idea," Jim said. "What's stopping him?"

Grant spoke without turning. "I got shot."

Stewart hadn't realized he was listening. Jim looked Grant over. "How long?"

"Fifty-five days."

He nodded, as if he understood something Stewart did not. He gestured toward the court. "Basketball is a great outlet for the guys, but it gives them a lot more than a chance to move their bodies and have fun. Every guy on that court has a tragic story, but we're all done with that part. When they're here, nobody's doing the awkward silence or feeling sorry for each other."

That was what Grant was looking at almost greedily. Stewart could see it now. The lack of strangeness. There was no set-apart feeling, either with the men in wheelchairs or anyone else in the gym. Everyone was normal.

"We've got kid's teams, too," Jim added. He smiled and waved at a child in a wheelchair on the other side of the court, holding a clipboard in hand and shouting some kind of instructions to a player waiting to shoot a free throw. “Our youngest player is five. The kids most often have lifelong conditions like spina bifida or cerebral palsy. Got any kids in your town in wheelchairs?” Jim asked.

“I don’t know.” Grant turned to him for the first time. “I never noticed any on the court.”

“They wouldn’t be on the court, now, would they? Not without someone inspiring them.”

Grant looked at his hands. “That wasn’t on my radar.”

Jim nodded again. “But it will be now. Being in that chair changes things, and change is not always bad.”

“You need legs to play basketball with kids.”

“Do you need legs to coach them?” Jim stood. “You want to give kids the message that they can overcome and make something of themselves, no matter what circumstances might seem to limit them, right? What better way to give that message than from right where you sit?”

A cheer went up as the final buzzer ended the game. Jim jogged toward the court, but then pivoted and ran in place, calling out, “Start that ministry of yours. Play ball. Find yourself a disabled kid or two to be your assistants. Think bigger than your original goal. Think God-sized and see what happens!”

“His team must be the one that won,” Stewart commented. Jim ran to the cluster of wheelchairs in the center of the court. He shook shoulders and slapped hands. Grant watched in silence so long Stewart found himself fidgeting. The bleachers had partially cleared, so he found a spot to sit, placing one foot on the floor and propping the other on the bleacher below him. “So...you ready to go get that steak?”

“No.” Grant looked down at his feet, then back at the men on the court. “I know why you brought me here, Stew. Everybody wants me to accept. To make the best of things and move on.” He took in a heavy breath. “I’ll try. I really will.” He ran his hands through his hair, then settled them on his thighs. Stewart wondered if his legs could feel the weight of his hands even if the nerves did not feel the touch. “Give me a few minutes,” Grant said, “then we’ll go meet those guys and talk with them, okay?”

One of the men shot the ball from half court. It missed the basket by at least ten yards. The others ribbed him as the team headed off the court toward the side. Stewart took in his own deep breath and let it out. "Okay."

She pulled up
a sleeve and
flexed a
non-existent
muscle.

Chapter Nine
Saturday Evening, January 24

Jean

Jean pushed Grant's chair until they reached the ramp leading to her front porch. "You're on your own here," she said, stepping away. "It's too steep and you're too heavy."

"Or you just have weeny arms," he joked and her heart smiled. Every smile, every laugh this week, gave her hope he was healing more than just physically.

"Not all of us can bench press three hundred on a good day."

"On a good day?" He took the ramp in two pushes and gloated at the top. "You couldn't bench press forty-five."

"You don't know that." She remained at the bottom of the porch steps, making their gazes almost level. "Maybe I've just let you think that so you don't feel badly that you're going to marry such a tough woman." She pulled up a sleeve and flexed a non-existent muscle. He laughed out loud. It sounded so good she wanted to cry.

Jean heard a door slam somewhere inside the house. "That's unlike Mother."

Grant turned his wheelchair toward the door. "I'm sure you noticed the extra car beside hers. Maybe she brought a boyfriend to meet you."

"Please," she begged, lifting her skirt to keep from stepping on the hem as she climbed the steps. "Don't add to the drama. More likely it's someone she's roped into doing something for the wedding."

She saw his frown. "The longer we delay, the bigger this whole wedding thing gets. We'll need to have it in a stadium if she goes much longer."

Jean paused outside the front door, not wanting their time alone to end just yet. "I never wanted a big wedding." She arched over his chair and put her face close to his. "If I had my choice, I'd walk over to that church across the brook right now." She pointed. "And I'd march down the aisle with no one there but you and God."

He circled his hand around her neck and pulled her face down for a long, lingering kiss. "I think there has to be a preacher present for it to be legal."

She smiled and gave him a quick peck. "You, God, and Stewart then."

He captured her mouth again. "Plus two witnesses."

Her lips smiled against his. "Brenda and Candy can be there, too, but that's it."

His smile reached his eyes. "Can they wear the dresses from Florence's wedding? It'd save money."

She burst out laughing and pulled away. "You just sucked the romance right out of that whole image."

He grabbed her hand and tugged her back toward him. When she was near, the teasing glint faded from his eyes and he regarded her seriously. "Would you really marry me like that? Now, as I am? Without all the fuss?"

She kept her face solid but knew her eyes gleamed with mirth. "I can't say I'd be okay with the dresses..." She put love into her gaze and her voice, palming his cheek with her hand. "But all the rest, yes, I would. Gladly."

His eyes held uncertainty. "Jean, really, would—"

Another door slammed inside and Jean turned from Grant when her mother's voice came through the closed door loud enough to hear every word. "How dare you accuse me of—"

"Accuse you?" a male voice yelled. Jean jolted. Who was inside? "I'm just stating facts."

"You can't put the blame on me," Grace Jameson shouted. "If you hadn't left, it never would have happened!"

Jean hadn't heard her mother raise her voice in years, not since...

She yanked open the screen door and grabbed the front doorknob. "Jean?" Grant questioned behind her. "Who is it?"

"If you hadn't driven me away, I never would have left!"

The front door opened from the inside. Jean jumped back. She stared at the man filling the doorway. His sandy blond hair and straight features, so like her own, were familiar yet strange. The way his sleeves were rolled up to his elbows and tie loosened around his collar brought hints of memories from somewhere far back in her mind.

"Jean?" the man asked. His face registered shock. His eyes glistened and he blinked twice. "My Jeanie Beanie?"

Jean, her hand still out from where she had reached for the doorknob, stood frozen and mute except for one word, after fifteen years more a question than a declaration of recognition.

"Daddy?"

Sunday Morning, January 25

Grant

He could do this. Grant set his jaw and nodded for Jean to open the door. He wheeled into the church foyer, his clammy hands slipping on the wheels. He had wanted to wait another few weeks before facing the crowd, before entering the building where Susan's funeral had been held, but Jean needed him. A glance her way showed pale skin and a mouth pinched tight. Since the night before, Jean had been in a daze. Right after her father had said her name, before they could have any kind of conversation, Grace had appeared, and the two commenced their shouting match on the porch. Finally her father had stomped down the steps with a promise to Jean to return after church Sunday when his former wife was no longer present.

Jean had questioned her mother, but Grace's mouth shut like a bank vault. She went inside and within minutes returned pulling a suitcase. "I won't stay here if he's coming back," she'd announced loftily. "I'll get a room at the hotel in town and—" A thought must have caught her by surprise, for she flushed, turned and dragged her suitcase back inside, but then rotated and came out again. "No. I'll stay. He'll probably lie through his teeth to you, Jean. Tell you all kinds of outrageous stories."

"Stories about what?" Grant asked for Jean, who had not moved through the entire exchange. She seemed congealed to her spot near the door.

"Never mind." With that vague, useless comment, Grace had done yet another one-eighty and disappeared into the house again, her suitcase wheels clanking over the threshold behind her.

The screen door banged shut and Jean stared. "What just happened?"

He hadn't been sure then and was still unsure now. All he knew was that Jean's father, after fifteen years of no contact whatsoever, was showing up after church that afternoon, and Grant was going to be right by Jean's side when she faced him.

How could the man have abandoned his daughter, then never even bothered to write or call? Grant added Charles Jameson's name close to Rod Carson's on his list of people he'd like to pummel.

Only now that he was confined, he couldn't do any damage unless a perpetrator came close and bent over so he could reach them.

He wanted a punching bag, but instead was offered a handshake by John Stanton, the new head deacon. "Great to have you back," the man said warmly. "You've been missed here at Brookside."

Grant murmured some kind of thanks, aware that Jean had moved behind to push his chair through the sudden throng around him. He accepted the handshakes and hugs, responded to the elderly ladies who teared up and patted him on the shoulder, and by the time they were down the aisle to their usual second row spot, he felt like he'd survived a run through a gauntlet of affection and goodwill.

"That wasn't so bad, was it?" Stewart came down the steps leading to the pulpit to meet him. "It's sure good to have you back, Grant."

He wasn't back, not fully, but refrained from saying so. He had promised Stewart he would try to accept, to move on. "Not so bad," he said, wiping his sweaty palms down his pant legs, trying to decide if he should go through the effort of transferring his body onto the pew or just stay in his chair in the aisle.

"If you're not feeling smothered by all the attention yet..." Candy approached with a huge smile. She wore a loud, crimson and cream swirled dress with a long black shawl draped over her shoulders and heels so high they had to hurt. "I saw Gladys pat you on the head and thought that'd be fun." She gave him two sisterly pats. "We're all glad you've back in church, and alive for that matter." He heard Jean gasp behind him but Candy charged on. "When I drove up that night and you had your head down in the dirt, and there was blood all—"

"My father is coming today," Jean interjected, her voice high. Grant did not mind the interruption. He had not thought of it until right then, but thus far, Jean had kept all their conversations short so no one had a chance to verbally relive the shooting or ask too many questions. He reached back for her hand in gratitude. She grasped it and held tight.

"Your father?" Candy was effectively distracted. "Are you serious? What does he want?"

"I don't know."

"What did he say?"

"Not much."

"What are you going to do?"

"I have no idea."

Candy crossed her arms. "This is like a bad soap opera script. You haven't seen him since you were ten and that's all you have to say?"

He looked back. Jean shrugged helplessly. What would she say when her father showed up that afternoon? Would Grace come and the two of them start yelling at each other and completely ignore their daughter again? His mind wandered through Stewart's sermon, and the moment the service was over, he benefited from Jean's nervous desire to leave as quickly as possible. Everyone had been kind, welcoming, and he had to admit it was good to be back among God's people in God's house, but still the weight of the sorrow and compassion in their gazes bore down heavy across his shoulders.

Back at her house, after difficult maneuvering through the furnishings in her living room, he sat beside where Jean perched on the arm of the couch and they waited. She tried to make casual conversation, but her thoughts would wander and they finally sat in silence, her hand in his, while Grace created a tempest of sound in the kitchen.

He heard the motor in the driveway, but Jean was up and nearly to the door before he had a chance to mention the sound. "He's here," she whispered breathlessly. "Oh, Grant, what do I do?" She put both hands over her heart and pressed hard. "How am I to bear this?"

His heart ached for her. He moved to her side. "Do you want to meet him alone?"

She looked at him almost wild-eyed and shook her head. "Please, will you come with me?"

"I'll be right beside you as long as you want me."

Her eyes glistened. She opened her mouth to speak but the door swung open and her father stared again, as if seeing her for the first time. Jean stared back. Neither spoke until Grace appeared from the kitchen. Jean's father glanced her way and frowned. "She's still here?" He turned his back on her and addressed Jean. "Will you come outside? I have some things I'd like to show you."

"He's twisting things, Jean. It wasn't my fault."

Chapter Ten
Sunday Afternoon, January 25

Jean

Jean closed her eyes and tried to collect the courage to voice the question she had waited fifteen years to ask. Would he give excuses about why he rejected her all these years? No reason was reason enough.

Wouldn't it be better not to know, if the knowing only caused pain?

Her father descended the porch steps and neared his car. "Jean?" he questioned when she remained on the porch. Should she tell him she was reliving the memory of watching him walk to his car with that same loping gait all those years ago, assuming he would return that night for supper like always, watching outside later as the sun set and the sky gave way to night, and her mother came out for the third time to insist she give up waiting?

"When I knew you weren't coming back, I wrote to you ever day for weeks." Jean walked down the steps, nodding back at Grant to let him know it was okay for him to stay on the porch. "Every time the phone rang, I prayed it was you. On my birthday, I just knew you would be there. I put on my prettiest dress and shoes and stayed at the door even after all my friends had gone to the table and were enjoying the cake." She felt tears gather as she approached his car, where he stood with the back door open, his face awash with feeling. "I let them open all the gifts. I don't remember even one of them. All I knew was that the gift I wanted most had not come."

"Jeanie Beanie," he said, his voice confused mixed with something else she could not discern. He reached into the backseat and pulled out a wrapped gift, long and rectangle in shape, tied with a ribbon that had long since been flattened. He gestured her attention to the inside of the car. She peered around the open door to see more clearly and her jaw dropped. Filling the floorboards, and then the seats to the ceiling were boxes and bags, all wrapped in cheerful paper, some yellowed with age, some new and shiny.

"What—I don't understand."

"I called, Jean, a hundred times. I wrote letters. Every birthday and Christmas for years I sent gifts that got returned unopened." He pointed at his backseat. "Even after I gave up sending them, I still shopped and wrapped gifts for you every year. I brought all of them, hoping you'd finally forgive me and be willing to see me."

"But I—" Her mind could not put the pieces together. "Mother said you didn't want to have anything to do with us. When I wrote or begged to call, she said you disappeared and she had no way to reach you. She said you abandoned us."

"He did abandon us."

Jean turned. Her mother stormed down the steps and put her hands on Jean's shoulders. "Come inside, Jean. Whatever he's telling you, don't believe it."

Her father slammed the car door shut. "I knew you were manipulative, Grace, but you stooped farther than I ever would have believed. How could you have told her I didn't want to have anything to do with her?" He focused on Jean. "I wrote. I called. I came to see you more than once." He turned eyes of fire on his former wife. "I was turned away at the door. Your mother—" He said the word with contempt. "—told me you hated me and never wanted to see me again. She told me that trying to contact you was only making things worse. That you were sick and if I really loved you I would stay out of your life."

"Jean was sick, horribly sick."

He did not blink. "I've talked with a lot of people since I came back into town, Grace. Her sickness was not because I left."

Jean watched the blood drain from her mother's face. "She desperately needed a man's influence."

"So you let in a monster."

"I let in someone who wasn't a coward who ran away."

His voice rose. "You let in an abuser, and I bet it wasn't hard for him to work you over with a few well-placed strokes to your ego."

Grace swung a palm to slap him but he caught her arm and held hard. They stared each other down.

"Mom?" Jean's call was frail in her own ears, too quiet to be noticed. "Mom?" she tried again. She felt a slight pressure against her right hand and looked to see that Grant was at her side. She took his hand in a vise grip and put force behind the air she expelled. "Mom!"

Her parents stopped to regard her.

"Is it true?" Jean asked. "All those times I asked and asked if I could find him, talk to him, see him—all those times you lied to me?"

Her mother's face was white, her father's red. "Jean," she said, touching her hair. "You were so miserable. I thought that—"

Jean pulled back. "You thought? Thought what? That it would be better for me to think my father didn't love me? To feel rejected for fifteen years?" She spoke through tears. "I wanted him at my graduation ceremony, at Grandma's funeral, in the hospital when they were doing all those tests. Did you know where he was all that time? Did you know..." She pulled in air and spoke around the disbelief. "You were going to let me walk down the aisle alone at my wedding."

Grace's hands rubbed the golden bangles around her wrist. "He's twisting things, Jean. It wasn't my fault. I—"

"The proof is right there, Grace." Jean's father opened the car door again and her mother's hands fluttered around her as if searching for some place to go. "I brought it all with me. The front seat is a box full of all the returned letters and records of every phone call. I kept it all in case I ever got the chance to take you to court and ask for custody." He put his hand on Jean's shoulder. "That chance never came, Jean. The law almost always sided with the mother back then. But I never forgot you, Jeanie Beanie. I should have been a man and made her let me see you. I should have—" He hung his head. "There were a lot of things I should have done differently, but I never, ever stopped loving you."

It should not have been awkward, but the moment was. Jean should have been able to fall into her father's embrace and have him enfold her with reassurances and all the things she wished he had said so many years ago. Instead she stood with her hand as tight as a tourniquet around Grant's while her mother disappeared inside the house. She reappeared not long after with her suitcase in tow and without a word climbed into her car and drove away. Through it all her father stood with his hand still on her shoulder, lines above his brows etched into his skin, his eyes on his shuffling feet rather than her.

Finally, after more agonizing moments passed, he said, "Well, should we take the presents inside?"

Activity would benefit. "Yes." She helped unload the piles of gifts and the three of them carried them inside, creating stacks several feet high on her living room floor right in the spot where the family Christmas tree had always been.

"I don't remember what's in them," he said once the last faded box had been placed. "I doubt many of them will be worth anything anymore."

"Shall I open them now?" Jean asked. It was daunting, the pile of gifts, what they meant.

He ran a hand through his hair. "To be honest..." He looked to Grant, as if hoping Grant would read his mind and speak for him. "I think that...no...I'm really tired." He wasn't looking at her again. "I think I'll go back to my hotel for the night. Let's save the presents for another time, okay?"

He did not wait for an answer or a goodbye. She stood in front of her stash of presents in baffled, stunned silence as he turned and quickly exited the house.

"He acted like he was trying to escape," she said to Grant.

It had not been her imagination, for Grant seemed as puzzled as she. "Maybe he was."

"From what?"

"I don't know."

She sat on the floor and reached for a box that had fallen from one of the stacks. She methodically removed the tape from the antique-looking paper covered in roses and ivy and opened a white clothing box inside. She moved the tissue paper aside to reveal a dress of satin and lace, ice blue in color, the perfect size for a small-framed ten-year-old girl. Under the dress lay a wand with ribbons dangling from the end, a set of clear plastic shoes meant to mimic glass slippers, and a silver plastic tiara. "A Cinderella dress," she whispered. "He bought me a Cinderella dress."

Grant moved his chair to be near her. She leaned until her head rested against his leg, the dress clutched tight against her chest. "All this time, all these years, he loved me and I did not know. Oh, Grant, of all the things I've had to bear, this one somehow hurts the worst."

Sunday Afternoon, January 25

Candy

"No way, Jose." Candy would have laughed at the phrase she'd said many a time during her childhood years had she not felt so irked. "Trust me, if I showed up at *Hot Town* with a stranger, Bradon wouldn't even bother to ask if she was a cop. I'll bring one when I come with the church ladies, but today, I have to do this alone."

"Last time Champagne was involved in your life, people died." Jose's voice held more concern than Candy had ever heard. It was touching, albeit frustrating. "Slash is getting out Tuesday, Candy. Don't think for a second this isn't all connected. It's too dangerous a situation for you to just walk in there."

"Too late to talk me out of that." Candy parked her old jalopy of a car and stepped out. "This world used to be my normal, Jose." She paused at the door. "But thanks for caring. Don't call me for the next hour. I'll be in touch."

She hung up with his continued arguments ringing in her ears. A few more and she might lose her nerve. She opened the door and Billy spotted her two steps into the building. His eager beeline toward her was more frightening than had he cursed at her appearance. Why was he glad to see her?

"Where's Champagne?"

She had hoped to get at least a hint of information before having to fake it. "Hi, Billy. Miss me?"

"You were stupid to come during the day." Billy rubbed his hands together like a greedy kid. "I've got the product. Are you ready to give me what I want?"

What did he want? And what was he trading for it? "Depends," she said, her stance easy and casual even as her mind scrambled like a squirrel in the middle of the road with a car bearing down on it. Either way she ran, she might end up road kill. "I want to talk to you about your girls."

He crossed his arms over his massive bulk. "Champagne already gave the conditions for her passwords." He glared and she knew he wished for the freedom to plant his fat palm flat across her face. "I should have known you'd want something for yours. Does Champagne even have any, or was she just playing me?"

"Oh, she has plenty." So Champagne was exchanging her passwords with Billy—or at least pretending to—but why? What had she told Billy that Candy had to do with any of this? "But then there's me."

He leaned against a support beam and Candy pictured it cracking under his weight and the whole building crashing down over them like it did with Samson in the Old Testament. "What do you want for your passwords?" he asked.

Candy's gaze traveled to the darkened hallway that she knew led to darker places of misery and evil. "I want Melanie and Star."

"No."

She shrugged outwardly while praying fervently, urgently on the inside. "Do you want the passwords or not?"

After a quick glance at the camera stationed in the far corner just under the ceiling joist, Billy grabbed her by the arm and pulled her across the room, past the stage, down the hall, and into the storage section of the building. "I'll make a deal with you."

Which sites had Champagne offered him? It had to be more than just his own for him to be this willing to negotiate. "I'm listening," she said. Make it worth my time."

His fingers squeezed around her arm. She'd have a bruise there in a few hours. "When you show up with Champagne for her little packets, I want my site that night. Then go do whatever dumb thing Slash set up to get the rest of the passwords she promised. When I have them all, you can ask Melanie and Star if they want to leave, and if they say yes, I'll let them go."

She snorted. "Don't assume I turned into an idiot the minute I left the life. You'll threaten them into saying they want to stay." Her hands went to her hips. "Do you actually know anybody that gullible?"

He chuckled. "I forgot you've been around a while. The little college girls I get in here believe anything." He opened the door and motioned her out, their meeting clearly over. "I don't blame you for not trusting Champagne, by the way. She's too savvy at this game for her own good. It's going to cost her someday."

She heard the threat in his words. Aware he had not come near promising Melanie and Star's release, yet also aware his fists had clenched and knew from memory that was the sign to stop pushing before things got violent, she made her way back into the main room and forced her legs not to run toward the exit sign. "I'll be in touch," she said, recognizing the irony that she had earlier said the same words to Jose, but with a much different feeling attached to them.

"Bring your little churchy friends with you next time," he said. "Looks less suspicious that way." He laughed. "I actually thought you'd gone over to the other side. Who knew they were a cover to get you back in here spying on me."

She was landlocked now. Until Champagne contacted her, she could not return, and Melanie and Star would be held tighter in Billy's iron grip than ever. Had she only made things worse for all of them? Digging her fingernails into her palms, focusing on the pain it caused to keep from blurting out a few choice Bible verses about oppressors right then and blowing her chance to find out what any of this was about, Candy sent one glance back at Billy, her most convincing plastic smile in place. Guys like Billy always believed such smiles were sincere; they never looked into her eyes to know they never reached that far. "Like I said, I'll be in touch."

"They'll be coming for you soon."

Chapter Eleven
Sunday Evening, January 25

Jean

Dear Jean,

You've probably already guessed that I've gone back home. Your mother hides behind lies. I run away. Neither of us deserves you, Jean. I hope you can enjoy opening the presents. I couldn't bear to stay and see them all again, but I will be back. I took off work for a couple of days. I'll call in the morning to see when would be a good time to visit again, maybe as early as tomorrow if your mother won't be in town.

Please forgive me, Jean, for everything.

Love,

Dad

P.S. Next time I come, I'll bring the doll house I built for your eleventh birthday. It wouldn't fit with all the other presents in the back.

Jean had the letter in the pocket of her gray pants, wrinkled from when she had crumpled it after reading it the first time. She needed to stop thinking about the letter and focus on Grant. He had sent her a text during the evening church service. He never interrupted church times unless it was important, and she had fought fear as she opened the message, only to smile wide at the news that the doctors had finally cleared him to be released—that evening if she could come get him. She had spread the news the moment the service ended, then rushed home to pick up a few food items to stock his refrigerator.

Her father's note had greeted her arrival, taped to the screen door. She had finally gotten a letter from him, but only because he had gone away again.

She drove to the hospital fighting tears. "God, I need to set my own feelings aside and make Grant's release from the hospital a good memory for him," she prayed aloud, searching for a spot in the parking garage. "It's going to be hard enough taking him to the new apartment. I don't want to add to his struggle by unloading my own."

Their church family had already moved his minimal furnishings and possessions from his former apartment to the new one, setting up his new rooms in as similar a fashion to the previous as possible. Jean had arranged all the details. She had tried to involve Grant in as much of the decision making as possible, but he finally declared that if it would be easier, she could just make the choices herself. He didn't really care.

"Did you tell him yet?" Candy asked two hours later from her spot in the passenger seat. Candy had met Jean at the hospital, along with Stewart and Brenda. Jean had suggested Grant ride with his brother. She needed a little more time to settle her emotions.

"No." Jean glanced in the rearview mirror, checking for Stewart's car behind her. "I hope I didn't make a bad decision."

"It was the only decision." Candy unhooked her seat belt when Jean parked in the second closest space to Grant's door. "Oakview isn't Charlotte. All the regular apartment complexes were full up except for upstairs options."

She watched Grant struggle from the backseat of Stewart's car onto the seat of his wheelchair, his jaw tight and face grim, eyes fixed on the sign that welcomed them all to the *Peaceful Lane Senior Center Complex.* "Looks like Stewart might have forgotten to share that bit of information until just now."

Jean remained quiet as they unloaded Grant's things from the hospital and took them inside, but Candy filled all the available space with noise. "I'm a nervous wreck about Tuesday. I want to carry a gun around in case Slash comes straight for me right out of prison, but I'm so jumpy I'm afraid I'd shoot the first person who came up on me unannounced." She held the door open for Stewart, Grant, and then

Jean. "Which is not such a great idea when you work at a coffee shop." She yelled toward the car, "You coming, Brenda? What's that you're eating?"

Brenda got out of the car and kicked the door shut with her foot. "Rainbow sherbet. I had Stewart stop by the grocery store on the way to the hospital."

"You're eating out of the carton? Way to branch out."

Jean looked back to see Candy close the door behind them and ask, "What's stuffed in your coat pocket? Wait, you're pregnant. I bet it's a jar of pickles."

"Nope. Salami."

"With sherbet?" Candy put her hand over her mouth. "I'm gagging here."

Brenda offered to share her sherbet, but no one was in the mood for a party. Jean could not decide if it would be better to have Candy stay and keep chattering, or to endure the silent awkwardness radiating from the rest of them.

Eventually, everyone else left and she faced Grant with uncertainty. "I thought Stewart had told you about this being...well..."

"And old folk's home?"

"This was the only handicap accessible apartment within twenty miles. And it's near the hospital." She hesitated. "And me."

He surveyed the kitchen where they talked. "I'll get over it." He turned toward the hallway. "It was just a shock." He shrugged but she could see how tight his muscles tensed under his sleeves. "Maybe there are some sweet little ladies here who will bake me cookies."

"In the meantime," she said, following him to the second area they had turned into a miniature living room, "I hope you don't mind, but I brought over all those presents." He could see that for himself, as Stewart had carried them in a stack at a time from her trunk before he left. They now filled the entire left corner of the room. "I was hoping I could open them with you?"

"Did you tell your dad where this place is?"

She dropped her face, an old habit so her hair covered her expression. "He's...he's gone. He left me a note." She handed it to him and when the silence lengthened, glanced at Grant. His face was hard.

Angry. She bit her lip. "Will you—will you sit with me while I open the gifts? I really don't want to go through them alone."

He took her hand and nodded. It was the first time he had touched her since they left the hospital. Perhaps her father running away was a gift in disguise. Her need might give Grant something to think about other than his own situation, at least for a while.

She sat at his feet and reached for the first gift. "No, wait," she said suddenly, rising and hunting down her purse. When she extricated her phone, she searched for a signal and said, "Hey, they've got a good wi-fi connection here."

His mouth quirked to the side. "For all those techno-savvy seniors."

She smiled. "You might be surprised." She found the site she wanted and soon had Christmas music playing throughout the room. "Now it feels more like it should." She resumed her place and chose a bright red bag with green tissue paper. "This looks like a Christmas gift. I'll start with it."

An hour later, they were surrounded by children's toys, little girl clothes, socks, music CDs, and costume jewelry. "All those years," Jean whispered. "All that time I thought I was abandoned and forgotten, he was wrapping presents."

Grant touched her hair with tenderness. When she whispered, "I wish I could cry, but don't think I can," he slid from his chair to the floor beside her. After stabilizing his body with his back against the couch, he pulled her into his arms. She settled her face into the curve of his shoulder, one palm against his heart. "Grant, I don't know what to do with it."

"All the presents?"

"No." She glanced at the mound of boxes, torn paper, and gifts. "I'll take the children's things to the women's shelter, and some of the other things, too. It's the love. I don't know what to do with the fact that I was loved all that time but never knew it."

His arms tightened around her. "I guess you can think of it as another gift that's been waiting, and now it's open."

"But where do I put it?"

He kissed her forehead, then rested his cheek against her hair. "Where it was meant to be all along. In your beautiful, soft heart."

She blinked away the tears that threatened to overflow. Now that she could cry, she realized she didn't want to. "It hurts there."

He held her without speaking for a long time, then shifted with an exhale that she knew meant pain. She sat up and moved out of the way while he worked to pull his body up onto the couch. "Well, then, you can store it away until you're ready to get it back out again."

She wiped her eyes and smiled. "You don't have much storage space in this apartment."

He crooked a finger at her and she bent so he could kiss her. "The freezer's empty. How about there?"

Choosing to run with his lighter mood, she crossed to the kitchen and opened the freezer door. "Actually, it's not. Brenda left her sherbet."

"Should we call her?"

"Don't bother." Jean shook her head. "By now she's probably moved on to pancakes with salsa on them or some other weird combination. Yesterday it was salt and vinegar potato chips with chocolate milk." She popped her head around the freezer door. "Want some of the sherbet?"

"After you mentioned pancakes with salsa? No way. What do you say we go out and meet our neighbors?"

She closed the freezer with a grin. "Are you being friendly, or hoping we'll find little old ladies with cookies?"

His smile was good to see. "Yes."

Monday Afternoon, January 26

Champagne

Champagne had to keep busy or she'd go out of her mind. Tomorrow night, she would be in Slash's room, knife in hand, making sure he understood she had ruined him completely. Then she would drive that knife into his heart and watch his eyes as the blood drained from his body and he died.

She was shaking like she had the first time Whip beat her, back when she was young and foolish enough to think she could be free if she was brave enough to escape. She had tried, failed, and got two broken ribs as reward. He had laughed over her, laughed as his boot crashed into her stomach, sneered in triumph at her pain.

Would she sneer when Slash suffered?

Champagne put her head in her hands. Would she even have the nerve to do this? She needed those drugs from Billy, something to calm her nerves even tonight as she waited.

With a sudden idea, she sat at the desk in her hotel room and pulled open her laptop, sliding aside the set of bottles she had bought for the evening. They might numb her enough to endure another sleepless night, but if she could get through Billy's surveillance and see if he left the building at some point, she might be able to sneak in—or convince one of the girls she had business there, enough to let her inside the door—and go find her packets. Billy would keep them in the storage room somewhere. He said he'd have them ready, so they couldn't be too hidden.

It was a long shot, but worth a try. She poured herself a drink and guzzled it in one shot, quick to put her gaze back on the computer. The camera showed the familiar scene of dancers rehearsing, plus a few early stragglers at tables, already drunk, blinking dizzily at the strobe lights. Billy was in his usual booth, counting money. They were going to have to pull the table up from the floor where it was screwed in and move it soon if Billy didn't stop stuffing his face. She imagined him getting wedged between the bench and the table so tightly he could not get free and laughed, thinking of all the ways she could humiliate him while he was trapped by his own blubber.

"They'll be coming for you soon," she said to the image. "After Slash, then the others, you'll be last. The big finale." She took another drink, then a few more, until boredom drove her to search through the past several days' history of surveillance. She had gotten tired of sitting and watching hour after hour, so had begun recording all the digital content, day and night, then searching through it in fast forward to find the evidence police would want.

"It doesn't matter," she told the computer, hearing her words come out a little too slowly. Was she getting drunk? No, she was too smart to get drunk. Not on a day like this. "I already have enough evidence. Don't need any more." But what else was there to do? Nothing on television was interesting enough to keep her thoughts from straying to tomorrow.

She waded through hours of boring daylight footage, until a familiar face came onscreen. Champagne's heart tripped, then beat double time. "Candy?" What was she doing at *Hot Town*?

Shaky fingers pushed buttons. Candy spoke with Billy too far from the camera for it to pick up their voices. After about five minutes, Billy looked up, straight at Champagne, and she pushed her chair back away from the desk. "He can't see you," she said out loud to herself. "He's just looking at the camera."

Champagne watched as Billy took Candy by the arm and dragged her out of site. He had headed toward the hallway and the storage room. Had he given Candy Champagne's packets? Had Candy told him Champagne was the one who really had all the passwords? Did he know everything?

She had to leave the hotel. Now. Before he came for her. There was no way she was letting him, or anyone, get to her tonight.

Swigging down the last of one bottle and stashing two more into a bag to take with her, Champagne hunted for her car keys and a few dollars in cash. "Can't use a card. Nothing traceable. Just in case." She tripped over a pair of heeled shoes, then checked to see if her feet were bare or not. "Flip flops on. Good. Gotta go. Right away."

She decided not to take the time to shut the computer down. If Billy came, it wouldn't matter if her computer was open and her files exposed. He could get everything off there, take the laptop itself, but in the end, only she knew the word he wanted most. Not a list of passwords. Just one. The name of the person she would kill for.

If Billy found her, tortured her, she might give in and say it. If only she had time to change it now, switch it out for a bunch of different passwords, hard ones that no one could guess.

She opened the hotel door, bottle in one hand, keys in the other. With one look back at the screen, she left with the words, "Candy, what have you done?"

"Long engagements are ridiculous."

Chapter Twelve
Late Monday Afternoon, January 26

Grant

Jean's father returned thirty minutes after Jean got off work on Monday, giving her time to pick up Grant at his apartment, but not enough time to clean up all the gift wrap they had left strewn across his living room the night before. He wanted to stay out of the entire scenario, but for Jean to leave that kind of clutter unattended was out of character enough to have him concerned. Having her father show up, leave, and come again had to be tough, and he wasn't going to let her go through it alone.

Charles Jameson carried in a large dollhouse which he set in the corner of the living room. "Built it from scratch myself," he told Grant, "as I did this house."

Jean exclaimed over the miniature structure, touching each tiny piece of furniture and noting similarities to the architecture of the family home. "I love it, Dad. Thank you." She appeared to Grant as if she would like to hug her father or perhaps be hugged, but of course Charles Jameson would not know the slight signals Grant had learned to read Jean's body language. She glanced his way and he winked. Her face relaxed into a smile.

Her father, after a short-lived attempt at small talk about the weather, unloaded a long rolled sheet, yellowed with age, that he had carried in with the dollhouse. He unrolled the paper across the dining room table and Grant wheeled over to see a set of blueprints.

"That's this house."

"It is." Charles slid his hands to the sides to flatten the paper. Jean went to the kitchen and returned with four mugs to hold down the corners.

"Are you planning some renovations?" Grant asked hesitantly. Jean's mother was forever trying to redecorate when she visited. It would not surprise Grant if Jean's father decided to change the house structure while he was in town. "I replaced a bunch of the planks on the porch floorboard that were weathered and creaking. I was going to repair the spindles that had started to rot, but didn't get to it before—"

Mr. Jameson was studying his paper, his index finger traveling through the house like it was on tour. "I've been marking the sections that will need rebuilding if you're going to make this house workable for your wheelchair."

Grant's throat tightened. He looked to Jean, who put her palm against her heart. "Dad, that's an amazing idea," she said, "but we don't have the money to make this house handicap accessible."

"Maybe not fully, but there's a lot you can do that will help." He gestured into the living room. "For starters, you can take out the excess furniture so there's more room for him to get around." He frowned. "And get rid of that stupid Oriental rug. Even if it wasn't ugly, it's like a speed bump right in the middle of the floor."

"But Mother made me promise not to—" Jean looked at him and flushed. She clasped her hands together in front of her. "You're right. I'll see if she wants it back, and if not, it goes in the basement."

"Should go to the dump if you ask me," her father grumbled. "Always hated that rug." He glanced at his daughter and quickly put his attention back on his blueprints. He cleared his throat. "Grant, while Jean moves things around inside, how about you and I take this out and talk over some of my ideas?"

"That okay with you, Jean?" Grant asked. "It is your house, after all."

She smiled her appreciation and came near. She leaned over, as if to kiss him, but stopped herself and instead put her fingers to the back of his neck, playing for a moment with the edge of his hairline where his hair curled at the ends. He shivered. She could do that all day and he would never get tired of how good it felt. "I think it's a great idea," she said. She did lean over then and pressed a kiss to the top of his head. "And I'm sorry I didn't think to clear things out more for you a long time ago. I guess I didn't want you to think I wasn't optimistic about you walking again."

"Optimism is great," her father put in, "but it will be quite a setback if he breaks his back trying to go up that makeshift, two-board ramp somebody set up over the stairs to the front door. That will be our first project. Did you keep the weathered boards you took up from the porch?" he asked Grant.

Grant turned his chair toward the door with a nod. "They're in the shed. At least twenty of them."

"Good. We can use any that don't have dry rot to build your ramp." He pointed at the plans. "We'll put it up the left half of the porch steps, leaving the right half for the regular stairs."

Grant gestured down at his legs. "We?"

Charles Jameson shrugged. "Can you still swing a hammer?"

"Sure can."

"Good enough. Let's get to work."

Grant soon found himself out of his chair and on the steps leading to the porch, multiple two-by-fours lined at his side and a hammer and nails within reach. As soon as he'd stepped outside, Jean's father had gone from a rather gangly and awkward middle-aged man to a carpenter in his element. Grant couldn't blame him. After fifteen years gone, it would be hard to take up the father role again. He did not seem to know what to do around Jean, but he knew his way around a set of blueprints and tools.

As they worked, Grant wondered aloud what had made Charles finally come back.

"I saw about the shooting on the news," Charles said, laying several boards in a row on the grass for the main part of the ramp, removing one that curled at the ends and replacing it with another. "The story ran nationwide."

"Don't I know it," Grant muttered. "I still get hounded by reporters sometimes."

Charles found three more boards to lay crosswise over the original row as joists and used his nail gun to secure them in place. After three or four of the sharp, popping sounds filled the air, the front door opened and Jean ran out, her face white. "Oh," she gasped when she saw the nail gun. "Oh, it's okay. Everything's okay."

Her hands twisted in front of her and her eyes were wide. Grant reached out but was too far away to touch her. "Jean, are you alright?"

"Fine." Her voice was thin and high. "It just sounded like—I thought—it doesn't matter." She pivoted and ran back into the house, letting the screen slam behind her.

Grant turned to ask Jean's father if he knew what Jean's puzzling reaction meant, but his gaze passed her garden, the patch still mangled from where he had fallen in the dirt and she had knelt and pressed towels against his back and head to staunch the blood. "The nail gun. It sounded like gunshots."

Charles looked over the piece of equipment. "It makes things go a lot faster, and easier."

Grant could hear chairs being slid across the floor. He pictured the scratches being made across the wooden finish, but was not going to say a word. "Faster isn't always better."

Jean's father set the nail gun aside and picked up the hammer. "Guess we'll go the old-fashioned way." He started pounding in nails, talking between strikes. "When I saw on TV what had happened, and that Jean had saved your life at the risk of her own, it was a wakeup call to me. Life isn't something we can take for granted, and I realized I could have lost Jean before I ever got to see her again."

He finished the joists and started nailing the old slats across them. "I watched all the news outlets, but none of them showed a picture of her."

Grant handed over tools as needed. "She was a potential target. It was dangerous."

He nodded. "Wise move, but it was killing me. I needed to see her to know she was okay. Finally, I decided it was time to come home. That was no quick decision, let me tell you." He asked for another three boards. "It's a lot easier to keep things as they are, even if the way they are isn't right."

Grant thought of Champagne, of the times they had offered her escape and she had chosen to stay trapped, and nodded. "Seems it is."

"But I'm here now, and I hope that doing this, making the house better for you, will be the start of making up for all the times I should have been here fixing things and wasn't."

Grant wanted to say that Jean would probably prefer time with him more than projects done for her. But people loved in different ways, and this was clearly his way of loving, just as Grant's purchase of the porch swing had been love, and ordering that pot fixed with gold for her. What had ever happened with that? The site said it would take a while to ship, but it had been months now. He should check the tracking, if they did tracking from China.

"Help me hold these boards upright for the side rails, will you?"

Grant positioned his body so he could assist. It felt good, working with his hands again. Maybe there were other projects he could help with around the house that he had not thought he would have the ability to do. None of this meant he was giving up on walking again, but like his physical therapist had said back when he was still in the hospital—and not inclined to listen—he should still live well now, with what he had.

He had his life, his faith, and Jean. And now it seemed he was getting a father-in-law, with a revamped house to boot.

"What else can I do?" he asked. "We've got some good daylight left. I'm ready to work."

Monday Night, January 26

Jean

Jean pushed Grant's chair through the tiny living room, right at the kitchen area, down the small alcove that pretended to be a hallway, to Grant's bedroom on the left.

"My muscles are going to be sore tomorrow," Grant commented. "Working with your dad was better than a therapy session."

"Did you see the second set of blueprints he brought, with all the changes he wants to make? I'm glad he wants to help, but I wish he'd listen about the money not being there to go all out like he'd like to."

"Neither of your parents seem all that great at listening."

She took her purse from where she'd hung it on one of the rungs behind Grant's chair and set it on his dresser, shaking her head as she dug for her car keys. "I don't want to think about that tonight. I'll get going before both of us get overwhelmed."

"Don't go yet." He reached out a hand. "There's something I want to talk to you about." He dropped his hand to the bed. "It may not be a good place, or the right time, but I'm not sure there is one."

"I'm intrigued." She approached his bed. "What do you want to talk about?"

"Sex."

The keys in her hand fell with a clatter. She bent to pick them up from where they landed on her right foot. She kept her face down as if that foot held great interest, and tried to say casually, "What about...it?"

He chuckled. "You still can't even say the word. I know there's no way to talk about this without it being awkward, but...I'm sure you've wondered. I mean, we are still planning on getting married. Jean...." He waited until she forced herself to look at him. "Come over here, please."

She moved toward him, but slowly, feeling like she had at age sixteen when she worked her first fast food job and some guy coming through the drive through told her she was pretty enough to eat. An armchair sat on the opposite side of the room under the one small window. Jean started to pull it toward the bed.

"No, Jean, come sit beside me. It's okay. I promise I won't bite." He grinned. "No matter how much I might want to."

"Grant, really. We shouldn't be talking about this here, in your room."

He grinned. "It's funny. If I wasn't paralyzed, people would think it was scandalous, you coming into my apartment late at night, coming into my bedroom and sitting on the edge of my bed."

"They wouldn't be the only ones." Jean sat down, but placed herself so far on the edge she had to put a hand on the mattress to keep from tipping onto the floor. "If you weren't paralyzed, I wouldn't be in your bedroom late at night. I wouldn't be in your apartment alone with you at all."

His grin spread. "Afraid I'd get too tempted?"

She ducked her head. "Not you."

His finger found her chin and nudged it upward. "Jean Louise Jameson, I do believe you're blushing."

She dared a glance at his face, smiled, then pushed his hand away. "Grant, for goodness sake."

"Okay, okay, I'll be serious." He folded his hands in his lap. "I don't know if you've talked to the doctors, but I have, and..." He twiddled his thumbs in circles around each other. "Now I'm the one feeling awkward. There's no other way to really say it than to tell you that I'm not sure, no one is sure, how, or if, things are going to work with me when we get married. With my body. I know we both expect and hope that this isn't forever, but I can't ignore the reality that it might be. I don't want you to go into marriage with false expectations." He stared at his hands. His thumbs had stopped rotating. "Truth is, Jean, I don't want you to be disappointed."

Her self-consciousness faded. Jean scooted fully onto the bed and put her hand over his heart. "I have thought about it," she said. "Do you remember when we first got engaged and I was the one having this conversation with you?"

His eyes met hers and he cocked his head. "No."

"With everything that had happened, with as scared as I was every time you touched me, I didn't know if I would be able to enjoy..." She paused. Gracious, they were almost married. She should be able to say it. "...the married part of being married." She smiled. "Do you remember how you responded?"

His hands unfolded and he lifted one to touch her cheek, the skin on his fingers smooth. His time in the hospital had not been one of inactivity, but it was not the hard work he was used to. Even his hands portrayed the change. "I told you it didn't matter," he said softly. "That we'd take it as slowly as we needed to. That we'd enjoy learning to love each other without expectations."

She nodded and her gaze was filled with love. "That's what I needed, and it hasn't changed." She shrugged. "Maybe we'll be on the same speed now. I knew it might take some time to be able to love you with joy as God intends, without my mind going to a dark place and taking that away from us, and it seems to me it's kind of the same with your body. It might take time, or it might not, but I'm not afraid of that journey, and I'm not afraid of traveling it with you." She mimicked his action, cupping his cheek with one of her palms. "I never traveled, at all. You know why. But now that I can, I think I'd be more the type to take it slow and stop often to see the sights, go exploring, instead of wanting to drive straight through just to get to the destination."

He tapped his finger under her chin. "Are you giving me a metaphor, my love? Saying we should enjoy the journey on our honeymoon, physically?" He laughed again. "Or are you telling me you want to go on a road trip like Florence and Doug?"

"Oh heavens, please no." She brushed hair out of her face and put a hand to her throat. "My ten minutes in Florence's camper was enough. The jostling from us walking around, when it wasn't even in drive, was enough to make me want to throw up."

He laughed. "That doesn't sound like a good honeymoon activity to me." He pulled her face toward his. "Let's wait on the nausea till you're expecting our first baby."

She felt herself blushing furiously and pulled away before he could kiss her. He smiled that smile that only came when he was teasing her and loving it. "Whatever happens, Jean Jameson, I have a feeling you and I are going to have a lot of fun on our honeymoon."

She tried pulling farther back so she could stand and escape to the bathroom, needing cold water on her burning cheeks, but he snaked one arm around her waist and with his other hand still behind her head, he leaned forward and captured her lips with his own. When she melted against him, he pulled back just long enough to whisper, "I love you, Jean," before kissing her again. When he released her, it was with a sigh. "And now you'd better go, before I forget that we're not married yet."

He folded his hands in his lap again and leaned back against the wrought iron headboard. "How many days until the wedding now?"

She had her hands to her cheeks. "Ninety-six."

He shook his head. "Long engagements are ridiculous."

She smiled. "It's barely more than three months. Most people wouldn't think that's a very long time."

His grin came back. "Most people aren't marrying you."

She fanned her face. "That, Mr. Henderson, was a very good line." She stood and caught herself arranging the comforter where she'd sat to straighten it again. "I hope you have sweet dreams tonight."

"I would if we were getting married sooner."

"You can talk to my mother about that."

"Now I'm going to have nightmares."

She laughed and flipped the light switch. The room went dark. "Oh, wait." She turned it back on. "You're not ready for bed yet, are you?"

"No, I'll stay up for a bit. Good night, Jean."

She glanced back at the man she loved, sitting on his bed in the sparsely furnished, undecorated apartment. When they were married, she would do her best to fill his heart and life with beautiful things, as she would his home. "Good night, Grant."

"I wish
I could have
said goodbye
to Candy."

Chapter Thirteen
Late Monday Night, January 26

Grant

"I've been waiting for you."

The voice was soft, hidden in shadows, as she was. Grant did not outwardly react to the words. Inside, however, everything began to churn. Rage built. He was surprised at the ferocity of it, how quickly it was rebirthed.

"Champagne." He did not need to see her. He still heard her voice in his dreams, where she held the gun that took his future, his present.

"You don't have any curtains on your windows," she said. "I watched you say goodnight to Jean. You smiled at her. You pretended you're okay." Her voice was slow and her words drawn out. "But when she drove away you came out here, looking up at the sky and hating the God who let this happen to you."

He looked into the darkness behind the trees lining the apartment sidewalks. Where was she? Why had she come to torment him? Or was this another one of his nightmares?

"Maybe you're not hating God." She sauntered into the light. He was surprised to see she was not dressed as she had been the night she deceived him and Stewart into getting their picture in the paper, or the night she had come to stay at Jean's house, broken and bloodied. She wore ragged sweatpants and a wrinkled t-shirt under an open-zippered hoodie. Her hair, wild around her face, looked as if she had slept in it and not bothered to check a mirror when she got up. In her hands was a bottle of beer wrapped in a brown paper bag like a bad cliché. With her other hand she steadied herself against a tree near the parking spaces along the sidewalk where he sat. Her voice slurred. "Maybe you're just asking God why."

She was drunk. He thought of turning his wheels and going inside, slamming the door behind him, letting her know there was nothing she could say that he wanted to hear. Except that it wasn't true.

"Or maybe you're looking up, just hating me, asking God to rain down wrath on your enemies. Me and Slash. Slash and me."

Bile rose in his throat and wanted to come out in bitter words, till his mind kicked in gear. "You're a wanted woman, Champagne. One phone call and you're in jail for life."

"But you didn't bring your phone, did you?" she slurred.

He grabbed for his pocket and realized she was right.

"I came...to tell you something...very important." The words sliding through her lips were barely understandable. She staggered toward him and pointed with the hand that held the bottle. "You...do you know that Slash gets out tomorrow?" She slid her hand to the right. "Doesn't matter. He gets out tomorrow, and I'm gonna get him. And after that..." She fell and landed on one knee, and had to try twice to stand upright again. "After that, they're all gonna come after me. I'm a dead woman, Grant." Her lips curled. "You don't have to pretend to be sad about that."

He wished his cranky neighbor was watching out the window and would call 911 for Champagne obstructing the peace.

"But when it's all done, when it's all over..." She pointed at him again. "I want you to know I did it. I did it aaaaall." She put her hands out in a wide, sweeping gesture, then had to use them to keep herself upright. "I did it all, it was me. I made it right." She wiped at her cheeks, and then looked at his legs. "As much as I could." Her reddened eyelids sagged. "And now I'm going to sleep."

She dropped there in the parking lot and laid her head down on her arm over the top of one of the concrete slabs that stopped absentminded tenants from driving into the apartment building, which according to the neighbor had happened twice the past year. Grant's fingers curled around the wheels of his chair. He turned slightly right, then left, battling his two options. Should he grab her first and somehow tie her to a tree or drag her inside so she couldn't get away? Or should he rush inside and call Jose, hoping she wouldn't wake up before he got back with a rope?

He jerked the wheelchair to the right, almost running into another human. "Jean!"

"Shh." She held a finger to her lips, her other hand on the arm of his chair to keep it from crashing into her legs.

"Jean," he whispered urgently, "call Jose. Call 911. Champagne—"

"I know." She held out her phone. "Jose is on his way."

"What are you doing here?"

Her cheeks flushed. "I left my purse on your dresser. You had me so distracted I didn't even notice until—"

"Hey there, Jean."

Grant jumped and turned. Champagne was still lying in the parking space, but had lifted her head and was regarding them both with a sleepy gaze. "I missed you. Can you believe that? It's true. No need for me to lie anymore." She waved at them. "I'm going to die soon, so might as well tell the truth. Last confession and all." She swung her bottle of beer. "You know, I wish I could have said goodbye to Candy. She was my only friend for a long, long time. She gave me a Bible, did you know that?" She took a swig from the bottle, then shook it, top down. "Iss empty." She tossed it and the bag into the yard. His cranky neighbor in the apartment to his left was going to love finding that tomorrow. "Told me to look for the prostitutes. Never had anyone say that to me about the Bible before. Read the book of John, she said. So I did. I found them. And Jesus. She said I would find everything I needed to know." Her voice became a wistful, painful sigh. "Even back then there were people like the ones I've met all my life, the ones who told me to straighten up, and even if I had straightened up never would have accepted me."

She rose to her knees. "They thought I was trash and said so. It's not like they were telling me anything I didn't know." She fell back again, scraping her elbow on the concrete slab. "But it still hurt. Still hurts." She rubbed her elbow. "You can cut yourself a thousand times, but it still hurts when someone else does it. I know. Slash made his mark on me."

She sat up and turned. "Have you seen it?" She lifted her hair. It was too dark to see much more than one thick line across her neck, but still it made Grant's insides clench tight. Jean shuddered beside him.

"Jesus wasn't like any of them." Champagne pulled her knees up to her chest and wrapped her arms around them. She laid her head down and Grant thought she drifted off until she mumbled, "But at some point, it's too late, right? People like Slash. People like me. People like Candy." She slowly lifted her head, confusion on her face. "But Candy—"

An unmarked police car pulled into the lot, lights off.

Champagne groaned. "No. No, no, no. I have to go. Tomorrow I have to fix it."

Jose exited the car, handcuffs in hand. Champagne started crying. "You don't understand! Jean, tell them not to take me in. If I'm in jail, I can't make it right. Slash is getting out tomorrow. Don't you know what he'll do if I don't stop him?"

Jose put her in the back of the police car, which was still running. "I'll call you in the morning," he said to Grant. "Thank you, Jean, for the phone call."

The car pulled away, the silence engulfing them both as thick as the darkness around them. Jean was the one to break it. "Grant," she whispered, "did we do the right thing?"

Grant stared into the bushes, where his neighbor would find a beer bottle the next day and probably blame him for it. "I don't know," he admitted. He suddenly felt weary inside and out. "I don't know."

Late Monday Night, January 26

Candy

Candy walked down the aisle of the empty church auditorium. "I need some time with You, Lord. Just You. No people. No distractions. No floor-to-ceiling windows that would shatter with one good bullet. I know You're everywhere, but *Jamaica's Place* is too full of memories tonight. I figured Your place would be better."

She stopped midway and retraced her steps, flipping on half the light switches to illuminate the front section of the building. "The atmosphere is nice," she said softly, "with the moonlight coming through the stain-glass windows, but I keep getting scary vibes that Slash is going to jump out from behind one of these pews." She shivered and rubbed her arms. "He's not even out yet. Lord, what am I going to do tomorrow?"

This time, halfway down the aisle she saw the box set on the third step leading to the pulpit. She had bowed there once, thrown herself down really, at that same spot the day she'd given her old life to Jesus and asked for a new one.

"Is that for me?" she asked God. "A sign? A present?"

With eager steps, she approached the box, looked inside, then heard the echo of her own laughter ring throughout the auditorium. "A box of broken pieces. Did I need more? Are You trying to tell me something here?" A laugh shot out again. "I already know I can't fix things. That's why I'm here, asking for help."

She picked up the box and on closer inspection recognized the contents. "This is Jean's," she whispered. "She showed me a picture of it the day after Grant ordered it. She was so excited..." What had happened? About half the pieces were edged in gold, and not the glitter kind Candy had tried to use. Who could have broken something so precious? "I need to call Jean. No, I'll go to her house." Had Jean brought the broken pieces here? Had she laid them at the altar, giving them over to God?

Candy sat on the front pew and held the box of shards in her lap. Brenda's borrowed church key, in her right back pocket, gouged into her hip. "Well, God, I came to talk to You about the people I love, the people I'm afraid for, but is this a message from You that I need to go find Jean instead? You know, it'd be a lot easier if You'd just speak down from heaven, or call my cell."

The phone in her left pocket rang, and Candy jumped clear off the pew and into the aisle. The box fell to the floor and clay pieces scattered. She dug into her pocket and answered the call, her voice shaky. "Ye-yes?"

"Where are you?"

She almost answered, "In Your house," but caught herself. God already knew where she was, so it couldn't be Him. "Who is this?"

"It's Jose. I know it's late, but can you come to my office tonight? It's important."

Candy dropped to her knees and used her free hand to begin gathering the turquoise shaded shards, carefully placing them back in the box. "You would not believe who I thought you were," she said with a breathless laugh at herself. "I'm at church and—"

"Candy, focus."

"Right." She crawled under the second pew where one of the shards had escaped. How did a piece of clay with only sharp edges roll like that? "We need to talk about Champagne, and Billy Bradon, and whatever they've got going on to—"

"Candy."

She stretched and got two fingers onto the last wayward piece. "Got you," she muttered, nudging it backwards until she could pick it up.

"Candy, can you get over here?"

She set the piece on top of the pile, stood, then bent over to pick up the box. "You're not asking me on a date, are you?"

"Candy..."

"Whatever. Anyway, about Champagne—"

"She's here."

Candy headed back toward the foyer and the light switches. "In Oakview, I know. That's what—"

"In my office."

"I'm coming already. Give me a minute, will you?"

"Candy, some days I think you are deliberately trying to drive me insane." Exasperation came through the phone. "Would you please stop whatever you're doing and listen to me for five seconds?"

She turned the lights off in the auditorium, tucked the phone between her cheek and shoulder, and pulled the church key from her pocket. "I'm listening, Jose."

"Champagne is in my office."

He had to be joking. "She came to see you?"

"No, she went to see Grant. Jean called me and I arrested her."

"I need to talk to Jean—wait, what?" Candy dropped the key. She reached to retrieve it and the phone fell from her shoulder. "Hang on!" she yelled. "Don't say anything important." With a flustered breath, she sat on the floor, set the box and key beside her crossed legs, and put the phone on speaker. "Did you say you arrested Champagne and she's in your office?"

"Yes. She says she has the passwords and more, everything we need to get Slash life without parole. But there's a catch."

Candy was already on her feet. She'd have to get the key back to Brenda, and the box to Jean, some other time. They'd be safe in the backseat of her car for now. "I'm on my way," she told Jose. She glanced back at the church before she reached her car. "Thanks," she whispered upward, then spoke into the phone. "Tell me everything."

He would
go see her,
the woman
of his
first wound.

Chapter Fourteen
Early Tuesday Morning, January 27

Slash

"See that scum?" Officer Davis pointed to a green line of mold inching its way up the drainpipe on the outer corner of the prison wall, just outside the door they exited. "That's you, Slash."

Slash did not pause to look closer, but picked up his pace to where Whip waited with his rusty old truck. His gaze darted right and left, wary of someone running forward at the last minute with enough evidence to send him back inside.

"Solitary got to you, didn't it?" Davis said without sympathy. "I wish we could have dug a hole in the dirt and thrown you in pitch black darkness."

Slash did not ask if he meant for sixty more days, or permanently. Just the thought of being confined in a dark and silent space again had sweat beading down his temples.

He faked his old arrogance. "I know you all hate me," he said. "No need to be indirect about it."

Davis' jaw clenched. "Don't we have good reason to?"

He had killed a sheriff. One of their own. "A lot of people have good reason to."

"How many, do you think?"

Davis was playing with him now? Trying to make him feel guilty? "Hundreds." He shrugged like it didn't matter, but their faces swam before his vision. Face after face after face. Some still alive. Some dead. "Everybody I've ever met maybe."

"Your mother probably doesn't even love you."

Slash stiffened. Fire returned to his veins. "Don't talk about her."

Davis chuckled. "Touchy subject?" He grabbed Slash's arm and pulled him onward. Whip saw them coming and started the engine. The truck belched smoke and gargled exhaust. "I bet you were a horrible kid."

"I was a good kid. I was."

"I'll believe that when I talk to your mother."

"Can't."

Davis eyed him. "Did you kill her?"

The fire inside spread. "No."

Slash could tell it took restraint for Davis to keep from shoving him forcibly into the truck. "You may be legally free for now," he said, voice hard, "but every guy in law enforcement here to Edison is waiting for the moment you slip up and we can put you away for good."

"Thanks for the warning."

Davis slammed the car door. "Not a warning. Just a fact."

Whip put the truck in drive and Slash did not have to tell him to speed once they left the parking lot. "He sure hates you," Whip said with a laugh. "It's got to dig under his craw that you've done every bad thing there is to do, but they can't get you on any of it."

He laughed again but Slash did not. Every bad thing. It was true. Those last days in lockdown he had read the Old Testament. The commands he had broken. The judgement he deserved. God's wrath was coming for him; he could feel it. The terror of it leeched all the courage from his body, soaked down through his bones to his very soul.

"What next, Boss?" Whip pulled up to the hotel where Slash had stationed himself and sold others, night after night, for so long. "How are you going to get those people who ruined your plan?"

Their names were still on his list. He should be reading them, strategizing how to devour their futures and destroy their hopes. But he just didn't care. What would more crime accomplish except to add to his huge, grotesque pile of sins?

Candy had accomplished her ultimate revenge. That Bible she had given him had not set him free. It had stamped out any flicker of happiness he might have had left in this life, and convinced him of his utter doom after death. She had destroyed him.

"Just drop me off," he told Whip.

"Okay, Boss." Whip was being extra nice, probably hoping for a job that would get him a fat handful of cash. "Say," Whip commented after glancing his way, "is that a Bible in your hands?"

Slash opened the truck door. "Get me a car and leave it in my space." He exited and took weary steps to the hotel's side entrance. Trash littered the walkway and old, torn cobwebs decorated the door corners like leftover Halloween decorations. He'd never noticed how ratty and old the hotel had gotten over the years. Like him, he supposed.

He locked himself inside the room kept under one of his fake names and immediately turned on the TV for noise. Tonight, he would open Candy's Bible and read the rest. The whole New Testament. Finish his condemnation by God and add it to his condemnation by all those who hated him here on earth.

Tomorrow he would get on the computer and get his life back. No, there was something else he needed to do first. He would go see her, the woman of his first wound. She was in that tiny town he had stayed away from for thirty years. He would go back and ask her why.

She would not answer. He knew that. But the going, remembering the pain, might be the only way to renew any life into whatever years he had left.

He needed that, because now, with no hope after death for anything but hell, this life, and the old pleasures of revenge, meager and pathetic as they were, were all he had left.

Tuesday Afternoon, January 27

Jean

Jean covered her yawn with her hand. What she wouldn't give for a mushy pillow and an air mattress to spread on the floor. She considered stretching out on the hospital waiting room bench, just for a ten minute nap while Grant was gone.

"That's the third time you've yawned since we got here five minutes ago," Candy said. "You need to get outside."

Jean shook her head. "It's therapy day. I need to be here."

Candy took her arm and pulled her to her feet. "You're not attached at the hip to the man." She cringed. "Which is a good thing, since you'd have a hard time fitting both of you in his chair. Come on, Jean. Grant will be in therapy for at least two hours. Let's go to a park."

Jean dragged her feet like a child. "Slash just got released from prison this morning. I'd think this is the last time you'd want to be walking around out in the open."

"I thought of that." Candy did not seem affected in the slightest by Jean's reticence. She pulled harder on Jean's arm until Jean's feet slid on the laminate flooring and she had to walk to keep from falling. "We can go to that little town outside Charlotte, remember? The one I told you that Slash hates and never goes to?"

"Do we have to?"

"Please, Jean. I'd go back to Jose's precinct, but until Champagne sleeps off her mega hangover, she's worthless as far as getting any information, and I'm going crazy not being able to find out what's going on."

Jean sighed as she swallowed. The antiseptic hospital smell was getting to her today. "Okay, but we have to be back by three so I can drive Grant back to his apartment."

"Good enough. That gives us enough time for a stop at the ice cream place on the way back."

Jean followed Candy to the elevator at the end of the long hall. "You didn't say anything about stopping for ice cream, too."

"You say that like I'm trying to sneak something bad into the agenda. It's ice cream, girl! We can get a huge four-scoop sundae to split and forget all our troubles."

"Till you get a stomachache from all that dairy."

Candy pushed a button and they started downward. "I'm going to start calling you Gladys if you don't let up."

Jean almost laughed but another yawn overtook her instead.

The elevator doors opened on the main floor leading to the parking garage. Jean pulled car keys from her purse.

"Could I drive?" Candy asked, hand out. "I don't trust you to stay awake. It'll take about forty-five minutes to get there."

Jean nodded gratefully. "You drive. I'll nap. How about that?"

Candy started up her car and the hum of the engine, and the lack of medical machines beeping, lulled Jean to sleep before they were out onto the main road. She was nudged awake by a somewhat gentle poke in the ribs. "Hey," Candy said, "we're here, in Millville. It's a tiny town. Don't blink or you'll miss it."

Jean stretched, already feeling refreshed. Candy pulled into a parking lot that lined a large grassy, fenced-in area containing a playground, lake and graveyard. "This is pretty," Jean commented as they made their way up the sidewalk beside the graves. "But kind of strange. I would feel odd bringing my children to play right next to a cemetery."

"I wouldn't." The sidewalk forked and Candy took the left branch into the graveyard, touching one of the larger headstones. It came up to her waist and was wide enough to showcase the names of a man and his wife, with a long epitaph on their lives carved into the stone. "When I was little we lived in a city, and the only grass for miles was in the cemetery. Grandma and I would walk there and feed the ducks in the lake. I'd go around reading the gravestones and wondering about the people's lives. Cemeteries have always felt really peaceful to me."

Wind whipped Jean's hair across her face. She pulled her coat tight about her. "Maybe today isn't such a good day for a walk after all."

"It does seem to be getting colder." Candy wiped a fallen dead leaf off Jean's shoulder. "We should—"

Her words halted to a stop with such a choking sound of sudden fright that Jean looked behind her to see what had caused it. Headstones lined the walkway, shadowed by tree limbs made barren by the winter cold. One man knelt at a grave, weeping. His coat lay on the ground next to his feet. A scar around his neck told of great suffering he must have endured. Jean's heart went out to him.

She jerked back when he pressed both hands onto the dirt over the grave, fisted them full of soil, and threw the soil at the headstone with a cry of hatred, or desperation, or both.

"Slash."

Candy said the word from behind her, just loud enough to reach Jean's ears. Jean immediately started trembling. "Are you sure?"

The man stood and Candy's voice held a fear Jean had never heard in it before. "I can't let him see me. I can't." Jean felt Candy grab the back of her shirt and pull tight. "Jean, what do I do? Help me!"

Slash wiped his hands free of dirt then put on his long coat. Watching him gave Jean an idea. "Hide behind the gravestone. Use your coat to cover your hair and shirt." Candy's hair was pale blonde and her shirt bright pink. Fortunately, her black coat would blend in with the shadows.

Candy jumped behind the gravestone and was covered in seconds. "What about you?" she whispered from her hiding place. "There's not enough room for both of us."

"Shh," Jean told her. "He's walking this way. I've never seen him before, so he won't recognize me."

Candy started praying out loud and Jean had to shush her again. She kept a hand on the headstone to keep steady as he approached. She should turn and look down at the grave, as if she had come to visit whoever was laid to rest there, but she could not tear her eyes away from this man, this evil in human form. He had trafficked Candy and Champagne. He was the reason the man she loved still at times had trouble knowing what wordless road signs meant or finding a simple word to express a thought. He killed Susan and Ian.

The lines of darkness from the shadows above crossed over the oily hair down to his shoulders, the broken nose, the scar circling his neck like a terrible necklace. He was not a large man, not intimidating aside from his wounds and the horrible knowledge of all he had done.

As he neared, Jean studied his face. It was not angry, as she expected. Only steps away now, she could see it was filled with despair.

He was in front of the headstone where she stood before he glanced at her. Jean had been holding her breath, praying Candy would keep calm, and if not calm, at least keep quiet enough for him to pass by without noticing either of them.

Slash stopped and stared at her. His face paled. Had he heard something? Did he somehow sense Candy was near?

Jean did not know what to do. She stared back at this man, this murderer, shocked, blindsided when he asked in a whisper, "Mother?"

Was his mother's grave the one he had visited? She heard a shift behind the headstone and tried to cover it with sound. "I'm Jean," she said.

"Jean." He continued to stare. "You look so much like her."

"Like who?"

He took a step closer. "The woman who destroyed me."

Jean's breathing had gone shallow. He was too close. She could feel Candy's intense need to run. Or she might just be feeling her own. "I am Jean Jameson," she heard herself say. "You put my fiancé in the hospital with a bullet in his skull and another in his back. He may never walk again." She heard anger and fear and pain in her voice, and did not mask them. "You killed my friends."

He staggered backward, as if afraid of her. "You're Jean," he said again.

She stood tall, on behalf of Grant, who might never stand again. "Yes."

He backed away from her until he was on the sidewalk again. "You're the reason my plan failed. Why I got put in lockdown." His eyes, wide and bloodshot, centered on her face. "Destroying me again. You *are* her."

Jean's heartbeat pounded in her ears, louder than the wind, masking the sound of Slash's boots on the concrete as he hurried away. She barely heard Candy's whimper from her hiding place, or her whispered question, "Is he gone?"

She watched until he was out of sight. "He's...gone."

Candy threw the coat off her head and came to stand close beside Jean. "What happened? You look like you've seen a ghost."

What had it meant? His eyes had been full of horror, and then something worse. Something evil. Suddenly, she was terrified, too. Not for Candy. For herself. "I didn't," Jean whispered, "but he did."

Once he
had her
home address,
the rest
would be
easy.

Chapter Fifteen
Late Tuesday Night, January 27

Slash

Jean Jameson. The TV had not shown pictures of her the night her fiancé was shot. The night she shot Monty and Jake. Was his mind playing tricks on him? Transforming his memories? It had been so long since he had seen her face. So long since she drove away that night, drunk, and ran into a tree, leaving the world before he had learned how to punish those who hurt him.

He had never missed the opportunity again. He had made them pay. Every person who hurt him, and many more. Every woman he marked, every woman he sold, was her.

But it was never enough.

If he got this one, this woman so like her, would that complete the circle? If he could run his knife across her neck, would it finally give him peace?

He shut the door to his hotel room, locked it, and dropped his head against the frame. There was no hope for real peace. It didn't exist. But if he could find some way to ease his torment, he had to try. He had no stomach for a night of searching online, contacting old connections, starting up the lucrative business of buying and selling bodies again. What did it matter? What good was money, or power, or even lust anymore?

His hired crony, Monty, had told him Candy and this woman, Jean, had gone to Bradon's club on some kind of charity mission for a church. Billy could find out which church, then Slash could send someone on Sunday to follow her. Once he had her home address, the rest would be easy.

He crossed the room to the computer. He'd send Billy instructions through their shared website, one of over twenty overlapping sites he used so each connection maintained a sense of power, but the ultimate authority over their business was retained and controlled by him.

He pulled up the *Hot Town* site. On the surface, it looked like a generic, cheaply-made website for a bar like any other. Behind the surface, though, were encrypted pages where Billy sold drugs and flesh. Slash put in his password. A window appeared: Access Denied. He tried again, then typed in the URL for a different site. Blocked. Click after click, he searched and found them all. Denied. Wrong password. Try again.

He slammed a fist against the computer screen, knocking the monitor half off the desk and against the wall behind it. He shouted curses, then sat down and forced his body to calm so he could think. Who could have usurped him? Who was smart enough to learn all his passwords and change them?

No. It hadn't been a hack. Slash remembered when he first created his plan of revenge against Candy and her religious friends. He had given Champagne the password to his master site so he could get a secure message to her from prison about a contact. Had she shut down all the sites? He'd had her beaten and left for dead. Dead women couldn't cough up passwords.

Years of work, all his power, was in the hands of a woman who might or might not be a corpse. Slash found his cell phone and put in Billy's number.

"You're out. Congratulations."

Billy must have number recognition. Slash wanted to ask, "Does your website still work?" but if he did, Billy would know he didn't have control over it any longer. If his contacts found out he was not at the top, he would lose everything.

"I need you to look up something for me."

A chuckle came through the line. "Back at it already, huh? No taking a vacation to the Bahamas to celebrate getting out of the clink?"

Slash wiped his upper lip. "Do you still see Candy, or Champagne?"

"Champagne disappeared right after you got taken in." Billy's smoker cough rattled through the receiver. "Candy, not lately. She was inspiring my girls to want to leave."

"Could you get her back? I need some information." Before she escaped, Candy had been the only one besides him who knew the passwords. Had she been the one, not Champagne, to change them all? Was she running his circuit on the sly?

"What'll it get me?"

Slash scratched his fingernails down the side of the phone, wishing it was Billy's face. "You know I always reward you well for your services."

"Yeah, but I've been doing pretty good on my own while you were gone. How about we talk about changing the percent ratio of my profits?"

So Billy's site was still live and accessible. Slash needed to talk to Candy, find out what she knew.

Any plan for Jean Jameson would have to wait. If Candy got wind he was getting close to Jean, they might both run. He had to find Candy, and soon, and until then maintain at least the appearance that he was still the king of his kingdom.

Bradon was getting cocky. He'd snatched up every morsel of power within reach like a rat scarfed down moldy bread. "Find out what I need and we'll talk." Slash would get what he wanted out of Billy, get his world back under control, then his talk with Billy would end with him fired, permanently, and Slash would find a more worthy, less ambitious pupil to take his place. Or maybe he'd just go to the Bahamas like Billy suggested and leave it all behind. He had plenty of money in his accounts. Yes, after he got his sites back, and dealt with Jean, he'd get his money and get out. Retire. Be done with all of it.

Billy's voice brought his thoughts back to the present problem. "Okay, I'm listening," Billy said.

"Get Candy back into your bar. When you know she's coming, call me. I'll tell you the rest then."

"Are you coming here?"

Billy knew better. Showing up in person was stupidity based on a vain need to have people know you were the source of their demise.

Slash never appeared on the scene unless it mattered. He hung up the phone. Let Billy be irritated. He needed the reminder who was in charge.

Slash was. Or he would be when he got those new passwords.

If Candy had them, had dared to overrun his kingdom, she would soon discover she had made a very grave mistake.

Wednesday Morning, January 28

Jose

Jose tapped his mechanical pencil against the desk and tried not to notice the heads that turned all along the precinct as Champagne sashayed her way to his office. "A celebrity on the red carpet couldn't have garnered more attention," he muttered.

"Most celebrities traipsing the red carpet wear more clothing," his secretary noted dryly, her own buttoned-to-the-throat paisley blouse, black jacket and loose pants in no way competition for the male dream in the flesh headed their way.

"Funny how those lines of scars down her face aren't putting any of them off much." Candy said. She leaned a hip against the side of his desk, her arms crossed. He didn't bother to comment that Champagne wasn't exactly dressed to draw attention to her face, but chuckled when Candy's sentiments came through her words. "You should have put her in an orange jumpsuit."

The two escorting officers flanked his new prisoner all the way to the chair facing his desk, then seemed in no hurry to leave. "Thanks, guys." Jose gestured them out the door. "I'll take it from here."

"Lucky dog," he heard as he closed the door to shut everyone out but himself, Sally, his trustworthy secretary of fifteen years, and the two women who might be their chance to get both Slash and Billy.

Champagne propped her legs onto the chair beside hers, exposing skin and smirking at the glances constantly coming through the windows separating his office from the rest of the precinct. "Sally, shut the blinds, will you? All that ogling is distracting."

"Gladly."

Champagne sat up straight once the show got canceled, looking slightly miffed that he wasn't staring in helpless adoration. Girls like Champagne weren't his type. He had no taste for the bold, forward kind. Give him a woman of substance and depth, the kind he'd have to search through layers to find her greatest beauty.

"Have a seat, Candy." Jose gestured to the chair Champagne had removed her feet from and once she was settled, tossed a manila envelope toward her. "I got this in the mail yesterday. You know anything about it?"

Candy looked it over. "No." She checked the left-hand corner, which bore no return address but did showcase a name. Candy looked at Champagne. "You sent this?"

"Figured if I put my name on it, he'd be sure to open it." Champagne's mouth puckered into a pout. "You messed everything up," she said to Jose. "I had it all planned out. Now I don't even know where Slash is. It'll take forever to hunt him down."

"He's at his hotel." Jose looked at the package from every angle. He'd had it checked out, but still asked, "There's no bomb in here, or arsenic, right?"

She glared at him. "Don't be ridiculous." Rubbing her head, probably still feeling the fringes of her hangover, she asked Candy, "Is he really back at the hotel? He didn't run?"

Candy's body language spoke tension. "Jose's had people tailing him since he left the prison."

"Sweet. You two might not have screwed everything up after all."

Jose cut open the package and dumped its contents on the desk. "So what is all this?"

She rose and rummaged through the pile. With her right hand she picked out a stack of three SD cards held together by a rubber band, and with her left, a CD protected by a plastic sleeve. "On here," she said, handing over the SD cards, "are over twelve hours of surveillance videos from twenty-one of Slash's highest paying connections. He lost a few back in that bust Ian did last summer, but there were plenty to take their places.

She raised a hip and perched on his desk. He wanted to tell her to get off but instead took the cards and asked, "Is this just regular surveillance—face recognition and stuff?"

"That would be a waste of my time and yours." She leaned toward him and he put his eyes down on the cards when gravity pulled her blouse to the point of distraction. "How about transactions with major drug players in Charlotte, pimps of minors in Edison, and secret black market dealings in supposedly respectable places here in Oakview?"

He reached for the CD. "And this?"

"Recorded e-mails and social media conversations. Backup evidence with money amounts and names."

"I'm impressed." He leaned back in his chair and crossed his arms. "What's the catch?"

‘If you
go blazing in,
it will ruin
everything.”

Chapter Sixteen
Wednesday Morning, January 28

Champagne

Champagne swung the right leg she'd crossed over her left, making sure she had her story straight before opening her mouth. "I want to be the one to take him down," she said.

"You said you were going to kill him."

Champagne ignored Candy and her comment. She leaned forward and looked Jose in the eye. "Let me be the one to walk into his hotel room, get a recording of him agreeing to pay me to get his passwords back, and then watch while your team comes in and cuffs him."

"We should just send in a team to get him. It's not safe you going in there alone."

"Then I'll take Candy with me." She stood. "If you go blazing in, it will ruin everything. He'd disappear before you could even get from the hotel lobby to his room. It has to be my way." She jerked the SD cards out of his hand. "Or no way at all."

Jose leaned back in his chair and crossed his arms. "Are we going after all of them on one big night, like the last sting?"

"No. Just Slash first, plus one random guy you can pick so I can get a video to use. I don't want to risk anyone catching wind of what we're doing and word spreading to him. After Slash, we can get the same agreement from the other connections, a few at a time, and take them down, too. Billy is last. I want him to sweat."

Candy inserted herself into Champagne's viewpoint and the conversation. "But Billy already knows you have passwords. He thinks I do, too. What will you do about that?"

Champagne thought fast. "We need to put him off. We'll plan a visit there to tell him everything is in the works to shut Slash down, which it is. Billy thinks I'm betraying Slash so I can transfer power to him. He needs to keep thinking that."

"What aren't you telling us?"

Champagne wished that for once Candy wouldn't be so street smart. She faced Jose. "I'm giving you everything you need to get Slash and over twenty other criminals. Do you want it or not?"

"I want it." Jose stood. "But I'm going to spend the rest of the day wondering what I've gotten myself into. I'll need some time to go through everything you've given me and see what else we would need, if anything. What day do you want to meet Slash?"

Champagne addressed Candy. "When do you usually visit *Hot Town* with your...friends?"

Candy was still looking her over with suspicion. "Saturdays."

"That'll work. Let's plan to visit Billy Saturday morning, and go to Slash's Saturday night."

"An undercover woman will be coming with you."

"To Billy's, fine." Champagne ran her fingers through the strands of her long hair. Funny, how many habits she had developed to distract men, things she did not even do consciously anymore, but noticed their affect. "But not when we go see Slash. He'll see through that one like glass."

Jose took his eyes off her and faced Candy. "Are you okay with her staying with you from Saturday morning until the evening?"

Candy was watching her. She could feel it even though she kept her eyes down on her swinging leg. With a tone that made Champagne wonder if Candy knew everything, Candy said, "I'm okay with that."

She closed her eyes. Saturday. In three days she would have her chance again.

"Until then, I hope you don't mind, but you'll be put under protective custody."

She met Jose's gaze. "You mean incarcerated."

"For your own protection."

She blew out a laugh. "That's rich. Thanks so much."

He held out his hand for the SD cards again. "Having this information makes you a target. I don't want anyone getting to this, or to you, before Saturday."

"You and me both."

"Then you won't mind a few days under lock."

She cocked her head and asked, "Hypothetically speaking, if I were to survive all of this, are you implying I wouldn't be sent back to prison when it's all over?"

"Not implying at all." Jose inserted the SD cards, CD, and other materials back in the mail bag. "You handing over all these wanted men would clear you of all charges and you'd be a free woman."

"I didn't even ask to make a deal."

He held up the bag. "You didn't need to. I don't know what your personal agenda is, Champagne, but if we get Slash this weekend, and even one or two of the others after that, I'm truly grateful to you."

She squirmed in her seat. Suspicion and even hatred she was used to. Gratitude? That was a new one.

"Let's get you squared away for now." Jose motioned for his frumpy-dressed secretary to usher her out of the office. "Get a written and recorded statement from her, will you? Oh, and Sally?" he called as they were leaving the room. "Next time you bring her in, make sure she's in a jumpsuit."

Saturday Morning, January 31

Brenda

Brenda turned sideways in front of the mirror. Stewart neared from behind, circled her waist with his arms, and rubbed her belly with love. "Are you sure you don't want to find out if it's a boy or girl?"

"I'm sure. I like surprises." She nestled against him until her watch alarm sounded. "Five minutes till time to go. I promised Candy I wouldn't be late."

"I really don't feel good about you going back to *Hot Town*, Brenda." Stewart turned her to face him. "Slash is out there somewhere. He targeted both of us last time."

She rubbed the scruff building along his chin. "We prayed about this, Stew. They need someone from church for it to look authentic. Florence isn't back yet, and now that Slash has seen Jean, she's at much higher risk for him targeting her." She didn't object when he pulled her tight into his arms. With a sigh, she buried her face into his neck. "If Candy and Jose succeed with their plan, a lot, a whole lot of women and girls are going to be set free and criminals who steal and sell people will be stopped from finding and hurting more victims." She lifted her head to look into his eyes. "Love me, pray for me, but don't hold me here."

She raised a hand to show him her fingernails, long and painted a soft shade of mauve. With a wiggle of her fingers, she said, "I've overcome so many fears, Stew. Today, I'm nervous but not afraid. I really believe God wants me to do this, and He will protect me."

He took her hand and kissed each of her fingertips. "I love you, Brenda. I'm proud of the woman you are."

She leaned in as close as her extended middle would allow. "We've both grown a lot since coming here, haven't we?"

He rested his hands on the sides of her stomach and grinned. "You more than I, I think."

She gave his shoulder a playful slap. "I really do have to go. Want to meet me at *Jamaica's* afterward? I have a feeling I'll need to unload, and talking with Candy is enjoyable but not always de-stressing. Besides, she'll have to go back to Jose's office with Champagne and the undercover woman to debrief or whatever they call it."

"I'd love to. We should enjoy spontaneous dates while we still can. I hear once a baby comes all that changes."

She hitched her purse handle over her left shoulder and headed for the door. "Well, that's a big topic...for another day. I'll call you. Pray, okay?"

She looked back. Her husband stood, hands in his pockets, glasses sliding down his nose, a smile meant to cover the worry that warmed her heart. "God has not given us the spirit of fear," she quoted.

"But of power, and of love, and of a sound mind," he finished.

He opened the front door for her as she said, "I'll take the power and love of God with me."

He shoved his hands deep into his pockets again. She had a sudden memory of the first time he asked her on a date. "Take my love with you, too."

She checked her watch, then stepped back inside for a long kiss. "Always."

"She's been
different
since he
came."

Chapter Seventeen
Saturday Morning, January 31

Grant

Through the window, though it was closed, Grant could see Jean giggling like a small girl, her eyes bright, her smile free from the stress of the past weeks. She lay on the floor, stomach down, a small doll in her hands. She bounced the doll from one foot to the other to make it walk toward the two-story dollhouse her father had built, now in a prominent position in the newly arranged living room. Melanie was beside her, Star on the other side, the three a trio of little girls in women's bodies. Off to the side, Melanie's daughter, Sapphire, opened box after box of Jean's other gifts, brought back from Grant's apartment. She squealed with happiness at each new toy.

It was nice that they had come to visit Jean on their day off. Jean's mother had called twice that morning to ask if her father was "still hovering in town," and her father had called to ask when her mother was sure to be away so he could work with Grant on more renovations. Jean needed a day off, a reason to play.

Grant watched the women, wondering how long it had been since any of them had played house with dolls. From what Candy shared of the girls' family lives, playing house might never have been something they would want to do. House was a place to run away from, not enjoy.

"Grant, I'm surprised you're out here."

Grant stifled a grimace before it became visible. Grace Jameson climbed the steps to the porch, her coat wrapped tight around her shoulders, the fur muff at the top circling her neck with elegance.

"It's freezing out here. Why don't you go inside?"

His first thought was to move his legs to give her room to join him on the swing, but his legs did not obey his command. He kept his eyes on his knees, fighting the frustration, but gestured toward the window. "Jean's inside with some friends. They're playing dollhouse."

"How delightful!" Grace stepped to where Grant sat sideways on the swing in front of the window and leaned over to look in, her perfume draping down to circle around him, tickling his nose and making him fight a sneeze. "I used to love playing house with Jean when she was small. We had such fun. I'm surprised she didn't tell me when I called to come sooner."

She made her way to the front door and her arm was out, ready to open the screen, when Grant stopped her. "Mrs. Jameson, why don't you sit out here with me instead?"

"But Grant—"

"If you go in there..." He hesitated, then decided to shoot straight. "It will mess things up."

She gave a tiny huff. "What could you possibly mean?"

He pulled in a deep breath, knowing he was about to probably break one of the first cardinal rules of what not to do with your future mother-in-law, and said, "This is the first time all week I've seen her enjoy something without any of the stress of me—" He waved his hands over his useless legs, then upward to include her. "—and you, and her dad. Please don't spoil it."

"But I—I—" Grace touched the doorknob, then let her hand drop. She turned and took the two steps back to the swing and sat on the end next to his feet. Again, he caught himself trying to move his legs, and again, he fought the helplessness and anger.

"She's been different since he came." Grace looked off into the distance, past the creek toward the church. "I knew it would be that way. That's why I didn't want..."

He waited. This was the spot where she would expect him to give some reassurance. After long awkward seconds passed, where he resisted the urge to look into the window and make sure Jean didn't know her mother was outside, Grace dropped her head and gazed down at her gloved hands.

"I just wish they both would understand. I was doing what I thought was best."

He prayed for wisdom, and opened his mouth and hoped what was coming out was the right thing to say. "It might help you, Mrs. Jameson, if for a few minutes you stopped focusing on your good intentions and thought about what you actually did."

She opened her hands, palm up, as if she had the answers written on the insides of her fingers. "All I did was—I just wanted to—" She curled her fingers into fists again. "I lied," she whispered.

He waited again, giving her time to think. A woman would probably jump in with some words to make her feel better, but maybe this was not the time for that. If it was, God should have sent her to a woman, because he had nothing to say.

"I lied," she finally repeated, resignation in her voice. "I lied to him. I lied to her. I told Jean her father didn't want to have anything to do with her. I told Charles that Jean hated him and never wanted to see him again. I thought she was so miserable because he was gone, and if he came back, it was just...it would just drag out the goodbyes, the separation, the—"

She stopped herself, and again he waited. "No, the truth is..." He was surprised to see tears slip through her lashes and make their way down her cheeks to drop onto her gloves. "I was jealous. Even when she was a tiny girl, they had this bond. They were so close. By the time Jean was born, Charles and I, we had our problems. I kept trying to fix them. I kept telling him, I kept...I kept..."

"Nagging?" he offered.

"Yes." She let out a mirthless laugh. "That's what he called it. And pushing, and a few other words I won't repeat. He was so stubborn, and I was so...selfish. But she adored him. He started avoiding me and spending more and more time with her. So when he left I thought everything would be fine. Jean and I would become best friends. We would be everything to each other. We didn't need him."

She started rocking the swing, probably without realizing it. "But then she was so sad. She would run out to the mailbox every day until I made her stop so I could check the mail first. She asked every night when he was coming home. I just knew if I let him stay in her life—" She put her hands up to her face. When she pulled them away, makeup spotted her gloves. "I hated him for still loving her so much when he had stopped loving me. So I lied. I lied and look what happened. I told myself it was justified. I told myself it was right, that I was doing a good thing. And when Rod Carson started showing an interest, that just proved to me that I was making a new life and she would be fine without Charles. Grant, what am I going to do? I can't go back in time." She stared at the smears on her fingertips. "What do I do?"

This time he did glance inside the window. Jean had rolled onto her side, grasping her stomach, laughing at something Melanie or Star must have said. He thought of all the wasted years, all the loss. Something deep within hurt for all the children who suffered when their parents made selfish choices. "I guess the first thing to do," he said, "is to tell God what you just told me. And then tell your daughter and your husband."

She sniffed. "Ex-husband."

He offered a smile. "Ex-husband," he amended.

She let out a feminine version of a moan. "It would be so...humiliating."

"Humbling," he corrected.

She glanced his way, mascara streaks under her eyes. "I guess I deserve some of that." She moved her hand to rest on the top of one of his feet. "If I did, and I'm not saying I will, but if I did, would you be there, Grant? I'd feel so much less...outnumbered...if I wasn't the only one not being...confessed to, I guess?"

He dipped his head in a nod. "I'd be honored."

She sat for a moment, then shook her head, lifted her chin, and brushed the fur around her collar, making sure it lay as it should. "Well then," she said briskly, then looked aghast at the stains on her gloves. "Oh, gracious. I'll never get those streaks out."

She pulled each finger free before slipping the gloves off her hands. "Well, I guess I'll just go shopping for a new pair then. Tell Jean I stopped by, will you? And that..." She paused on the stairs. "I'm truly glad...that she's having a good day."

At that, he gave her a genuine smile. "Thank you, Mrs. Jameson."

She responded with a nod, then made her way to her car. He wondered if she would be okay, until he saw her glance in her side mirror, gasp, and frantically start digging for tissues to wipe the mascara lines from her face. "Yeah," he muttered. "She'll be fine."

Late Saturday Morning, January 31

Brenda

Brenda tried not to think of it as a wasted trip when Billy told them with a smirk that Melanie and Star both had the day off. There was no question he was keeping them out of reach. Why he had their group come at all was still a mystery. It probably had something to do with Candy and Champagne, and long ago dark secrets Brenda did not want to know.

Her job was not to figure out the ins and outs of a criminal system like Billy's. She was there to minister to the women he employed, and be a believable cover. According to Candy, Billy's women were all prisoners to some extent, so there were more women in need there than just Melanie and Star.

She smiled at the three young women who had joined her, Candy, Champagne, and the undercover stranger from the police station at the table, wishing Florence was back from her honeymoon. Florence would have put the women at ease with her motherly ways, and her chocolate. Brenda should have brought some.

"We're having a special study for women at our church starting Sunday," she said, sounding to her own ears like a kid with no confidence. "We'd love for you to come. We could pick you up if you don't have a ride."

The long-haired, long-legged Barbie across the table, dubbed Dreamgirl, scoffed. "Why would I want to go to church?" she asked. "We all know about your church, about the guy they caught who was a deacon. And it's not like we haven't seen our share of church people in here, right?"

Brenda felt her forehead break out in a sweat at the heads nodding around the table. "Well, we are all sinners and have a fleshly nature..." she started, but faded out. "Have you really had Christian men come in here?"

One snickered. "Guys who *call* themselves Christians anyway." She leveled Brenda with a knowing smile. "Sometimes even a priest or a big-name pastor. Never seen your husband in here though."

Nausea raged an unpleasant path from Brenda's stomach up into her throat.

"Give her a break, guys," Candy ordered. She looked Brenda in the eye. "Men come in here from every type of situation you can imagine. You're right that we're all sinners, but as far as guys like Rod, there's more to it than that. It's an acting game."

Brenda winced. "A game? How can anyone exploit someone else and think it a game?"

"It's easier than you'd think." Candy sighed, then Brenda was surprised to hear her chuckle. "Slash sent me to a tree-hugger meeting in Asheville once. I went in and watched them all doing yoga while some main dude made a big speech about oneness with the universe. They had a 'sound healer' come in and bong on wooden planks and stuff, but then I up and said I had a faster way to be healed of the 'commercial imperialism' the guy talked about." She chuckled again. "I told a big personal story—totally untrue of course—about how I used to be rich and unfulfilled, but then I became one with the universe and got away from everything. And then I pulled out my bag of coke."

Brenda gasped, but the girls laughed. "What'd they do?"

Candy plopped her feet up onto the table and leaned her chair back on two legs. "The speech guy and the sound healer kicked me out, but enough of the crowd followed me that it turned into a very profitable night, especially after I convinced them that Buddha liked the stuff."

Champagne looked impressed. "Buddha did drugs?"

Candy shrugged. "I don't know a single thing about Buddha," she said, "except that his knees had to hurt, sitting cross-legged like that all the time."

Brenda shook her head. "I'm sorry, but I have no idea what that has to do with Rod Carson."

"Don't you get it?" Candy dropped her chair back to the floor, pulled her legs from the table, and sat up straight. "Predators look for easy prey. If a guy can come to a place where there are lots of kids, and people don't ask a lot of questions, and they assume everybody is there for God or community service or whatever, the predator hits the jackpot. Back when I didn't know Jesus, I had no qualms faking a mantra or belief to get a sale. You wouldn't believe the lies I told."

"I would," Champagne quipped, and the girls laughed again. When they quieted down, she added, "But she's right. A predator enjoys the challenge of deceiving all the adults while he preys on the kids. And where better to find trusting adults and lots of kids than a church, or school, or summer camp?"

Candy must have seen the tears Brenda felt developing for she sobered and put a hand on her arm. "What I'm trying to say is that the church is not producing these guys, Brenda. Those kinds of predators are drawn to places where they can do sick stuff without getting into trouble. And, I'm sorry to say it, but in a lot of churches, even if the guys do get caught, they get a spiritual slap on the wrist and then everybody gets told to forgive and forget. Wouldn't you pick that rather than, say, a school with heavy background checks and a written response plan to abuse?"

Brenda dropped her head onto her folded arms on the table. "I get your point," she murmured, her words floating around her in the small space inside her arms, her breath thick and musty with revulsion. "But I wish I hadn't heard a word you said. I wish I didn't know. How do I not look around church from now on and wonder who is a horrible person targeting our children?"

She heard a voice from the other side of the table. "See? That's why I don't want to come to church. What if I see some guy who was in here the night before?"

"Go up to him and knee him where it hurts," Champagne offered. The laughter was more forced this time, and sounded to Brenda like inside-out tears.

"Predators like Rod do exhibit predictable behaviors, Brenda," Candy said. Brenda did not look up, but she listened with everything in her. "Go home and google grooming techniques of child abusers, or something like that. Once you know the signs, they're easier to spot than you'd think." Candy must have stood because her voice came from higher up, and a chair made a rude, scratching noise across the floor.

"I've got something to say," Candy declared in her loud announcer voice. "I've met some men who called themselves Christians and even went to church who did terrible things. Women, too. But I have never met a genuine follower of Jesus Christ who would harm another person purposefully, especially the young and innocent. Since I got saved, I've gotten to know Jesus. He's no pale wallflower guy who walks around in a robe and hopes everybody does nice things. He's a warrior who sets captives free and makes whips to drive out guys who exploit poor people. He fusses at disciples who don't want to take time for kids, and he talks to women like us when everybody else is waiting for us to be condemned. Every man or woman who truly follows Him is changed from the inside out, and none of them, not one, would be okay in a place like this unless they were trying to help people be free."

Brenda looked up with hope only to see Dreamgirl clap her hands slowly and, if Brenda had a guess, with sarcasm. "Big speech from the woman who said she was great at faking mantras to get people to buy in. What are you trying to sell us, Candy?"

Champagne pushed back her chair. "I'm going to the bathroom."

Dreamgirl stood and said goodbye. One of the other girls joined her.

"I'm right, aren't I?" Candy asked softly. Her gaze remained on Dreamgirl's retreating back, openly revealed in her cut-out dress. "Nobody who truly loves Jesus could ever give in to this kind of thing, could they?"

The last girl stood. "Candy, can I talk to you outside for a minute?"

Candy's gaze took in Billy sitting across the room at his booth, then drifted to where Champagne had disappeared down the hallway. "Okay, but just for a minute."

Brenda watched them go. Billy got up and crossed the room, following Champagne's route down the hall. Alone now except for the policewoman, who was busy texting on her phone, with nothing to look at but that hateful stage, Brenda dropped her head back down onto the table and let the tears fall.

*‘Billy
asked me
to distract
you.”*

Chapter Eighteen
Late Saturday Morning, January 31

Candy

"I know it's cold out here, but I didn't want anyone to overhear us." The girl nodded toward the door. "You know how Billy is."

Candy did not mind the frigid temperature as it meant getting away from the look in Brenda's eyes for a few moments, but she needed to get back so she could talk to Billy. "Yes," she said, "I know how he is." Candy did not bother to say she knew more than this girl would want to imagine. "I don't remember you from before. If you're new, it will be easier to get out." She took off her coat and wrapped it around the girl's shoulders. The girl was in a tank top and miniskirt, and her fishnet stockings did nothing to cover her legs from the January chill. "And if you want any advice from someone who knows, get out now. Today. While you still can."

Too cold or too weary to protest, the girl wrapped her small frame in Candy's coat and nodded. She told Candy her parents were separated. She had been lonely and bored at home and met a great guy on the internet who said she could have the modeling career she'd always wanted. A familiar story. Candy already knew the end, but to this girl, it was brand new.

"So here I am now." She put her fingers up in quotation marks. "'Modeling' at night for losers who pay to put me on the internet." She wiped at her eyes. "Even if I do get out, get a decent job, I can't ever get those pictures back. They'll be out there forever, telling me what a mess I've made of my life."

Candy could not deny the truth of what she said. "Please listen to me, um—" Candy rubbed her hands up and down her arms. "What is your name?"

"Maria."

"Maria, I know right now you're scared to leave because of what might happen, but believe me, it will only get worse. His stack of threats to hold against you—photos and debts and drugs and secrets—will pile higher until you have no hope of digging yourself out. Come with me today and I'll get you to a safe place. We can have someone contact your family, and—"

The girl backed away and Candy sighed on the inside. How many times would she hear the same line? I want to get out, but not today. I want a better life, but I need a little more time. A little more money.

Why didn't people choose freedom when it was offered to them?

She realized she had not been listening to Maria, who was stepping to the side, toward the door. The girl slid Candy's coat off. "Thank you," she said, offering a small smile. "For the coat, and for listening. I really did want to talk to you, and I really do want to get out of all of this." She tugged the door open and a welcome gust of warm air rushed out, absorbed too soon by the cold. "That's why I didn't mind when Billy asked me to distract you for a few minutes." She pointed inside. "He wanted to talk to that girl you brought with the stage name. He's looking for somebody and thought she might know where he was."

The girl tugged her tank top down over a bare section of midriff. "I hope I didn't cause her any trouble," she said, but Candy was already inside, running down the hall, calling Champagne's name.

Late Saturday Morning, January 31

Champagne

Billy peered through one of the small windows set in the double swinging doors of the stock room. He held the right door open a crack, angling his head to the right and then left. Champagne knew he had full view of Candy's table. It was an intimidation tactic, meant to swell her sense of unease as she waited for him to speak. The dread creeping across her shoulders let her know that, unfortunately, knowing about a tactic did not keep it from working.

"So she really is working with you," he said softly, his gaze still out on the main room. Champagne heard laughter, nothing suspicious. What was he looking for? Or was he just dragging this out? She would have thought he would be in a hurry. "I thought you were bluffing." His head turned and his eyes, when they found her, were full of purpose. "I wonder if you know more than you are admitting."

She recognized that look, had seen it too many times. It always preceded pain. If he thought she knew all the passwords, and he had her to himself there in the stock room...

Act fast, think faster, she told herself. The mantra, taught to her by Candy after a client had used Champagne's stiletto heels to beat her with, put a smile of confidence on her face and a saunter to her step as she made her way around Billy's girth and put a hand out to pull the door shut, closing them in. *When you're desperate to leave, make him think you want to stay.* "I wish I did," she said. She lowered her voice to a whisper, some of her full-body tension lessoning when he had to bend down to hear her. Anything that got him more to her level was an advantage. "Well, since you made me those packets, I might as well tell you..." She bit her lip, as if unsure she should reveal a secret, then smiled up at him. "You always get our secrets out of us anyway, right?"

He chuckled. His massive belly bobbed against her. She forced herself not to back away. "You girls are all the same," he said, putting his hand up to rub her shoulder, then the back of her neck. It was a subtle sign, but he knew she would catch it. "You try to keep secrets, but nothing passes by Billy." The chuckled died to silence and his hand squeezed on her neck. "Talk."

She told her pulse to calm before he could feel it raging through her. Instead of backing away in obedience to every instinct of self-preservation she had, she stepped forward, brushing up against him. She leaned in close, making her voice conspiratorial, drawing his attention to her full lips and away from the fact that the motion had pulled her out of his grip. "Slash betrayed me. Now I'm returning the favor. I've chosen you and I don't want to regret it. I need to know you're with me and not with him."

"Did you bring the password for my site?" he asked. She pulled a slip of paper from inside her top and handed it over. She had changed all the passwords earlier that day at the precinct. Jose, now with access to the *Hot Town* site, would be able to see and record everything Billy did from today on. Worried such thoughts might reveal too much on her face, she touched the door, her way of escape, tapping it with one long fingernail as if pointing toward Candy on the other side.

Billy was not watching her. He pulled out his smart phone, checked the paper again and pushed letters and numbers. "Back in," he whispered and his low laugh sent chills down her spine. "I'm starting to like you, Champagne."

She pushed the door outward a foot and looked into the room. The table was empty except for the undercover woman and the church lady, who was crying. Where had Candy gone? She closed the door and turned to Billy. "Where's my payment?"

He led her around a set of shelves filled with standard stock: napkins, plastic silverware, cups, cases of beer. Past another line of shelves, mostly empty except for a few stacks of papers in manila folders, he stopped at a filing cabinet, reached around to the back, and pulled off a small magnetic case. Champagne shuddered. It was a perfect hiding place; she never would have felt around behind anything in that shabby room, too fearful of living creatures that might have set up camp there.

Billy opened the case and set one small and two tiny plastic bags of powder onto one of the empty shelves. "The blue one is for the person you need to take a nap. Put this in a diffuser and she—or he—will be out like a light for as long as it runs. Just don't put it in until you're leaving the room. It works fast."

"And the other two?"

He picked up the larger of the two white packets. "This one is yours. You said you needed courage, so I added a special bonus." His smile down on her was anything but pleasant. "You'll love it."

"It's a lot bigger than the one for Slash."

"Don't worry." Billy put the smaller packet into her palm. "This will be enough to get Slash high and keep him there for at least an hour, long enough for you to get access, send me what I need without him knowing it, and get out." He added the larger packet. "I added some filler to yours so you'd be able to tell them apart."

She wasn't buying that. "Why didn't you—"

Candy's voice, shouting her name, came down the hallway like a car alarm. Champagne snatched the last bag and opened the door wide. "I have to go."

He shut it, blocking her way. "You'll send the other passwords as soon as you get them from Slash, right there from his room. No waiting."

"Yes," she promised. "I'll contact you."

Billy's strong hand wrapped around her upper arm. "Don't forget," he said, curling his lips to expose teeth, like a wolf would, "you don't want to make an enemy of me."

"I know it," she whispered. She pocketed the drugs, then forced a smile. "We're not enemies, Billy. We're partners now."

He scoffed but opened the door. "We'll see."

She escaped into the hallway and almost barreled into Candy, who grabbed her arm, breathless. "Are you okay? Where's Billy? I need to talk to him."

"I took care of it." Champagne started down the hallway. "Let's go."

"But—"

"Trust me. It's done."

The storage room door swung outward again and Billy appeared. Candy opened her mouth but Champagne pulled her toward the main room. "Candy, I mean it. We need to leave." She glanced back. Billy nodded at her with a slight smile.

Champagne shivered deep within. Everything about this was wrong. She turned away. "Let's get your friends and get out of here."

"Keeping what happened inside will eat you alive."

Chapter Nineteen
Saturday Afternoon, January 31

Candy

Candy handed over a set of linens and showed Champagne Jamaica's guest bed. "Feels like old times, doesn't it?"

Champagne looked around the clean, cheerful room. "Not at all."

"It was a joke. You're mega uptight."

"Aren't you?" Champagne dumped the sheets onto the bed and left them there, marching to the stairs in that jittery way she had when she was nervous. "We're going over to meet Slash at midnight tonight. I'd think you'd be a wreck, too."

"See these?" Candy motioned to verse after verse drawn with permanent marker onto the wall leading down the stairs to the café area. "I've spent weeks hiding these in my heart. I won't say I don't feel any fear, but I know where that comes from and am rejecting it. God is going to be with us tonight."

"With you anyway." As usual, any mention of God had Champagne wandering off, searching for a distraction. "Or He might just stay here if He knows I'm going to be with you."

Candy smiled. "No chance of that." She opened the small refrigerator set up in the kitchen area near the walk-in cooler. "I'd say make yourself at home, but neither of us have much experience in what that means. Eat whatever you want except the stuff for sale, unless you want to pay for it." She smiled again. "Whipped cream is free."

Champagne peered over her shoulder into the fridge. "Pretty bare. You on a diet?"

"Hardly." She closed the fridge. "Just a lousy cook. Let's order pizza. I invited Jean and Grant to stop by before she drops him off at his apartment tonight. Maybe we should bake some brownies. I have a box mix around here somewhere."

Champagne got all jittery again. "You invited people over?"

"I know you'd rather avoid it." Candy went in search of the brownie mix. "But you really need to face them, Champagne. You need to ask forgiveness and receive it. Keeping what happened inside will eat you alive."

"Say, what's this?"

Candy returned to the café area to see Champagne pick up a package left on the counter. She let Champagne change the subject. Jean and Grant would get there soon enough and she couldn't avoid it then. "It came just before I left for *Hot Town* this morning. I thought it was from Jamaica but she lives in Atlanta."

Champagne checked the label. "This is from Michigan. Got any friends there?"

"Not that I know of."

"Where's a pair of scissors? Maybe it's food."

"You really are hungry."

"I'm making up for all those times Slash rationed me down to one meal a day to keep me slim."

Memories, unpleasant ones, came flooding back. Candy closed her eyes. "I hope it is food then," she said softly. "And you can eat it all."

Champagne missed the moment, busy pulling large bags of powder from the box. "Candy, you aren't—this isn't—is it?"

"I'm not dealing drugs on the side, if that's what you're asking." She stomped to Champagne's side and dumped the box's contents onto the counter. "Good grief, Champagne, do you think I'd have a bare fridge if I was pushing this much dope around town?" She examined the different bags, then found a brochure. "Say, this is the stuff to do that Kintsugi thing—fixing broken pots with gold. It's the materials to make the real paste."

Champagne picked up the bag of golden powder. "So you're saying this is real gold?"

"And it's expensive. Really expensive." Candy looked for a note or some kind of explanation. When she did not find one, she circled the counter and pulled out her box of broken mug shards, and the box of pieces from Jean's bowl. "Who would spend that kind of money so that—oh."

"What?"

"Florence." Candy knew her smile was big. "She and Doug must be in Michigan, or were when she found this. I had told her about Jean's pot. God bless her."

Champagne was digging through the boxes. "Some of these blue-green pieces already have gold lines. This boxful looks a lot like the bowl Jean was going to get as an engagement present."

Candy's gaze shot to Champagne. She knew Jean's house had been bugged for sound, but had Slash put a camera in there, too? "How did you know about that?"

Champagne shrugged, but her face flooded with what looked like envy, or perhaps regret. "I was spying on them. Wanted to see what they were like when they thought no one was looking." She picked up a piece and held it up to the light. The gold flickered like tiny flames. "Is this hers? Who broke it?"

"I don't know. I thought I'd try to fix it, but the glue I used on these mugs wasn't worth anything, and the glitter looked terrible."

"This just proves my point, you know."

"What point?"

Champagne repacked all the boxes and stacked them. "Some things are too broken to be fixed. Jean's pot was beautiful, fixed like it was with gold, but now it's broken again."

"So it can be fixed again."

"By who? God?" Champagne pulled the boxes into her arms. "Seems to me like God's been doing a lot more breaking than fixing with all of you lately."

Should she say it? Candy tapped the highest box in Champagne's arms to get her attention. "And yet we have peace and joy, and you're full of fear and hate. What does that tell you?"

Candy was not surprised when Champagne pretended not to hear. "Let's see what we can do with these mugs, but not here. I wouldn't want to get sticky stuff on the counter. Let's go up to your room." She stopped at the bottom of the stairs. "By the way, do you still have one of those diffuser things?"

Candy took the highest box so Champagne could see up the stairs, and at the top used her foot to open the bedroom door. She nodded toward the end table next to the bed. "Right there. Why?"

"Could you run some calming oil or something? We've got hours to kill and I'm about to go crazy, and I doubt you have anything to drink in this place."

"Sure I do." Candy grinned. "Lots of coffee. Water, too."

Champagne rolled her eyes. "Let's stick with the oils."

Champagne had never liked Candy running her diffuser, said it sounded like a kid gargling mouthwash, but maybe it was the only alternative to alcohol she could think of. "We could pray."

"Oils."

"Okay." Candy went rummaging through her stash and set the diffuser to dispense the smell of lavender into the air. She joined Champagne on the room's one large rug, but then rose to her feet again. "You know I'm no good at following instructions." She found her phone under her bed pillow and waved it at Champagne. "How about you mix that stuff up while I go order a pizza?"

"Get a two-liter to go with it. Something with lots of caffeine."

Candy left Champagne studying the little booklet that came with the gold dust—detailed instructions gave her mental hives—and went downstairs to grab a couple of plates and napkins. She should open a can of veggies. "Hey!" she yelled up the stairs. "You want some corn? Or green beans?"

"I want a beer," Champagne yelled back.

"Corn it is, then." Candy chuckled as she opened the can and searched for a microwave-safe mug to heat the vegetables in. It was nice having someone around. Things got too quiet at night.

"Just a few more hours, Lord," she whispered as the mug whirled in circles in the microwave. "We're going to get him for good this time. I just know it." She couldn't tell if her heart was racing more out of excitement or fear. "Keep us safe, Father, please. Especially Champagne. She's as stubborn as a teenage mule and has to stay alive until You get through to her."

She remained downstairs to pray until the pizza arrived, then carried it and the now-cold corn precariously up the steps to her room.

"Wow," she commented once she set everything down and could see Champagne. "You're good."

"I used to like doing puzzles when I was a kid."

Champagne had organized all the pieces into their correct piles, most lined according to where they needed to attach to other pieces, had the paste made, and was already holding two larger shards of Jamaica's favorite red mug together to dry. She didn't look up, but asked casually, "When did you say Jean and Grant were coming over?"

"Probably not till late, but if Grant's had a bad pain day, it might be earlier. I put the brownies in to cook. We should save them some."

"Good idea." Champagne set the glued pieces onto the newspaper she had laid across the carpet. She stood and arched her back. "Do you have any toothpicks? Some of these pieces are so small, the brush they gave me won't work."

"I think so."

When Candy returned, toothpicks in hand, Champagne was waiting for her at the bedroom door. "Thanks." She pointed back into the room. "You can set them near the paste. I've got to go to the bathroom."

Candy put the toothpicks where requested, then sat on the bed. No sense giving herself an aching back sitting on the floor until Champagne came back and showed her what she could do without messing things up. She'd probably get delegated to holding pieces while they dried, which was fine with her. "This lavender smell is nice," she yelled, "but it's a little weird mixed with the brownies cooking downstairs. I think I'll unplug it for now, okay?"

She stood and reached for the cord, but the room swam before her eyes and she fell back onto the bed. "Whoa, I just got really dizzy for a sec." She'd better lay down until it passed. "I guess I shouldn't have just had whipped cream for lunch." She stretched out on the bed, which suddenly felt like heaven, or at least a cloud, something soft and mushy. Champagne appeared at the door, but her image waved like a bad illusion. "So what do we do next? I'm...ready to..." What was she ready to do? "Help...ready to help."

"You'll help best by staying right there," Champagne said. Candy watched in slow motion as Champagne pulled in a deep breath and held it, then came into the room just long enough to collect the pieces to Jean's bowl and carry them in one of the boxes back to the hallway. "I'm sorry, Candy, but you knew from the beginning what I had to do."

Candy tried to shake her head in protest, but found she could not move. The image of Champagne faded and Candy's vision darkened along the edges. Why had she ever believed Champagne was willing to just put Slash in jail? She should have told Jose to have a set of guards there to keep watch on Champagne's every move. Her mistake—trusting an old friend—was going to cost a life.

Just as
she lifted
the knife
high...

Chapter Twenty
Saturday Night, January 31

Slash

Slash shut the door to his apartment and locked it. Every contact he had was hounding him for access to their sites again. He could only bluff his way through the lie for so long. Eventually, they'd figure out he didn't have access to them anymore. He had to get those passwords, and soon.

He turned and tossed his keys toward the bed.

Champagne caught them.

"Hi, Slash," she said, smiling at his slack-jawed lack of response. "Surprised to see me?"

He did not have the energy to pretend he had any of the old power, or even to put his shoulders back and stand up straight. "What are you doing here?" he asked.

She stood, slowly, in that seductive way he had taught her. "I'm here to kill you," she purred. She propped a foot up onto the bed and slid a long knife out of her left spiked-heeled, black leather, knee-high boot. Her methods were calculated and his heart pulsed faster, not because of the skin she exposed, but from how her hand shook as it held the knife in his direction. She was frightened. A scared person could be more dangerous than a calm one. "Have a seat," she ordered. "I need a drink."

He placed himself on the bed near the headboard. When she turned to look into his mini-fridge for the alcohol she knew would be there, he studied the two small packets on the side table. "What are these?"

She glanced back. "A little courage, courtesy of our old friend Billy. The bigger one's mine. The clear one is for you. I figured after all those days in prison, you'd be feeling pretty deprived."

Desperate would be a more accurate term. Now he was going to have to kill Champagne, and right there in his hotel room. That would be a mess to cover up, and he wouldn't even enjoy it. "Champagne, go home. You don't want to do this." He reached for the first packet. Courage he could use. Oblivion would be even better. He set up both sets and had them ready as she finished chugging a shot of whiskey and found her way to the one chair in the room.

She held a second shot in one hand, the knife in the other. Crossing her legs, she swung one boot back and forth, her words already beginning to slur. How much had she drunk before she came?

"You've never killed anyone before, have you?" Slash asked. Maybe if she got drunk enough, she'd pass out and he could call Whip to come drag her away and dump her out back. The last thing he needed was a dead prostitute with a slash on her neck found in his hotel.

"You'll be my first." She held out her shot glass as if in toast to him. "The man I once loved. The man I now despise. You will never find my little sister. You will never hurt one more girl. I am going to dig this knife into your already dead heart and kill the rest of you."

He used the small packet of heroin from the clear bag and looked longingly at the larger packet she'd brought for herself. "Am I supposed to try to buy you off?"

"Nope." She shook her head, sloshing whiskey over her lap. "Don't want money. I could have gotten plenty of it, you know. I have your kingdom. Every connection you have would have paid for those passwords on your sites. Big bucks, too."

He started sweating. "Why didn't you sell them?"

"Who wants money when you can have revenge?" Champagne laughed behind him, a high-pitched sound that scraped across his nerves as if she had stretched them over shattered glass. "Go check your computer," she said. "I've got it all set up for you."

If he pulled up his sites, he might be able to bluff his way into getting the passwords out of her while she was drunk. He sat at his desk and clicked on the mouse. A screen emerged with some kind of surveillance video on it. He started to close the window but Champagne said, "You'll want to watch that." He checked the time on the video. Two minutes, fourteen seconds. He could spare that. "Have another drink," he told Champagne and clicked play. He heard her stand and approach, but then his focus transferred entirely to the video on the screen. The neon sign beside the building flashed in the darkness, illuminating raindrops, like a scene from an old, badly-filmed mafia movie. One exposed bulb above the Exit door gave a halo of light that reached down to a torn mat soaked with grime and rain. The door opened and a man stepped onto the mat and into the light. Slash recognized Black Jack Ransom, one of his massage parlor owners, who had a lucrative business in his back rooms selling underage girls to high profile businessmen and politicians in the greater Charlotte area. Three police cars swerved into view of the camera, lights flashing. Jack retreated into the darkness of the building, but emerged again with his hands up. Behind him, one hand on his collar and the other pushing something against his back, appeared Jose Ramirez in full uniform. The smug expression on his face when he looked up at the camera sent Slash into a spiral of red-hot anger.

"The same thing is going to happen in your clubs and brothels and massage parlors all over the city and every town you've touched. You're done, Slash."

His hands were shaking. "You're dead, you know that, don't you?"

She came up behind him, close enough that he could feel the heat pulsing from her body. She leaned over. "I know," she whispered, her breath brushing against his neck, "but I win."

Her hand ran down his hair, a gesture he had done to her a thousand times. He turned to stone and his heart pounded in his ears. She slid her hand up under his hair and to his neck and squeezed, just as he would do, especially right after he had marked them, to remind them they were his now, forever.

Her hand froze on the back of his neck. He knew why. When she lifted his hair, he snapped her hand away and stood, too quickly. The drugs made his vision blur, but he could still tell her face held shock.

"You have it, too," she whispered. "The slash. Who gave you yours?"

"Go away, Champagne," he ground out. "Get out of here while you still have the chance."

"No." She swayed and fell onto the bed, nearly cutting herself with the knife. With effort, she regained her footing. "I have to go to the bathroom. Don't go away."

Should he kill her now and get it over with? But then how would he get his passwords? She shut the door to the bathroom and Slash eyed the bigger bag's contents. Courage. The more the better. Champagne would probably pass out in the bathroom. If not, he could call Whip to come give her a few punches and take her away.

He had found what he needed.

Saturday Night, January 31

Champagne

Champagne poured the shot of whiskey down the sink drain and stared at herself in the mirror. The bloodshot eyes and dark circles weren't from alcohol, just from the lack of sleep trying to work up the nerve to actually do this. Pretending to be drunk had given her some time. Slash found drunk people disgusting and wouldn't lower himself to deal with them personally.

She splashed water on her face, then after drying off reached for the Bible she'd stowed in her purse. Candy had told her to read it. She had not read far, but had taken to holding it at night to help her sleep, like a child would a stuffed animal. "Who brings a Bible with them to a murder?" she asked the woman in the mirror. The face hardened. "Not murder. Justice. The police won't ever get him. I'm the only one who can."

Just as quickly, Champagne watched her face crumble into despair. She lowered her head to avoid the sight and heard herself pray, "If there's another option, I'm listening."

No voice came from the sky, or even from outside the door of the dingy bathroom. What had she expected, that Candy and the preacher would come barging through to give her another chance? That God would somehow come down and give her a miracle?

She'd hoped to be strong enough to save the drugs for afterward, to help her forget, but she needed them now.

Champagne took a deep breath, put the Bible back into her purse, and opened the bathroom door. She remembered at the last second to drop her shoulders and loosen her walk to appear drunk again, but it was unnecessary. Slash lay sprawled on the floor, arms out to his sides, unaware of her presence.

She rushed to the side table. "You were only supposed to take the small packet. You jerk!"

Even now, he was stealing from her. She seethed over this final injustice until she noticed how completely inert he had become. This could be a good thing. Now was her chance. He would not resist. Probably wouldn't even feel it.

She set her purse on the bed and the shot glass on his desk near the computer that had overseen her life for long, horrible, terrifying years.

Gripping the knife with both hands, she stood over the body of the man whose death would allow her sister to live free. "For you, Emily," she whispered.

Just as she lifted the knife high, Slash opened his eyes, looked at something over her head, and shrieked in horror.

She whirled, knife out in defense, searching for whatever he had seen.

"Neither of them are responding."

Chapter Twenty-One
Saturday Night, January 31

Grant

The stairway in *Jamaica's* was curved, but only slightly, as if the building had ambitions of antebellum décor but did not have enough room to succeed. Grant rolled toward the counter but did not see lights on any of the coffee burners. "What's that beeping? If Candy was home, you'd think there'd be hammering."

Jean headed for the kitchen area. "Sounds like a timer of some kind, like an oven."

"That would explain the burning smell."

His fiancé smiled. "Candy probably forgot she was cooking and took Champagne to the store or something." She made her way into the kitchen and called out, "It's the oven. Looks like what would have been brownies." The beeping stopped and Jean returned, her eyebrows creased. "The back door is unlocked. She wouldn't have left it like that if she'd gone out. I'll just run upstairs to her room and check."

Grant moseyed around the counter and considered making himself a cup of coffee. If Candy had been downstairs, she would have offered him a cup of whipped cream with a spoon, and likely a burnt brownie to go with it.

Jean appeared at the top of the stairs. "Grant, Champagne's not up here, but there's a full pizza box, a bunch of broken mug pieces all over the floor, and Candy is asleep."

"That's really strange."

"I'm going to wake her up and we can search the rest of the upstairs. Can you look around down there?"

"Sure." Grant gave up thoughts of brewing a cup and started a search of the downstairs areas where Champagne might hide. Why she might want to hide, he had no idea, but he checked the stock room and the large freezer room, then turned his chair and pushed back toward the stairs. "Jean," he called out. No answer. "Jean," he said louder. "I think she's gone."

He called her name again, several times. A rope of concern knotted in his gut. "Candy?" he yelled. "Jean?"

If he had his legs, he could find out if she was okay in thirty seconds, fifteen if he took the stairs two at the time. Here he was, helpless at ground level, nothing but his useless legs and a chair in a building with no elevator. At least this time he had his phone. Yanking it out of his pocket, he dialed Jose's direct line.

"Something's wrong," he told Jose. "We're at *Jamaica's Place*. Champagne's gone. Jean went to wake up Candy—she said she was asleep—but now neither of them are responding."

"I'll be there as soon as I can."

Grant didn't bother with a goodbye. He stuffed his phone back into his pocket and launched his body off the chair and onto the first steps. Using his arms and shoulders in a military crawl, he dragged himself upward, belly down, legs dangling. He climbed, step by painful step, yelling Jean's name every few seconds until he ran out of air and energy for anything but moving upward, arm over arm, pull after pull. Twenty-two steps.

Jean had once told him the most terrifying part of the night of the shooting had been having to sit beside him while he lay in a pool of his own blood, waiting helplessly for the ambulance to come.

Would he find Jean in a similar scene? He had heard no shots, but Slash had enough money to access the latest, most high-tech weapons, and silencers.

Slash. He pictured the jagged line of red, like raw meat, on the back of Champagne's neck. "Jean!" he shouted. His arm slipped. He fell several steps before grabbing onto the stair rail to stop his descent. With a cry, more from the pain in his mind than his body, he hauled himself back up the space he'd lost and on to the final, agonizing feet to the landing. "Jean! Answer me!"

At the top, dreading what he would see, needing to see it anyway, he continued his prone crawl across the floor, but the cloth on his long-sleeved shirt slid across the surface of the tiles. "Jean!" he shouted, pausing only to jerk his sleeves up so he could use his skin as traction. How long would it take for Jose to get there? "Jean! Where are you?"

He had never been upstairs in *Jamaica's Place*. A quick glance up from the floor revealed one door to the left, one to the right. He chose the closer one. If it turned out to be a bathroom, he would pass it and keep going. "Jean! Candy!"

He heard a door open downstairs and Jose's voice. "Grant, what's your location?"

"Up the stairs, first door on the left." Either Jose had made good time or Grant's crawl up the stairs had been dangerously slow. Jose's feet pounded up the stairs behind him. They reached the door at the same time. A look inside revealed Candy on the bed, looking peacefully asleep, but Jean's body was draped over Candy's legs in an unnatural position, as if she had fallen there.

Grant cried out her name, terrified, anguish at his own inability to reach her bringing tears to his eyes. He crawled into the room, but a hazy smoke in the air made him cough. "Where is that coming from?"

Jose covered his mouth and nose with his shirt and searched the room with his eyes. "In the corner. See that thing puffing out smoke?"

Grant's answer was another cough. He was feeling lightheaded. He rolled onto his back and used his own shirt to cover his airways. He couldn't help anyone if he passed out and they had to drag him downstairs. Then again, he couldn't help anyone as he was now anyway. "God," he groaned, "why have you left me like this?"

Jose gripped the cord attached to the diffuser and pulled, then took the pillow from under Candy's head. Her head flopped onto the bed, but Jose did not notice. He waved the pillow around the room, then opened a window. "I think I got it mostly out of here, enough for us to breathe anyway. Champagne must have put something in the diffuser. I have no idea how long it will take for them to wake up. They are breathing, right?"

Again, terror gripped Grant's heart. He turned his head and stared hard, until the soft rise and fall of Jean's chest pulled the fear from his own. If Champagne had killed the woman he loved... He closed his eyes tight. It was unthinkable. "How long do you think she's been gone?"

"Well, if I was the type to know about these smelly things, I might be able to tell. My wife has one, but your guess is as good as mine. Could be minutes, could be hours. But I think we both know where she's gone." He dropped his shirt from his face, tossed the pillow back onto the bed, not quite hitting Candy's head, and spoke into the radio on his shoulder.

Grant sat up and dragged himself toward the bed. He reached for Jean's hand, draped off the mattress and almost touching the floor. Seeing her like this, unresponsive to his voice or his touch, was frightening in a way he had never experienced. Was this how she had felt when he was shot? Was this why she said it didn't matter if he couldn't walk, that he had trouble remembering things? Wouldn't he feel exactly the same if she had been the one shot?

He rubbed her fingers with his own. Damaged, he had called himself, but were they in opposite places, he would never think of her that way. That was what she had been trying to tell him all along. "I understand, Jean," he whispered, kissing the soft skin on the back of her hand. "I understand."

"I got people on the way to Slash's apartment," Jose said. "One way or the other, something's going down tonight. I need to be there." He looked over their three bodies, all incapacitated in their own way. "You okay with staying here with them until the EMTs arrive with the ambulance? They'll need somebody to tell them what happened when they wake up, and get their statements."

Grant agreed and Jose ran from the room. Grant knew there was no point objecting. Gone were the days when he could insist that he wanted to be there, to go get Champagne himself and help drag her to jail, with one more mark on her already long list of reasons for him to want her put away for life. He knew she had gone to kill Slash. She had as much as said so. Unless it was another lie, and all of this was an elaborate plan for her to join forces with him again and continue the evil that defined their world. He had learned the hard way not to believe anything that came from her mouth, no matter how sincere she sounded at the time. But if she was going to kill Slash, Grant was not sure he wanted to think about how he felt regarding the possibility of

Jose not getting there in time—or how he would feel if Jose did get there in time to save Slash's life.

He worked to lift himself onto the bed so he could move Jean to a better position so she wouldn't be uncomfortable when she woke, hating the fact that, when help arrived, he would need as much assistance as the women beside him. "God," he prayed out his anguish, leaning over Jean's form, the soft breath coming though her lips reassuring his thundering heart. "I want to be able to protect her, but I know that was no guarantee even when I was well." He sighed. "But I am able to love her and be there for her. I want to be strong again. I want to know that I still have purpose even if I don't have my legs. Help me learn how to live with this new reality of who I am, to accept what is, while still working for what can be. And I need help learning how to not be bitter, because I am."

He dropped his head to rest next to Jean's. "I know that every day I let this darkness eat away at me, it's worse than my muscles wasting, and it hurts Jean and everyone else I love. I can fight the paralysis, but I don't have the strength to fight the anger in my soul at what Champagne has done." Jean started to stir beside him. "I don't have much else to say, God. Just help. Please. I need You. I give up trying to do this on my own."

Grant's heart leaped when Jean opened her eyes. She saw him and smiled, then fell back asleep. He pulled her body close against his, his hand on her beloved face, before closing his own eyes and whispering against her hair. "Stay with me always, Jean. I love you."

Saturday Night, January 31

Champagne

Nothing. Champagne pressed a hand against her racing heart. It was nothing. Slash was hallucinating, screaming in terror about visions seen only within his own mind. The extra dose from Billy must have been a large one; Champagne had never seen Slash like this.

"Hell is waiting. She is waiting for me there." His shouts were enough to wake anyone in the rooms beside, below or above him, but Champagne knew no one would complain or even respond. Slash's section of the building was protected by the invisible code of treachery and blackmail. Anything that happened in his room, no matter how barbaric, would not be reported. She knew; her own screams in this very room had been ignored. Now his would be, too.

"She has the knife!" He cried like a child, rolling to his side and whimpering, his hands up around the back of his neck. "Mommy, don't! Please. I didn't mean it."

"Your mother did that to you?" Champagne asked the question aloud but Slash was too far gone to hear it. He thrashed and wiped his hands on the carpet, as if trying to clean them. "It hurts, Mommy. It hurts. It hurts." His voice turn to a menacing growl. "No one will ever hurt me again. I'll make them pay. They'll all pay."

Champagne had never heard the child's plea in Slash's voice, but the low tone of threat he'd just used was familiar and filled her with dread. She climbed onto the bed and pulled her legs up out of reach, holding her knife out, shaking with such force she finally dropped it on the sheets to avoid cutting herself.

"Shut up, Slash," she yelled. "Stop it."

"She's in hell waiting for me with her knife. There's no escape. No escape! I deserve it. I killed and raped and sold them." His voice lulled into the rolling tones of a high, but no happiness, however false, could be heard in it. "I earned hell. I punished and cut them. Stole their futures. I did it all. Broke the commands. Shook my first at God. Traded my soul for lust and power." He kicked at the air. Saliva streamed from the sides of his mouth.

"Stop it!" Champagne put her hands over her ears. His words were every nightmare, every beating, every hope he'd stripped from her. "Be quiet!"

"I'm doomed. Condemned forever." He moaned and thrashed against the base of the bed, knocking the lamp and clock from the nightstand. They crashed to the floor. The light bulb in the lamp sent a wild stream of light across the wall as it descended then shattered, leaving Champagne in darkness made so much more terrifying by Slash's shrieking.

"Turn it on! The light. I need the light!"

Unable to bear the dark any more than he could, Champagne scrambled from the bed and felt her way to the opposite wall, as far from Slash's flailing body as physically possible.

"Don't condemn me to the darkness. Please! Have mercy. Mercy!"

She groped past the desk, blindly knocking items to the floor, uncaring what broke on her way to the light switch next to the door. "You're the last person on earth or in hell to deserve mercy."

"I know." His voice was hollow, the sudden awareness in it so frightening Champagne hesitated, her finger on the switch. She had left her knife on the bed. If she turned on the light, would he attack her before she could reach it? She paused, sweat streaming down her back, her whole body trembling.

At a crash of sound, she jumped and turned on the light. Slash must have tried to stand. He lay sprawled over the broken lamp, his hands thrusting out along the carpet into the jagged pieces of the light bulb. Sharper than knives, slivers of glass sliced lines across the skin of his hands and arms. He screamed, but Champagne knew it was not from any pain, nor from the red blood smeared across the lampshade where he gripped it.

Champagne leaped over his body and onto the bed, too close to her knife. Her momentum carried it into the air. It sliced across her leg and she cried out, but the sound had no chance of being heard over Slash's guttural, animal moans of despair.

She couldn't kill him like this. Yet how could she endure waiting through this agony that might last all night? Billy hadn't told her how much he'd put in the bags. It could be hours before Slash was lucid.

Another cry of despair and fear pierced the air and singed through her skin to her very soul. She clamped both hands over her ears and screamed until her throat was raw. He continued to shout his sins and condemnation, and his terror at God's certain wrath.

God. Champagne held the bedsheet against the cut on her leg with her left hand and clutched her purse with her right. With frantic, urgent movements she searched for the Bible she had carried with her everywhere since she'd found Emily, like a talisman to protect her and Emily from evil. She had read Emily the stories of Jesus. Emily liked the one about the children best of all. Where was that? Luke, it was in Luke. She found the passage in chapter eighteen, the page folded at the corner and the story circled next to a smiley face Emily had drawn in the margin.

She read as loudly as her voice could project, screaming Jesus' words to His disciples about letting children come to Him and not stopping them.

"Jesus." It was not a shout or a curse from Slash's mouth, more like a yearning cry. He threw up on the lamp and carpet around it. His hands slid the lampshade aside. He slipped on the muck and fell into his own filth. "Jesus, help me. Save me from her. From myself."

Champagne wanted to spit on him. How dare he ask for mercy now? She tried to increase her volume to drown out his, reading on in the Bible verse after verse, chapter after chapter. Slash's rants became moans, then as the minutes passed, the moans turned to weeping. He rolled in his own blood and vomit, unaware of his stench.

Champagne read on. For what felt like hours she read, through the corrupt trial where Jesus was framed, through the mobs shouting to crucify Him, through His own disciples running away or pretending not to know Him.

Nobody was good when it came down to it. Everybody looked out for themselves.

Champagne had not noticed the quiet, so absorbed she had become at the cross, until she read about the thief at Jesus' side. *"Then one of the criminals who were hanged blasphemed Him, saying, 'If You are the Christ, save Yourself and us.' But the other, answering, rebuked him, saying, 'Do you not even fear God, seeing you are under the same condemnation? And we indeed justly, for we receive the due reward of our deeds; but this Man has done nothing wrong.' Then he said to Jesus, 'Lord, remember me when You come into Your kingdom.' And Jesus said to him, 'Assuredly, I say to you, today you will be with Me in Paradise.'"*

"That's me," Slash said from the floor. "I deserve to die. You did nothing, but You died in my place." He wept again. "Mercy, Jesus. Forgiveness."

She ignored him, the fury festering deep at his gall, and kept reading. When she reached a point where Jesus appeared after rising from the dead, and greeted the very disciples who had run away like cowards with the words, "Peace to you," she could not go on. She dropped the Bible and put her head in her hands.

"Peace," came the whisper from below at her side. She looked. Slash lay on his back, arms out, eyes upward. "Peace to you. He said it." His breathing lengthened and rattled as if his chest had no room left to expand his lungs. His next words came out a sigh. "Peace to me."

She waited for him to breathe in again. He tried. Air gurgled in his throat. She dropped to lay on the bed where she could not see him, hating the silent pauses that stretched between breaths almost as much as the screaming.

Champagne knew the moment he died, heard when the last ragged bit of oxygen left his body. Her own body lay inert, eyes open but unseeing, while her mind clawed destruction into her soul.

Had anyone walked in, Champagne knew that by all appearances she would look as dead as the man on the floor, until she roused herself enough to whisper, "I hate you and I envy you."

"We found her knife at the scene and her fingerprints all over the place."

Chapter Twenty-Two

Early Sunday Morning, February 1

Jose

Jose did not know if Candy would rejoice to hear of Slash's death or just go numb at the news as a way of setting it aside until she could process it. He was no counselor, and wished he could have sent one in his place, but this information should be delivered by a friend.

She stood at Susan's grave. He smiled when he saw her lips moving. What would she be telling Susan on such a morning? The sun had barely begun its climb onto the horizon. It bathed her in gold, a true natural gold, unlike the glitter that had bordered her face when he met her at *Jamaica's*. He never had asked how that had gotten there.

She seemed to sense his presence and turned her head. Her soft smile spoke a chosen peace, an impressive feat considering all she had been through in her recent and distant past. He had never encountered anyone like her, so transformed, yet still so the same.

"You're smiling," she said, her voice softer than normal, perhaps to match the soft sounds of the morning and the softer light of dawn. "Does that mean good news?"

"I was smiling about you, not the news, I'm afraid."

Candy went completely still. "She killed him."

"No." He saw her shoulders drop in release of tension. How would she respond to what he had to say next? "We found her knife at the scene and her fingerprints all over the place, even a small amount of what is likely her blood on one of the sheets, but there were no knife-marks or other wounds on Slash's body except cuts from a broken light bulb."

She blinked in slow-motion. "Her knife was there, but she wasn't?"

He shook his head. "By the time we got there, no one was in the room except Slash."

She was looking at him with her head cocked to the side and her hands deep in her pockets, much like a child when told something too advanced to compute. "You arrested him then?"

Again, Jose shook his head. He looked out across the field of gravestones honoring the dead, marking the passing of so many lives. How had they all died? Young and from violence like Susan? Old, surrounded by loved ones and friends, with a word of hope to bade goodbye?

"Slash overdosed on heroine, Candy. He's dead."

She stared at him for a full minute, uncomprehending. Then a jolt of shock shot through him like the jagged electric current of lightning when she let out a wail of grief unlike any he had ever heard and collapsed to the ground.

Of all the reactions—relief, bitter joy, open hostility—he never imagined this. She heaved in deep, shuddering breaths and sobbed. He dropped to the ground beside her. "Candy, it's okay. He's gone." He pulled her to sit beside him, their backs against the smooth rear side of a marker. "He can't ever hurt you again."

She curled up against him and wept into his shoulder. She cried so long and so hard her tears seeped through his uniform shirt and undershirt and onto his skin. He had an arm around her and patted her shoulder with an awkwardness due to lack of practice. He wished he had thought to bring some of her women friends with him. They would know what to say, how to help.

He knew neither, so sat without words while she cried until her tears were spent and her breathing came in short hiccup sounds. She wipe her nose with her sleeve. "I loved him once," she said, her voice raw and vulnerable. "He promised me the world. Said he would take care of me. I put every dream of my heart in his hands and he crushed them to dust." She wiped her nose again, this time with her other sleeve. "I don't know why I'm falling apart like this."

How would a friend respond? "I guess it's okay to grieve what should have been."

She glanced up at his face, her eyelids swollen, her eyes deep wells of suffering. "I miss my grandma," she whispered.

She lay her head against his shoulder again. "Thank you, Jose." He wrapped both arms around her, sheltering her from the wind, keeping her body off the cold granite stone. They sat together among the graves, quiet, still, and at peace.

Late Sunday Night, February 1

Candy

"Am I intruding?"

Jean sat sideways on the second step leading to the church altar, her legs bent at the knees, her long blue skirt draped over her and down the stairs like a waterfall onto the floor. She had been leaning with her arms folded on the top step and her head down on her arms. At the sound of Candy's voice, she raised her head. Her eyes were slightly reddened, but when she saw Candy, she smiled softly.

"I'm glad to see you, Candy. We haven't had much time together lately."

It was a kind and polite thing to say, but Candy never could tell when people meant what they said or were just being nice. "I can see you were praying. I don't want to interrupt."

Jean looked upward. "There's room at God's throne for the two of us." She dropped her gaze to the step where her hands rested. "I was giving things over to God."

Candy joined her on the steps, sliding Jean's skirt to the side so she wouldn't sit on it. "I needed to come and talk to God about Slash."

Jean nodded in understanding. "The night Champagne got arrested, I came here just before I went back to Grant's apartment. I left a box here on the steps, full of broken pieces of something that mattered." She rubbed the carpet on the steps first one direction then the opposite, watching the fibers appear to change colors as they caught the light. "I came back the next day and the pieces were gone."

So it was Jean who left the box. "Do you want them back?"

That peaceful smile crossed Jean's features again. "Stewart probably has them. It has turned into a good lesson. I thought I was handing over a thing, letting it go, admitting I couldn't fix it." Her upturned face looked to Candy like a painting of a truly holy person. Something about her profile as she put her gaze toward heaven was beautiful in a fully spiritual way. "Tonight I came to give over more broken pieces."

Candy surveyed their surroundings. "I don't see any."

Jean shook her head. "They don't show. They are the broken pieces that make up the people I love. I'm giving God my parents." She turned to Candy. "I wanted them to behave in a godly, mature way, but they didn't. I had been agonizing over trying to figure out why they made the choices they made so I could forgive them, but my broken pot made me realize that broken pieces are broken pieces. Regardless of why, they need fixing, and I can't fix them."

Candy pictured the box of mug shards she had gooped over with glue and gold glitter. She thought of Slash and Champagne and Melanie and Star, even that new girl, Maria, who wouldn't leave when Candy offered her a ride out. She shook her head. "Don't I know about not being able to fix things."

Jean's gaze was far away. "I can't change my parents, any more than any of us could change Champagne, or you could have changed Slash. I thought understanding was the solution, but God is showing me that forgiveness and understanding aren't the same thing. Neither is responsibility. I'm not meant to carry them or their faults. That's not what forgiveness is."

Candy pictured Slash's face. "What is?" she whispered.

"Letting go." She gestured to empty air on the step, her hands forming a shape as if holding a box. "I left broken pieces here, thinking I would show them to God and ask Him to show me how to fix them. But they're gone. That's what I need to do with the people I love and those I need to forgive. I don't need to tell God about them and ask Him to show me how to forgive. I need to give them over, lay them on the altar and let Him take them." She rubbed the carpet again. "Even Rod. I need to leave him at this altar and walk away free for good."

Candy let the thought sink in. After a time, she reached into her back pocket for her wallet. "I've been carrying this around for a long time," she said, opening the wallet to reveal a small piece of paper covered with names. "I used to read through these to remember who to blame for my problems. After I came to Jesus, I kept it to pray for them, but I've got to be honest, seeing this paper hurts, every time." She set the scrap carefully on the altar steps. "Slash. A police officer who turned the other way. A girl from *Hot Town* who turned me in one of the times I tried to escape. The first guy who beat me. The boy on the streets my first weekend who...." She felt the old churning, the old pain.

Jean touched the paper, tears gathering in her eyes. "So many names. So many people to forgive."

Candy tore the paper until individual names lay in a small row across the step. "Every one of these people are better off here than carried around in my back pocket. Like you said, we can't fix them."

"Can you give them up?"

She took one last look, gathered the pieces into a pile, and tossed them forward, shouting upward, "Here You go, God. I let them go. I forgive." She smiled. "That felt truly freeing." Her smile spread. "I think I'll leave them all there." She was going to say Pastor Stewart would be confused when he saw them all over the steps next time he came into the church, but then she remembered her previous visits to this same altar and laughed. He would know who had been there.

Jean rose gracefully from her spot and crossed to retrieve her purse from the first pew on the left side. She brought it back and pulled out a small zippered pouch. From there she extricated a set of photographs. Looking at Candy with her own smile, she threw the pictures with the words, "Here you go, God. I let them go."

The pictures floated to land on the platform, steps, and Jean's skirt. The moment felt like a prayer—a strange one, but sacred. Candy bowed her head. "Amen."

‘Billy wants to kill her.”

Chapter Twenty-Three
Monday Morning, February 2

Candy

"Candy, get over here. Right now."

It was all Jose said before he hung up. Candy called back as she sped to the precinct and left at least a dozen questions on his voicemail. Had he found Champagne? Had they figured out where Slash's drugs had come from? Was somebody else dead and he didn't want to tell her over the phone?

"You're going to take years off my life, man," she announced the moment she entered his office. "What's the deal?"

He simply motioned her over to his computer.

"You're not usually this stoic," she remarked, using a new word she'd learned from Jean last week. "Have you not had your morning coffee yet?"

He pointed at the screen. "Read."

She stood behind his chair and leaned over his shoulder. "Oh, praise the Lord. You heard from Champagne! Where is she?"

His frown did not waver. "Read," he said.

She scanned the social media message conversation.

Jose, I have something. It's big.

Champagne? Where are you?

Don't ask me that. I've been texting with Billy all morning. He's planning a kill. I think it might be one of Candy's friends.

Why did he contact you?

He didn't. I have Slash's phone and computer. He thinks I'm Slash.

"That's right," Candy said. "No one knows Slash is dead. You arrested Whip, right?"

Jose nodded. "And no one else had access to the room or the information. We put the word out that there was a robbery, but nothing about a murder."

"You think it was murder? Not an overdose?"

"Originally I thought overdose, but the autopsy showed more than heroin in his bloodstream. He was poisoned." Jose's face was grim. "Candy, you were drugged so Champagne could go there that night. Who do you think the drugs that killed him came from?"

She would have dropped into a chair had there been one nearby. She fell to sit on Jose's armrest and leaned her body weight against his shoulder to keep from falling to the floor. "But..."

"She says she didn't do it."

Candy was glad she hadn't put on any makeup. Her eyes would be running with mascara by now. "Do you believe her?"

He scrolled his computer mouse farther down the internet conversation. "I'm not sure. Read on."

Come in and let's talk.

No way. I'm staying out until I can prove I didn't kill Slash.

Who did?

Billy. The packet with the overdose was meant for me. Jose, Billy thinks I'm dead. He did it as a favor, a way to get in with Slash.

"I wouldn't put it past Billy." Candy realized she was almost sitting in Jose's lap and stood to her feet. "He hates Champagne. She isn't scared enough of him. And he's wanted Slash's power for a long time."

"That fits with the rest of what she says." Jose leaned his elbows on the desk and put his weight forward, as if unconsciously trying to get closer to Champagne, or the truth.

Candy read on:

He wants to do a trade. He wants passwords to all of Slash's sites. Says it's time for Slash to retire. I guess Slash botched up one of Billy's human trafficking sales a few weeks ago. Wouldn't let the transaction go through because the girls were too young.

"Never thought I'd hear that about Slash." Candy teared up again. Why was she crying all the time lately? It's not like he was her father or her husband or anything. He was her owner.

She shook her head, trying to shake free of her thoughts. "Anything else farther down?"

Jose skimmed the rest of the conversation. "She says Billy is going after someone Slash wants killed, but either she's being really vague or Billy didn't give her enough information. Said stuff about some women who is like Slash's mother, and he needs to bring her in alive so Slash can mark her before he kills her." He rubbed his face in his hands. "These guys are sick."

Candy touched the back of her own neck. "You don't have to tell me that." She paced around the desk in what little room the office provided. "Someone like his mother..." She thought through friends, old conversations, incidents. Her mind went back to the day Slash was released from prison, the day that—she felt the blood drain from her face. "Get up," she told Jose. She took his chair and typed as quickly as her two-finger pecking would allow.

It's Candy. Are you there?

She waited, breathing hard. When nothing happened after ten seconds, she pulled out her phone and punched in Grant's number. A message popped up just as he answered.

I'm here. Candy, I didn't kill Slash. I couldn't do it.

"Hello?" Grant asked the second time.

"Grant, Jean's in danger. You have to take her out of town, far away, as soon as possible."

"Candy?" Grant's voice rang with confusion. "What are you talking about?"

"Billy wants to kill her to get in good with Slash."

"Slash is dead."

"He doesn't know that. He thinks Champagne is dead and is trying to get Slash to trade his passwords for Jean's life."

"Why would he want to kill Jean?"

"I don't have time to explain right now!" Candy couldn't type and talk at the same time. "Call me back in twenty minutes, but call Jean first and make sure she's okay!"

She went back to poking keys, but finally slapped at the keyboard in frustration. She stood and pushed Jose toward the chair. "You type. I'll talk." She ignored Jose's grumbling and dictated fast.

I believe you. Billy's talking about Jean. How did you know it was one of my friends?

Billy said he was doing Slash a favor, but he would enjoy giving you a good kick in the gut while he was at it.

"A kick in the gut?" Jean was the closest friend Candy had ever had. A barrelful of words Candy did not say any more wanted to spill out. "We have to get him. I'm tired of people going after my friends." She put her hand on Jose's shoulder and must have squeezed hard because he winced. "I'm going to say a message and you tell me if you have a different plan."

"I've got no plan," he said, putting his hands over the keyboard to type. "I'm still trying to figure out how Jean is like Slash's mother."

"I'll tell you everything later." She spit out words and Jose kept up with her, not objecting to any of them.

If you're still on our side, put on hold everything about our former plan to shut down Slash's other connections. Keep Billy thinking you're Slash and agree to his plan, but ask him to wait a few days before he goes after Jean. We need some time. Stall somehow. We'll keep recording everything we get on the live feed from Hot Town and you keep all those texts on Slash's phone. After we get Jean safe let's set up a transaction point and snag him.

He hit the button to send the message and they waited. Jose moved her hand. "You're about to break my shoulder."

"Sorry." She leaned over to stare more closely at the computer and tapped her fingernails on the desk. "I'm nervous."

He grabbed and stilled her hand. "Yeah, I caught on to that."

She glanced back at his deadpan face and smiled. "You know, if I wasn't me, I'd probably develop a rather serious crush on you, Officer Ramirez."

He considered her. "I'm not sure what to say to that."

She could not tell if he was insulted or complimented or what. She laughed a little. "Don't worry, you're safe. I'm done chasing guys in this life."

He smiled. "Planning on chasing them in the next?"

"Oh stuff it." She glanced back at the computer. "Something's coming in."

I'm in.

"Praise God." Candy felt she could breathe again. "I've got to call Grant. No, Florence."

"Isn't she on her honeymoon?"

"She's getting back sometime this week." Candy rounded the desk, already searching for Florence's contact information on her phone. "Besides, this is life and death. She won't mind."

"How is she going to help?"

"She has access to...um...helpful resources."

He chuckled. "You know if I pried, you'd tell me. You can't keep a secret to save your life."

"That's why I'm leaving your office right now." She held the phone to her ear. "Florence, that you? Are you having a nice honeymoon? That's nice. Listen, we've got trouble here. Big time. I need your help and need it quick."

Monday Evening, February 2

Grant

Grant tapped his knees with the brochure. It still seemed strange to him that his legs could not feel the movement. "We need to talk about this trip Florence wants us to go on."

He watched Jean bite her lip and scrunch up her nose like she did when she couldn't decide about something. "I still can't figure out why she thought it was so urgent. I mean, she called us from her honeymoon trip."

He said nothing about Candy's phone call, Billy's plan, or the danger Jean was in. "Maybe there was a special deal on the treatment right now."

"It's in Europe. That would mean a plane flight, taking taxis, a foreign country. Would we really want to consider it?"

Grant lifted his shoulders in a shrug. "She says it would all be paid for. It would be a waste not to give it a try, don't you think?"

"I've never been anywhere. I wouldn't know what to do, how to get places." She rubbed her nose with the palm of her hand. "And this idea of them putting an implant in your body? Are you okay with that?"

"If it works, I'd be okay with just about anything. I did some research after she called on the electrical stimulation approach. It doesn't work for everybody, but..." He ran a hand through his dark hair. He had to convince her. "Florence said she'd pay to have a trained nurse travel with us. You wouldn't need to worry about my catheter or what to do if something went wrong."

"Just the thought scares me." The porch swing where they sat rocked faster, her nervousness coming out through her feet. "She said they've had huge success with the implants, or even the devices that you stick on the skin instead of going in surgically, but..."

He was sitting sideways on the swing, too far away to reach her on the other end beside his feet. He put his arm on the back of the swing and beckoned for her hand. "But what?"

"What if it doesn't work?" She looked off into the woods bordering her yard. "Would it be worse if we tried and it didn't help than if we just kept things as they are?"

He followed her gaze. They had played football near the brook, walked together from the house to the church up the hill, sat on the log beside the water and Jean showed him where she had dropped the key to Rod's office all those years ago. This trip would be for her, but he could not help wondering at the possibilities. He had heard of the treatment, had pondered if it would be worth trying, but it had been too expensive to even consider. "If there's a chance, Jean." His voice came out husky and more vulnerable than he wanted it to be. "I want to take it."

She took one of his hands in both of hers. "I just don't want you hurt."

"Devastated and depressed like before, you mean."

Her eyes teared. She nodded.

He leaned as far forward as he could with his legs extended like they were. Looking her in the eye, he said, "If you're willing to go with me, I will commit to giving this trip, and the results, to the Lord. If He chooses to make the treatment bring improvement of any kind, I'll praise Him. If he doesn't..." Grant made sure he meant the words before he said them. "I'll still praise Him, and I'll accept it."

A tear spilled over onto Jean's soft cheek and he wanted to wipe it away. He lifted his legs at the thighs and dropped them off the edge of the swing, then angled his body sideways so he could sit beside her. She did not wait for him to touch her, but encased his torso in her arms and buried her head against his heart. He wrapped his own arms around her slight form and held her close, resting his cheek against her silky hair. "Come with me, Jean? It will be a challenge, a trip like that, but it will be full of hope."

She lifted her head and blinked away tears, her eyelashes dark with the moisture. "Ten days at least, Florence said. That's such a huge expense with having to get three hotel rooms."

He kissed her. "Three?"

"One for you, me, and the nurse."

"Hmm, maybe we could hire a nurse over there. I'll talk to Florence about that." He tasted her lips again, so soft against his. "As for you and me, we could elope before the trip and save all kinds of money."

She smiled. "And it would make other things much more convenient. I could get my passport with my married name and not have to change it later."

"See there. Getting married now just makes sense."

She laughed and snuggled against him. He looked across at the church again, the place where he would promise to love her for the rest of his life. "Jean?"

"Hm?"

"Remember what you said about not wanting a big wedding? How you'd marry me now if you could?"

He felt her head move against his chest in a nod. "Mm-hm."

"Did you mean it?"

"Mm-hm."

He pulled in a deep breath. "Then let's get married. Now."

She sat up. "What?"

"You already have your dress. We could call Candy and Brenda. Stewart's at the church right now studying. We could be standing in front of the altar in half an hour—you and me and God."

"This isn't funny, Grant."

"I'm not being funny."

"What about my mom's big wedding? She'd be devastated if she found out we got married behind her back. She's already scheduled the caterer, paid for the invitations, everything."

"We wouldn't have to tell anyone. Your mom could still have her big party, and you'd get to wear your dress twice. You could consider it a renewing of our vows."

"What about my job?"

"You can call up your boss and explain." He grinned. "She's got a soft spot for me in my wheelchair."

She touched his cheek. "She had a soft spot for you before the wheelchair. I think it's the dimples."

"Think of it, Jean." He took her hand, turned it over, and kissed her palm. "It would be our wedding. Just ours. Not half the town. Just us and God. If that's the way we both want it to be, why shouldn't we? And look." He picked up the brochure. "We'd get an all-expense paid honeymoon."

"But what about when we came back?"

"Well, I guess for a couple of months, we'd have to keep it a secret. Maybe you could sneak over to my apartment every once in a while and spend the night."

"Grant!"

He could see she was blushing, even in the dark. "Jean." He took her other hand and pulled both to his heart. "Will you marry me?"

"Tonight?"

"Tonight."

She swallowed. Bit her lip. Smiled. "Yes."

Had he been upright and on his own two feet, he would have picked Jean up and swung her around. As it was, for the first time since the shooting, even the thought that he couldn't did not mar his joy. He pulled out his phone. "I'll call Stewart and Brenda. You call Candy. Let's see if we can get any of them to believe us. But remember to tell her it's a secret."

She put a finger over her smile. "My lips are sealed."

His kiss was long and full of promise. "So is my heart."

If ever
there was a
foundation for a
lifetime love,
they had it.

Chapter Twenty-Four
Monday Evening, February 2

Candy

Candy joined Stewart and Brenda at the altar. "I came as early as I could." She smoothed wrinkles from her rayon dress. The style was from back in the nineties, but it was the nicest dress she had. "I didn't want to give anyone time to come up with a bridesmaid dress for me, or worse, ask me to wear the one from Florence's wedding."

Brenda laughed and it made her belly bounce. Candy couldn't resist rubbing it. "You're so adorable. Like a big ladybug."

Brenda scowled. "Candy, I love you, but get your hands off my stomach."

Grant wheeled into the auditorium from the side entrance, looking more than handsome in a three-piece black suit. Candy wondered if he was able to dress himself, but figured it probably wasn't tactful to ask. Stewart shook Grant's hand like an officiator, hugged and congratulated him like a brother, then looked across at Brenda with a smile. "Grant needs a best man. Should we decide the baby is a boy and you come stand on this side?"

Brenda's response was quick. She must really not like having her belly touched. "I owe you," she murmured as she passed behind Stewart to join Grant.

Her husband winked at her. "I'll remind you of that later."

Grant tapped the arms of his chair. "So...my wedding?"

"Oh, right." Stewart started down the aisle. "Be right back."

Candy watched curiously as Stewart disappeared through the double doors leading to the foyer. "Is he going to walk her down the aisle?" She looked at Brenda, who shrugged, then at Grant, whose widened eyes were fixed on the doors Stewart had just reopened.

Candy turned, gasped, and her eyes filled with tears. The doors had opened and Jean entered, radiant in a white satin dress with a simple cut and no bling. It suited her perfectly. Her hair hung long and loose down her shoulders. Her face shone with love.

Grant's hands gripped his armrests. He seemed to be struggling to control his emotions, and Candy understood why.

Jean was in a wheelchair.

Stewart pushed Jean's chair slowly. Candy tip-toed over to Brenda and whispered, "We forgot to bring some music."

Brenda wiped her eyes. "I don't think either of them have noticed."

Jean rolled the last few feet herself, then reached out her hand once she was beside Grant facing the altar. "I'd rather sit beside you than stand alone."

His jaw worked. Candy felt like an intruder upon a sacred moment. The church was always a special place, but this setting, with moonlight coming through the stained-glass windows like a blessing from God Himself, felt truly hallowed.

Stewart took his place and Jean and Grant promised to love and to cherish, in sickness and in health, together until death.

The words were so much more powerful when people actually meant them. Candy had seen plenty of weddings, thrown-together ceremonies in bars or clubs, people intending to keep the vows they said, but everyone knowing there was no real commitment behind them.

Candy had watched Grant love Jean from a place of fear into freedom. Now Jean was loving Grant through pain and disability. If ever there was a foundation for a lifetime love, they had it. "Those two renew my faith in humanity," she whispered to Brenda.

"Shh."

"Marriage is hard work," Stewart was saying. Candy had never heard that at a wedding before. People usually only talked about the good stuff. Stewart probably considered himself a realist. "The Bible says without Christ we can do nothing, but with Christ all things are possible. A marriage founded on Jesus will succeed and last, and be full of joy." He joined their hands and quoted, "A threefold cord is not quickly broken. Have God at the center of your marriage, and nothing on earth can separate you."

Candy's eyes stung. This moment, so simple, had a beauty and holiness that rose above things like decorations or a big cake or fancy music. Grant slipped his grandmother's delicate, feminine ring on Jean's small finger. She put a simple gold band on his. Jean and Grant had already proved, each of them, a sacrificial, Christ-like love for each other. The world she had known, so fueled by lust and greed, consumed but did not satisfy. What she was seeing now was something higher, love as God intended.

"I now pronounce you man and wife." Stewart clapped Grant on the shoulder with a grin. "Little Brother, you may kiss your bride."

They tried maneuvering, with laughter, to get their chairs close enough. Finally, Jean stood from her chair, took the two steps that separated them, and sat on Grant's lap. She took his head in her hands, with a smile rubbed his nose with her own, then kissed him.

Candy told Brenda there was no word to describe that kiss other than sweet. "And not in a patronizing, sickening, too-much-cotton-candy way," she said, "but a happy and good sweet, like lemonade on a hot day."

Jean smiled up at her. "Lemonade. I like that."

"We should go somewhere to celebrate," Brenda said. "There wasn't time to bake a cake or anything."

"You go right ahead." Grant put his arms around his new wife. "We're going to the creekbed where I proposed."

Jean kissed her husband again. "Am I allowed to be glad that we can't go on that motorcycle of yours?"

Candy winced, but Grant actually smiled. "Don't rule it out forever, my love. I'll be back on Chachie someday, and there's a spot on the seat behind me that's just your size."

Her lips curved. "Brenda, if you go somewhere, bring me back a huge piece of cake, will you? I need to change my size."

Grant laughed out loud. "Come on, beautiful. Let's go have a reception for two at the lake."

Jean stood and rounded Grant's chair to push it. "Don't forget, we have to stop by to talk with Florence about our honeymoon trip."

Candy had turned to go but did a double-take back at Jean. "Please tell me you're not borrowing her camper!"

Monday Night, February 2

Grant

The streetlight was their moon, the real orb eluding visibility by hiding behind a patch of clouds. Grant carried Jean's large bag, one of those with side pockets all around it for who knew what, on his lap as he wheeled around the back of the car and onto the grass beyond the guard rail that edged past the bridge over the creek. He wouldn't think about how much nicer the view would be could they walk down the hill to the actual creekbed, as they had the last time they had been there. No black thoughts were allowed, not tonight.

He found a spot near the slope, locked his wheels, and started rummaging through the bag. "What all did you get when you stopped at the store?"

His new bride closed her car door and walked toward him, her dress billowing out with each soft step. The smile curving her lips made her beauty shine, and the thought that she was his now flooded him with more feeling than he knew what to do with. He set the bag to the side and opened his arms. She came willingly, settling her small body as near his as the chair would allow. His one arm encircled her waist and he reached his other hand up around her neck to tangle his fingers in her hair.

"Jean," he whispered. "My wife."

She put her lips against his. Her kiss ran deeper, exploration and desire in it, and that flood of feeling already surging through his veins blazed hot in a way he'd not dared allow before.

She pulled away and when he reached to draw her back to him, a teasing glint filled her eyes and she edged out of reach. "I need to set up our wedding reception." She giggled and for a moment he thought of Florence's face when they had dropped by after the wedding. She had promised to keep their secret, and laughed with delight, her cheeks jiggling, when they handed her the brochure and asked if she would set up the trip for them as soon as possible. Tomorrow, she'd promised, and hollered into her living room for Doug to stop watching the game and call a travel agent immediately. She had clapped her hands like a little girl and hugged Jean at least four times before they left. He smiled at the memory. His Jean, who once avoided touch of any kind, had embraced her warmly and with love. That had been good to see, but he had felt jealous, wanting those arms around him instead.

"Jean, come back."

She had set out a blanket, and on it, from the depths of that bag, had pulled four flameless candles, a bottle of sparkling cider, a small circular package with an assortment of cheesecake slices, paper plates, napkins, and plastic forks. "I'm not my mother," she said, dropping to sit on the blanket, the skirt of her dress floating out around her and covering the plates and napkins, "but I think this will suffice." She sent him a cheeky grin. "She's been preparing for years and I only had an hour or so after all."

"You're magnificent." He slid from his chair, trying not to be gangly and uncoordinated as he dropped onto the blanket and put his legs straight out, then crossed them so he could sit without falling over. "This is the best wedding reception I've ever attended."

"Me, too." She scooted closer to his side and tucked her skirt under her curved knees, revealing the plates again. "Want some cider? I forgot cups, so we'll have to drink out of the bottle." She removed the top and held the bottle out to him. "Would you like a taste?"

He touched her face, ran his thumb over the full swell of her bottom lip. "Yes," he said, hearing the husky tremor in his voice. She smiled and her eyelids shuttered closed as he neared and kissed her. He could not shift his position while his arms were full of her, but she did, slipping closer and wrapping her arms around his neck, pressing close. His whole being pulsed with life, with love, with desire God-blessed and free to enjoy to the full.

She must have put the bottle down somewhere, but he did not bother to ask where or if she had closed the top. It could be pouring all over the blanket or on the legs of his suit. His mind, his heart, both were full of better things, as were his arms. He was filled with her.

"Jean," he spoke against her skin, her name his joy. She ran trembling fingers across the line of his jaw, down his neck, across his collarbone where he had loosened his shirt. He shuddered at the pleasure of her touch.

"Grant," she whispered, "I—"

Headlights found them. A car raced by, startling Jean. She lurched out of his arms with a cry of surprise, falling to the side and knocking him over, like they were two bowling pins. He chuckled from where he lay as she scurried to right the bottle of cider, which now was indeed spilling all over the blanket, one hand keeping her skirt out of the puddle while she then collected the candles, plates, and forks, and tossed them haphazardly back into the bag. "I didn't realize there'd be people out here at this time of night," she said breathlessly. "Our special reception shouldn't be out in public. Let's go home."

He knew he was grinning like an idiot. The car was long gone and chances of another passing by were slim to none, but her embarrassment at being caught in his arms was just plain fun. Her cheeks were bright spots of color and she refused to look him in the eye as she collected the rest of the items, except the wet blanket, and returned the full bag to the backseat of the car.

He swallowed his laughter enough to say, "Should we go to my apartment or your house?"

Biting her lip, she helped him climb back into his chair, then tipped the blanket so the cider could run off into the grass. "Well, these days I never know when Mother is going to show up at the house."

His laugh burst through. "To my apartment then, please, Mrs. Henderson. I, too, would prefer our reception to be private."

By the time they reached his front door, Grant had gone from anticipation to a near-teenage brand of nervousness. "I wish I could carry you over the threshold."

She waited for him to unlock and open the door, then said, "I have every intention of you carrying me across the threshold, Mr.

Henderson." She placed herself on his lap. "If I tuck my legs up, I think we'll fit."

He rolled forward to the door frame. "If you tuck your legs up enough to fit, I won't be able to see over your dress."

Her laugh was contagious. "You don't need to see, so long as you didn't leave anything on the floor just inside the door."

He wheeled them inside, clumsily maneuvering down the hallway, laughing with her as she used her feet and hands to keep his chair from running into the walls on either side. "I need a bigger apartment." At the open door to his bedroom, he stopped, winded. "Jean, I want to start our marriage being more honest than I'd like to be. I know you want to know how things really are, so I have to admit to you that today has been long and active, and I'm really worn out."

She stood at once. "Oh, Grant, I'm sorry. I didn't—"

"No, I'm fine. Just tired."

She circled to stand behind his chair and pushed him into the bedroom. "Let's get you into bed so you can rest."

"Jean, it's our wedding night. I was just wanting to ask if we could save the reception until tomorrow sometime."

"Oh." She flushed. "Well, just the same, if you get ready for bed you can relax and put your legs up at least. I don't want them swelling and you having to take extra meds tomorrow."

He hated the intrusion of his disability on this moment, this night, but it was there, a part of their marriage as long as he was. She helped him through his nightly regime of pills, then busied herself at something in another room while he finished his bathroom routine, changed, and placed his body into bed, two pillows behind his back so he lay at an incline and could see the door.

Eventually, she appeared in the doorway, all beauty and softness. She turned out the light in his room and the light from behind in the hallway silhouetted her form, making her face unreadable. She crossed to the bed, each step making his senses more aware, and sat on the edge facing him. "I want to start our marriage honest, too," she said, so quietly he barely made out the words. He had taken her hand with one of his and was reaching around her with the other. "You said...you said we could go slow, no expectations, right?"

He checked her face, her eyes, for signs of the old fear, but saw none. "Right." Just in case, he moved to the side until he no longer touched her.

"Then may I do something I've wanted to do for a long, long time?"

His mind ran to several things he had wanted to do for a long time. He tried to guess her thoughts, but came up blank. "Please do, my Jean."

She bit her lip, that full bottom lip he wanted to taste again, then surprised him by climbing onto the bed on his left side, between him and the bedroom wall. "Your dress will get all rumpled," he said.

"I know." She came toward him on her knees, white satin flowing around her, until she was by his side. She touched his face, her hand soft against the stubble developing below his cheekbones. "I love you, Grant Henderson." She settled her body beside his and nestled her head into the curve of his neck. Her palm rested against his heart and her sigh was one of pure contentment.

His arm wrapped around her slight waist and pulled her more fully against him. His other hand stroked her hair, the strands as smooth as the satin of her dress. Her skirt draped over his legs. He could not tell where she ended and he began.

"As it should be," he whispered.

She lifted her head. "What is?"

"You and me. One."

She moved her hand up to his shoulder and rested her head onto his chest, her ear against his heart, and nodded. He felt her breathing deepen. She had told him once it was always hard to fall asleep. The night was when she struggled most. Yet here, now, his wife slept peacefully in his arms.

His wife.

He held her close, whispered, "I love you, Jean. Always."

Then he, too, closed his eyes and slept.

"You'll
tell me
when Jean
gets back,
right?"

Chapter Twenty-Five
Tuesday Afternoon, February 3

Florence

Florence squeezed her husband's hand as they walked the cobblestone path to her old home. "Our trip was fantastic, Doug, but it's nice to be back in Oakview."

He gave her a quick peck on the cheek, making her blush. "You visit with that crotchety old sister of yours. I'm going to call Henry Redding—see how his fishing trip went." He put a hand on her shoulder. "And stop worrying about your new dress," he said with a loving smile. "Gladys may hate it, but I think you look great. Like a huge avocado."

He meandered back down the bath and she shook her head. The man was adorable, but if his life depended on it, he couldn't pay a compliment without it sounding like a backhanded insult.

With a glance back at the camper where Doug stood talking on the phone, Florence clasped her hands together and felt the excitement rise. She couldn't wait until that evening. Brenda was going to put Alice's big black bag, holding nearly half the money Alice had left, on their home's dining room table. Florence and Doug were invited to supper and she imagined Pastor Stewart's face when he opened the bag and saw seventy-five thousand dollars in cash right where his plate usually sat, with a note from an anonymous donor.

She was having the time of her life with Alice's money. She needed to remember to call Jean's father before the day's end and set up a time for her to send construction workers to renovate Jean's house so it would be accessible for Grant's chair. "Until he learns to walk," she whispered. Would the treatment in Europe be a success, or yet another in a long string of disappointed attempts?

She was praying at the door when it opened from the inside.

"So you're finally back," Gladys said, little Sapphire by her side in a pink dress covered in frilly ruffles. "What is that all over your dress? Pineapples?"

Florence smiled. "I had a wonderful trip. Thanks for asking."

Gladys pulled her into a stilted hug. "I'm glad you had a good time. Come in so Sapphire and I can see your pictures."

Florence greeted the child, but when she ran ahead into the living room, Florence commented quietly to Gladys, "I thought Billy wouldn't let her stay anywhere but that awful day care."

Her sister nodded. "He changed his mind all of a sudden and said Melanie could let her stay with me during the day. I just know something fishy is going on. I think he's making a plan to do something bad to Melanie and Star before we can help them escape. Melanie has been all sorts of secretive about some big job he wants them to do." Sapphire skipped back toward them and Gladys pulled her close to her side. The little girl hugged Gladys around the legs and smiled up at Florence. "And she keeps tearing up every time she looks at—" Gladys pointed her gaze downward. "—someone. I don't like it. We need to get them out. And soon. Can't you use some of Alice's money to bribe somebody?"

"Candy's working on some plan with Jose."

"Well, they need to plan faster. Where is all that money from Alice anyway?"

"The big bag is at Doug's place now."

"You mean your place."

Florence tilted her head. "Goodness, your right. I'll have to get used to that. The bag is at our place. I'm returning a huge bulk of it to the church to replace all Rod stole from them. I've already used a chunk to hire that super lawyer I told you about, and he made sure Rod was served justice. That was worth every penny. Another pile is going to get set aside for a summer road trip."

"You can't use that money to go gallivanting across the country. It's supposed to be helping people, not funding your vacations."

Florence shook her head. "If Candy were here she'd say don't get your panties in a wad, Gladys."

"Well, she's not, and that's vulgar."

Florence smiled. "Anyway, it's not a vacation trip. Doug and I will be going to find the other four girls Rod abused and see if we can help them."

Gladys led the way into the kitchen, where Florence's mouth dropped open in astonishment. "Did a tornado come through here?"

Sapphire's laugh rang like bells. "We played with clay." She held up a pink blob. "I made a kitty!"

"Oh, that looks..." *Like a kitty that found the wrong side of a meat grinder.* "It's very creative."

Sapphire proudly showed her other creations—a giraffe, airplane, and a purple hot dog with a green bun. "And then we made a cake with real strawberries in it!" She held up pudgy fingers. "I ate two pieces."

What a transformation this child had made in Gladys. Her kitchen was a wreck, but her face had gentled in a way Florence had not seen in many long years.

"When we get the day care set up, you should volunteer some," she told Gladys. "It would get you more time with Sapphire."

"No need." Gladys swiped the edge of the cake pan and licked frosting off her finger. Florence nearly fell over from the shock. "As soon as we get them away from that Bradon character, I'm going to have Melanie and Sapphire move in with me. Someone needs to feed this child healthy meals, and I doubt her mother knows how to do more than open a can of pork n' beans."

Florence wanted to point out that two pieces of cake for an afternoon snack fell far below the healthy line, but instead she slid her own finger across the pan and tasted the frosting. Cream cheese. Her favorite.

Gladys looked her over. "I hope you washed your hands."

Florence laughed. "I missed you, too, Gladys."

Doug opened the front door. "You about ready to go, love bug?"

Gladys mumbled something about lovesick teenagers, but wrapped a section of cake in tin foil and handed it over. "I suppose that man has someplace to take you. Call me later. We can plan to come over and see your pictures another time."

"I'd like that." Florence hugged Sapphire with the hand not holding the cake, then started toward the door.

"Before you go," Gladys asked, "do you know when Jean and Grant will be coming back into town?"

Florence slowed to a stop in the hallway. "Why do you want to know?"

"Melanie and Star have gone to her house a few times over the past weeks. For some reason Billy doesn't mind them visiting her. I don't know why he likes her better than me. But Melanie said she tried to visit the other day and of course Jean's house was empty. She asked me where Jean was and when I told her she was off gallivanting in Europe somewhere, she wanted to know when they would be back. Said she needed to see her about something important."

A subtle glance at Doug confirmed Florence's fears. The concern furrowing his brow made her turn them both toward the door before their faces told Gladys more than she should know. The danger to Jean had not passed, even now that Slash was dead. "Let's go," Florence whispered to her husband. "I don't know when Jean's getting back," she tossed back to Gladys, keeping her face averted, "but I really hope that treatment they're trying on Grant works."

"Sticking a box inside a person just isn't natural," Gladys said behind her.

"Neither is deodorant," Doug quipped, "but I'm sure grateful for it."

Florence giggled while Gladys huffed in the background. "Do you want to come with us to Alice's?" she asked her sister. "I can't wait to see the improvements."

"I don't know how you can go into that place at all." Gladys followed them to the door and stood in the entryway as they left. "It's full of years of evil and unhappiness."

"Yes, but that's the point. I hired men to come in while we were gone and transform the place. What was once used for evil will now be used for good."

Her husband gently pinched her cheek. "Hope they cleaned up that mess you made when you ransacked the place."

She smiled at the memory. "That was first on their list. Then next was to completely gut Rod's office and his bedroom and turn them into indoor playing areas for the children. Some of the house will be the same as before, for whoever we find to live there as cook and housekeeper, but most of it will look and feel like a modern, professional day care, a place of hope that's going to help people like Melanie find a better job for themselves and their little ones."

Gladys surprised her by putting her hand on Florence's arm. "It's a good thing you have done, Sister. A good thing Alice has done." She waved goodbye when they made their way to the camper filling half the road off the driveway. "Later in the week, when Sapphire comes over, I'll meet you there and you can get a three-year-old's vote on the new look."

Florence waved back. "That will be fun."

"And you'll tell me when Jean gets back, right?"

Florence smiled and waved again, but mumbled under her breath, "Not if I can help it." She turned to her husband. "After Alice's, we need to go see Jose."

Tuesday Night, February 3

Jean

Jean thanked the male nurse and walked him to the hotel door. "See you in the morning."

"Call my room if you need me during the night."

She smiled her thanks, shut the door, then crossed the room to flop onto the bed next to Grant. "What a trip. I like what I've seen of Europe so far, but I'm exhausted. I can't imagine how tired you must feel."

The big appointment was at ten in the morning, less than fifteen hours away. The doctor would assess Grant's X-rays, MRIs and CT scans, come up with a plan for their ten-day treatment, then start with either the cold laser therapy or the electrodes with the remote. Jean did not know the details. Normally she would have researched every aspect and known every possibility, but their hopes had been dashed too many times. At this point, she would just pray for the tiniest improvement, and try to be strong for Grant no matter what happened.

"It was no picnic." He hadn't said so, but the flight had been a challenge, possibly more of frustration navigating such small spaces and rushing from one airport terminal to the next than physical pain. He lay semi-reclined on the bed, pillows behind his back, his head against the headboard and eyes closed. The weariness she felt lined his face also.

She lay against his side and nudged her head up into that perfect space where his neck curved into his jaw, made just for her. "How about you relax and I give you the best foot rub of your life?"

She felt his smile against her hair. "That sounds nice, but I'm afraid the effort wouldn't be appreciated as much as it should be since I wouldn't be able to feel it."

Her head shot up. "Oh, Grant, I'm so sorry. I wasn't thinking."

He ran a hand through her hair. "Don't apologize. It makes me feel good that you forget sometimes I'm paralyzed. That's not all I am to you."

She kissed him. "I could write a list of all you are to me, but you'd fall asleep before I could get halfway finished."

"How about you write me a list on the plane flight back when we have nothing better to do."

She blushed. "Are you saying you have something better to do at the moment?"

His fingers played with her hair, sending shivers of delight all through her. "Are you nervous about tomorrow morning?"

Should she be honest? She dropped her head and her hair fell to cover her blush. "Not as nervous as I am about right now."

Those fingers of his tugged her hair away from her face and drifted over her skin. How could something feel so amazing and be so frightening at the same time? "Talk to me, Jean," he whispered. "I'm listening."

She bit her lip. "Well, I've been thinking about our wedding night."

"Was that just last night? Seems like it was a week ago. A lot has happened."

"Not that night." She felt her face flaming. "The one that's still to come."

He cocked his head, but she saw when he caught her meaning. His mouth spread into a grin. "You mean the married part of being married?"

How could she not smile back at him, even as she put hands to her burning cheeks? She looked away from him, at the wall, at the chip in one of the ceiling tiles, at the headboard, which needed a good refurbishing.

He cupped her face in his hands and turned it until she had to look at him. His grin had not faded. "I adore you, Jean Jameson. No, Jean Henderson now." His thumbs made soft trails along her cheekbones. "I've been thinking about our wedding night, too."

"I should certainly hope so."

He laughed out loud. "Will it help you talk if you don't have to look at me?"

"Yes."

He dropped his hands and folded them in his lap. "Okay. Go ahead."

She felt like a child, but just couldn't look him in the eye. She curled her legs crossways and stared at a picture on the far wall, a non-impressive painting of bananas and apples in a wooden bowl. Her mind processed the colors and shadows, the illusion of depth and texture, while her heart raced and told her to run and her spirit told her to stay and tell him.

After long moments, she closed her eyes and said, "I don't want it to be dark. If I can't see you, I'm afraid when you touch me, I'll see him."

"That makes sense."

He said it so...so calmly, as if she was being practical and reasonable rather than childish and demanding. She did look at him then, but her eyes filled and his image went blurry. "But when it's all bright like this..." She gestured to the overhead light. "I feel completely self-conscious and don't want you to look at me and see all my flaws."

"Your flaws?" He took her hand and kissed it. "Jean, do you have any idea how long I have wanted to look at you? And I can't remember even once worrying about any flaws."

"Oh goodness." She scooted off the bed and stood, waving her hands in front of her face like her mother did when she couldn't think of what to do but had to do something. "Did I tell you that Florence called me and told me Rod got life in prison without parole? It feels so good to know he's locked away and can't ever hurt anyone again. I'm going to enjoy not having my heart jump anytime I see someone with his build, or hear a voice like his. Knowing he will never show up back in town, or be the voice on the other end of the phone, is such freedom."

"She did tell me, and I'm glad." His voice was full of love. "Jean, come here."

She swiveled to face him, hands clasped in front of her. "I know I'm being ridiculous, Grant, but I'm so nervous I can't stand it."

"What do you think about candlelight?"

She stopped fidgeting. "What?"

"Candlelight. It's a good compromise between the lights being on or off, and I hear it's pretty romantic." By then she had come close enough for him to touch. "And it's like the sunset. You're at your most beautiful when we watch the sunset together. Your face gets covered in gold."

"Grant," she breathed out. "You amaze me."

"We'll get some candles tomorrow after the appointment. For now, though, sit beside me. I've got an idea."

He'd said tomorrow. She felt the knots in her stomach untie and the tightness in her chest ease. "Just a minute." She found the switch for the bedside lamp and clicked it on, then turned off the large ceiling light. "That's better." Climbing over where he stretched out on the near side of the bed, she curled up beside him. "What's this idea of yours?"

"Remember when you asked me to help you learn to enjoy being touched?"

They had sat on a log by the creek near her house, a yard apart, and slowly, with anticipation, excitement, and yes, fear, she had placed her hand down on the log. He had positioned his next to him. Little by little, their hands had moved toward each other until they finally touched. She still remembered that feeling—an impossible mix of joy and trepidation, of the desire to move closer and the equal desire to flee. "I feel exactly the same way now."

"But we kept practicing, and now you don't even flinch when I hold your hand."

"I love holding hands."

"See, then it worked." He held her hand easily, almost in a friendly manner. "So now we need to practice on the rest of you."

"Oh my."

He grinned. "And though I wholeheartedly like being touched by you and have no hesitations whatsoever, I think we should practice on me, too."

At that she smiled. "I read in some magazine once about making a chart and marking from one to ten how much you like or dislike being touched in different areas."

"That sounds fun. Got a marker? You can skip the chart and just write numbers all over me."

She laughed and rose to find a notepad and pen. "And how would we explain that to the doctor tomorrow?"

"I'd tell him you were marking your territory."

"Think I'll stick with pen and paper." She drew a stick figure on the first page. "Let's start with your arm." She ran her fingernails from his palm to his elbow, then from the inside of his elbow, which received a high number, up to his shoulder. This was good. Analytical. Precise. Contained. She traced his collarbone and he closed his eyes and sighed. She marked that spot with a star. Her fingers traveled up to his neck.

"Mm, that feels really good."

"Really?" She put a hand to her own neck. "I can't stand anything touching my neck."

He looked her way. "What about here?" His hand found her collarbone and the line he drew with his fingers across her skin drew out a sigh of her own.

Grant took the notepad from her hand and looked it over. "That's not me," he said, tossing the paper off the bed. He pulled her to him. "I'm over here."

"But if I don't write it down, how will I remember which places you like best to be touched?"

His chuckle was low and curled her toes. "I'll be happy to remind you anytime you want." His one arm went around her waist and his free hand circled her neck and ran up into her hair.

"What are you doing now, Grant Henderson?" she whispered.

"I've decided it would be nice to make out with my wife. If she doesn't mind, that is."

Jean's heart filled and overflowed. Her body—she didn't know what was going on with her body, but whatever it was, it was good. "She doesn't mind." She moved her face close. "Not one bit."

‘I don’t know that I’d trust Gladys with an assignment like that.”

Chapter Twenty-Six
Wednesay Afternoon, February 4

Candy

Candy paced the tiny area around Jose's desk. "Billy is a jerk, but he's a smart jerk. We've been able to watch him in that main room and even hear him thanks to the bug Champagne put under his booth, but I still have no clue what he's planning or how we're supposed to stop him."

Jose, looking infuriatingly calm, sat at his desk and skimmed through the digital history from *Hot Town* for the third time that afternoon. "We know his pattern has changed with Melanie and Star, so they probably have something to do with it."

"From what Florence said, it sounds like he wants to use them to get to Jean."

"Do you really think he plans to deliver on his promise to give Jean to Slash—or rather Champagne posing as Slash—unhurt?"

Candy thought hard. "Honestly, I don't know. If I had to guess right this moment, I'd say he's planning to double-cross Slash somehow, but he needs Slash's passwords first, so he has to have some leverage to trade. If Jean is all he has, yes, he'd keep from harming her. But the poisoned drugs he gave Champagne means he's not playing it safe anymore. He's getting either desperate, or power-hungry enough to not be careful. That makes me nervous."

Jose spoke low and she almost did not hear him. "Nervous enough you wouldn't want to ask Jean to volunteer as bait?"

She shook her head so hard her dangling earrings almost flew out of her ears. "Don't even think it, Jose. We're not getting Jean anywhere near this. Even I wouldn't put a foot in *Hot Town* at this point. Billy has a line. I've only seen him cross it twice, and both times people died.

Champagne's drugs, and the texts he's sent to Slash since, are without question across that line. He is really dangerous right now. We need to be careful."

"I hear you." He steepled his fingers and rested his chin on them. "But I'm not comfortable sitting back and letting this all play out."

"Neither am I." She checked her reflection in the window behind Jose's desk. "It's a shame Jean's so tiny. I'd dress up and put on a wig and we could set up a showdown if it would get this over with."

"A showdown. Do you think that's what Billy is planning for Slash?"

Jose's secretary entered the room, coffee mugs in hand. She offered one to Candy, who made a face and shook her head. What she wouldn't give for a cold Diet Coke, or even a bottled water. Why did everybody have to be into coffee? "Doesn't it feel weird, talking about Slash like he's still alive?"

Jose nodded while he blew into his cup. "Do you still think Champagne is with us, enough to stick it out to the end?"

"She wouldn't be handing everything over like she has if she wasn't. I think she really wants to prove she didn't kill Slash."

"Which is ironic since that was exactly what she had planned to do."

"Yeah, we girls can be complicated sometimes."

He smiled at her. "Sometimes?"

She wasn't going to announce it to him, but he had a really nice smile. "If we could get through to Melanie or Star, we could figure this mess out, but Florence says Melanie won't even tell Gladys what's going on. They can tell she's scared, though, too scared to talk."

"Do you think Gladys could get a bug onto Melanie's clothes next time she came to pick up her daughter? We don't have any like that on hand—too expensive for small-town stuff—but for this I could order one in."

"I don't know that I'd trust Gladys with an assignment like that. She might not be able to keep it a secret."

"Says the expert secret keeper."

She kicked at his leg, but purposefully missed, enjoying the secretary's look of horror at her familiarity. "I can when it counts." She resumed her pacing. "I want to get to Melanie but can't. Billy wants Melanie to get to Jean but—" She stopped, whirled, and sat on the edge of Jose's desk. She reached for his mug and took a sip of his drink. "Oh, that is so gross." She shoved the mug back into his hands. "Jose, do you have any experience in construction? Never mind, that won't even matter. Boy, have I got a great idea!"

Wednesday Night, February 4

Jean

Dinner had likely been delicious, but Jean did not remember tasting much of it. She wheeled Grant toward the hotel elevator. "I still can't wrap my head around what I saw today."

Grant did not seem to have heard her, perhaps too absorbed in his own thoughts, which were surely as overwhelming as hers. They had followed the doctor at ten that morning to one of the center's rehabilitation rooms, where they met Carlos, a car accident victim who lost all feeling from the chest down. For over two years, he worked to regain muscle control with no success. The doctor showed Grant a model of the small machine he had implanted into Carlos' back, then Carlos showed them the remote in his hand. "Go ahead," he'd said, handing the remote to Grant, pointing at a button on the right side. "Push it."

Grant pushed the button and Jean jumped back when Carlos sat up. "How did you do that?" she asked with a gasp.

"The electrodes jolt the nerves into sending messages to the brain for my muscles to move." He shrugged. "I don't know really how it works; I just know it does."

When the doctor led them onward, once they were out of earshot, Grant asked the question that was also on Jean's mind. "Is he able to walk?"

"Not Carlos," the doctor said. "We don't have the technology to go that far yet on a paralysis as complete as his. For cases like yours, however, we've seen a higher success rate than any other treatment." They'd ended their tour in rehab room number three. "We'll start with the cold laser today, and see how your body responds. Later in the week, we'll talk about options with the electromagnetic treatment."

Jean's thoughts came back to the present when Grant's chair got stuck on a ridge in the hotel hallway carpet. He rocked back and forth to get over the hump, saying, "I wanted to ask him to stick one of those machines inside me right then and see if it would work."

Jean walked forward to step on and flatten another ridge two yards ahead. "I would feel the same way."

He caught up with her and reached to cover her hand with his own. "I'm really glad you're here with me."

She leaned forward to wrap her arms around his shoulders and place her cheek against his. "Me too." Just outside their hotel room, she stopped his chair facing a bench set on the opposite wall. She walked to sit on the bench, carrying the bag of candles they had stopped to buy on the way back, but ended up pacing, back and forth, turning every three or four steps. "I want to talk to you before we go inside."

He grinned. "I gathered that."

"It's the candles." She set the bag on his lap and went back to pacing. "I want tonight to be so special, but I've got these things I feel like I have to tell you, but I don't want to ruin the moment with all my silly insecurities." She pivoted and faced him, soldier-like. "So I'm going to stand here and say them, so that when we go inside, nothing bad goes inside with us."

He took a look down both sides of the hallway. No one was in sight. "I think that's a great idea. Shoot them at me."

She winced. He had no problem joking about shooting, but she still wasn't there yet. "I'm really skinny. Dad used to call me a green bean."

He threw his head back and laughed. "Jean, how old were you when he called you that?"

She shrugged. "Ten, I guess."

His gaze ran down her frame then back up to her eyes. "I will never call you a green bean. I promise."

"I have knobby knees."

Eyebrows went up. "What do knobby knees look like?"

She tugged on her hair self-consciously. "I don't know. They're just...knobby."

"Is that why you wear skirts almost all the time?"

Had he never noticed that she never wore anything that revealed her legs above the calf? She nodded and sat on the bench, running her hands down her flowy skirt, making sure it was covering what it should.

"I have to say that makes me totally curious about your knees now, but whether they are knobby or not, whatever that means, you should know I have a thing for long legs, and yours are long and slender and very, very attractive."

She stared down at her legs. "They are? Really?"

"As is your willowy figure and that very desirable curve you have right at your waistline. Jean, don't you know by now that I think you're beautiful and I'm one hundred percent attracted to you?" He wheeled forward so he could dip his head and catch her gaze. "Are you not attracted to me or something?" He grinned. "Are you worried about my knees?"

"Goodness, no, but you're an incredibly good-looking man. Everywhere we go, women stare at you." She bit her lip down over her smile. "And then glare at me. I'm just—"

"Jean." He took both her hands and the change in his tone caught her attention. "Have you not noticed that since I got put in this chair, nobody stares at you with envy anymore? They stare with pity now."

She tilted her head. "I hadn't thought about it."

"And I love you for it. You see me beyond my chair." He rubbed the backs of her hands. "And I promise I will see beyond your knobby knees."

She checked his face, saw he was teasing, and pulled her hands away, pretending offense. "Are you ready to hear the twenty-three others?"

He looked longingly at the hotel room door. "This is not how I'd hoped to spend our wedding night, Jean."

She smiled and stood. On her way by his chair, he caught her and, with one more quick check down the hallway, pulled her down into his lap to kiss her. She struggled free, laughing breathlessly, and put the key in to unlock the room. "As Gladys would say, 'No more shenanigans like that, mister' until we're inside and I've lit those candles."

He chased her inside, but when she turned on the light, he detoured and turned the switch off again. She started to ask why when the flickers of gold caught her attention. She turned full circle. Her mind stalled, but her heart responded. "Grant, how—when—?"

The room was a paradise of soft light, music, and rose petals. At least thirty flameless candles, in tasteful clusters, graced different areas of the room, sending delicate light onto the vase of red roses displayed on the desk, the two long-stemmed yellow roses on her pillow, and the white rose petals strewn across the bed. She did not know where the music came from, but the violin rendition of Canon in D was subtle perfection. Draped across the edge of the bed was an elegant nightgown of white satin, but of much thinner material than her wedding dress. Even lying there, it begged to be touched.

"Red for love," Grant said at her side. He picked up one of the roses on the pillow and offered it to her. "Yellow for friendship." She took the rose in one hand and touched the nightgown with the other. "White for purity."

She closed her eyes against the tears. "How did you do all of this? I was with you all day."

He pulled an envelope from his back pocket. "I have friends in creative places, some who love you very much." He handed the envelope to Jean and she sat on the bed to open it.

> *Dear Jean,*
> *Grant asked me to do whatever it took to make this night totally separate from anything you had ever experienced. He wanted to make sure there were no bad associations, only good ones. I called Candy and Brenda and we brainstormed. I hope we chose well. We all want you to be happy, Jean, to love and be loved as God intends. Don't let any memories from the past or fears from the present stop you from enjoying every moment with abandon.*

Jean blushed, wiped her eyes, and read the end aloud.

God loves you with an everlasting love, and Grant's love is not far behind. We all love you, too.
Very sincerely,
Florence

"She even guessed right about the candles."

Grant took the second yellow rose off his pillow and set it on the nightstand. "That was Candy's suggestion. Brenda picked out the nightgown. Florence..." He wheeled to the mini fridge and checked inside. "Florence stocked us with sparkling cider, croissant rolls, a jar of blackberry jam, and several dessert options, all chocolate of course."

"And the roses," Jean added.

He took a petal from the bedspread and rubbed it down her cheek. "The roses came from me."

The nightgown slipped to the floor, unnoticed. Jean sat in her husband's lap and hugged him for a long time. When she pulled back, it was to touch his face. She ran her fingers in exploration across his eyebrows, down his temples and over his chin, loving the stubble collecting along his jawline. She brushed over the rounded curve of his cheeks, prodding her fingers into his dimples when he smiled at her. Her journey ended with his lips, fuller than most men's but just right for him. Her fingertips traced the line of his upper then lower lip.

He sighed, eyes closed. "How is it possible you can affect me like you do, Jean?"

Why had she been worried about her skinny legs and knobby knees? This man was her love for life. God had created her for him and him for her. She touched her lips to his and he pulled her into his arms, her heart against his, her pulse thundering and body coming alive.

If Florence planned to ask upon their return if Jean had followed her advice, Jean knew she would never have the nerve to give an answer to another person. Inwardly, however, in her own heart, she answered Florence's question that moment as the candles flickered and the music faded into the background. Yes, she would enjoy every moment with abandon. She would love and be loved as God intended. This night, their night, would be filled with nothing but goodness, touched by nothing but love.

In the beginning he offered an exciting job, high pay, plenty of attention.

Chapter Twenty-Seven
Sunday Night, February 8

Champagne

Billy was bluffing, but why?

I'm close to getting Jean for you, his message had said.

She texted back. *How close?*

Close enough to want a guarantee that it will be worth the risk I'm taking.

She knew for a fact that Jean was safely out of the country. Had been for almost a week. Did Billy plan to have someone fake being Jean to try to pull one over on Slash? She had already sent him passwords for the two extra sites in his area, massage parlors he had promptly taken over and started sucking dry of profit. That was his reward for supposedly killing her. If only they could capture him today, this minute. She couldn't wait to see his face when she showed up at his arrest. If Jose let her, she'd be the one putting the cuffs on his fat hands.

A guarantee? she texted. *What do you want?*

Three more sites now, the rest when she's handed over.

Champagne rose from the dingy hotel chair and crossed to look out the window. She had to think for a moment to remember what city she was in. Since Slash's death she had wandered place to place, moving on every few days, hiding her trail just in case either lawmakers or criminals were after her. Baltimore was a long way from Oakview. Those mind-numbing bus rides had almost lulled her into feeling safe, every hour the wheels turned taking her farther away from danger.

But every text from Billy brought it right back into her palm.

She hated him almost as much as Slash.

I think I'm the one who deserves a guarantee. How do I know you're going to come through? I could be giving up sites for nothing.

How about I throw in two extra girls?

Champagne felt sick. *I don't need two girls.*

Sell them, then. They'd be 100% profit.

Who are they?

Just a couple of troublemakers who need to learn a lesson. They're friends with Jean. I'll use them to rope her in, and if you have enough muscle with you when we meet, you can take all three.

Champagne lowered the arm holding her phone and stared out the window at the street below. A dumpster sat open near the opposite building, more trash around it than in it. The wind picked up an empty water bottle and carried it down the alley. A homeless woman pulling a shopping cart full of aluminum cans captured it and added it to her pile in the cart.

If Champagne went along with whatever Billy's plan was, would it speed things up? Stop this endless waiting? He had to be talking about Melanie and Star. Candy had already told her they were in deep and scared. Why did he want to get rid of them?

Send me a photo of the two girls and I'll send you one site.

Not enough.

I'll send another if you tell me how you're going to get Jean, and when.

No, too risky.

"You mean you don't have a plan because she's not around," Champagne said to the phone. "You're such a liar, and that's about the nicest thing I can say about you." She tossed the phone onto the hotel bed. Let him get nervous waiting to hear from her. Let him marinate in the uncertainty, wondering if Slash was mad and would back out of the plan altogether.

She watched the homeless woman sort through the trash bordering the dumpster until the phone beeped. "That didn't take long." She picked it up and checked the message. A photo image covered the screen. It was Star, barely clothed, in a provocative pose. Knowing Billy, he had a hundred such photos, most of them worse, and would use them as weapons. He would threaten Star, say he'd send them to her mother, splash them all over the internet, put one on the front page of her hometown newspaper.

His threats were effective. Of course none of this was part of the initial package. In the beginning he offered an exciting job, high pay, plenty of attention. It was only after those first photos that the other jobs were required.

Champagne rubbed her hands over her face. She needed something else to think about.

My password?

She wanted to call Candy and tell her to take over with Billy, that she couldn't take it any longer. *You said two girls.*

Trust me, the second is even better.

Melanie appeared on Champagne's screen next, her beauty beckoning, though anyone looking closely at her face could see the hollow emptiness in her eyes. This one had to be recent, a session forced on her. Billy had probably threatened to do something bad to Melanie's little daughter. Girls who had anyone they loved were the easiest to use.

She punched in a link to a website Billy would want, then sent a second message with the password. Next she forwarded the photos, link, and password, along with an explanation, to Jose and Candy so they could start monitoring that site and add to the massive pile of evidence already obtained against Billy.

Before they could respond with questions, Champagne shut down the phone, Slash's old phone, and tossed it across the room. The carpet cushioned its fall. "I wish you'd break," she said to the phone. "In a million pieces."

She glanced near the fallen phone to the mug shards she had taken from *Jamaica's Place,* the broken pieces of Jean's precious bowl kept in a box next to the bed. Even if the stupid phone had broken, it would not compare to the fractured pile of shards her life had become.

No, not her life. Herself. Her very being was broken.

She leaned her head against the window and murmured toward the homeless woman, "Even you have more purpose than I do. If we do get Billy, and all the others, what then? What is the point of my life after that? What will I have to live for, except more failures and hopelessness and nightmares?"

She shouldn't think about that right now. First, she needed to help get Billy behind bars, and do so without Jean getting hurt. It was the least she could do for a woman who had suffered so much because of her.

Champagne sat on the bed and picked up the pieces to Jean's bowl. If she tried, could she fix it?

If only she could repair Grant's broken body.

She laid the materials for the Kintsugi paste out on the bed and read the instructions for the first time since the night Slash died. As she worked to restore the broken vessel, she murmured with regret, "I'm sorry, Jean. I'm truly sorry."

Wednesday Morning, February 11

Jean

The light turned red before they reached the intersection. Jean did not mind being required to stop for a moment. She reached across to hold Grant's hand. "That was quite the reception you got at the airport. I can't believe so many people came out at six in the morning to welcome you home."

"To welcome *us* home." He turned her palm and rubbed the lines with his thumb, making her shiver. "I'm still a little dazed from all the questions."

She smiled and shot out ones they heard at least twice:

"How did the trip go?"

"Did you eat snails?"

"Did the treatment work?"

"Is there a doctor here who knows how to do it?"

She grinned. "And my personal favorite from Gladys: 'You didn't let some quack doctor put a box in your body, did you?'"

He laughed. "I don't think she appreciated my humor that garage doors were going to open in every neighborhood I drove through from now on."

The light turned green and Jean had to drive on. "I think Stewart was disappointed you opted to not have the implant done and focus on the laser therapy with external electrical treatment instead."

"I tried explaining, but when he started rubbing his glasses on his shirt, I knew I'd lost him."

"Was that after you talked about 'flexible arrays combined with laser probes,' or when you mentioned the mylien sheath on your nerves was damaged and that might be causing the pain more than just scar tissue and inflammation at the injury site?"

"Okay, so the medical jargon gets confusing, but it could have been worse. I could have gone on about neurogenic bowel, or how if I could get my quadriceps activated and gain rudimentary ambulation, I might incorporate usable cells back into my neural network." He shifted in the seat, using his hands to move his legs. "I sure am glad to be off that plane, and will be even more relieved to get onto the couch in my apartment where I can put my legs up. It feels like somebody burning brush just walked over and laid a big pile of it in my lap."

She glanced his way with concern. "I'll hurry."

"It was good to be able to tell everyone that I've gained two more inches of feeling down my waist, and that the laser treatment has an eighty-seven percent success rate with my level of injury." She wondered if he was putting on an act for her sake when he concluded, "Someday I'm going to be able to take you up on that offer of the world's greatest foot rub, and enjoy it."

"Sure," she said, matching her tone to his, light and hopeful. "I'll start with your head tonight, and every day we can move a little farther down till we wake up your feet."

He had released her hand to adjust his legs, but took it again. "It was genius on Florence's part to tell you in front of everyone that you should live temporarily at Alice's house to help set up things for the new day care. Now you can live with me at the apartment without raising any eyebrows. Everyone will assume you're at Alice's."

"And it will be safer, too." Jean glanced his way again. "Why didn't you tell me before about Billy and the danger? Were you afraid I would be stubborn about staying at my house?"

"No." He let go of her hand and reached across to put his palm on her thigh. "I didn't want to ruin your honeymoon with bad news."

At the next stoplight, she angled her body and faced him. "Did it ruin your honeymoon?"

"No, ma'am, Mrs. Henderson," he said. "My honeymoon was amazing in every way." They shared a secret smile. "And speaking of, I hope you brought all those flameless candles back with you. I think they'd look great all around my bedroom."

She only had time for one quick kiss before the light changed. "Fortunately for you, Mr. Henderson, I was thinking the same thing."

Their route to his apartment went through town. "Jean, there's the park." Grant pointed. "Could we stop for a minute?"

She slowed but her voice held concern. "But you're hurting and need to get your legs up."

"I can hold out for the time it takes to say hi to the kids." He yelled a hello and waved out the window as Jean drove past the basketball court. A chorus of joyful shouts preceded the ball being dropped and forgotten as the group of children raced to the parking area.

"They're happy to see you." Jean pulled into a space and cut off the engine. "You haven't been here since the accident."

His voice went low. "And I'm ashamed of myself. To be honest, I'd still like to avoid people and all the pity, but with these kids, staying away has been selfish."

Jean smiled at the boys running full speed toward their car. "You might find children the perfect people to be around. They aren't the pitying type." She grinned at him. "Kids are, however, openly curious. Be prepared."

He opened his door and when she brought his chair from the trunk, before Grant could even start to shift his body from the passenger seat, he was surrounded by boys and a bombardment of questions.

After volleying at least ten, with so many more coming it was impossible to differentiate who they came from, Grant held up his hands in surrender. "Okay, let me get into my chair, get to the court, then you can take turns asking questions."

Most of the kids took off running for the court. Only two remained behind. Jean asked their names. The smaller of the two, Simon Boyles, watched in fascination as Grant switched to his chair. The other, Damien Evans, asked Jean if they could push him.

Jean knew Grant disliked being pushed, felt it made him look helpless or lazy, but after a slight touch on his shoulder and nod from her, he relented.

Each of the two boys took a handle and they worked together to give Grant a far-from-smooth ride to the basketball court. The moment his wheels hit concrete, Damien was ready with his question. "Did you break your legs? I had a cousin break his legs when he fell out of a tree. But you don't have casts."

"How come you have to use that?" Simon asked of the chair.

A young bystander walked up and touched one of the wheels. "This is a really big stroller."

"It's not a stroller, Nicky," Damien said, shoving the boy's shoulder.

"It is so," the child argued. "See? He even has a big diaper bag hanging off the back, just like my little brother's."

Damien told Grant to ignore Nicky, then asked, "What happened to you? We thought you moved away."

Simon put himself in front of Grant's legs. "Did you not want to play with us anymore? We missed you."

Jean was surprised to see Grant's eyes fill with emotion. "I'm sorry I stayed away so long. I got shot and felt pretty bad for a long time."

"Is that why your legs don't work now?"

Grant nodded. "But I'm working hard to teach them how to work again. You can pray for me about that, okay?"

"Okay." Simon wedged between Grant's knees to stand closer to him. "But until you can walk, will you still play with us?"

Moisture filled Jean's eyes when the boy threw his arms around Grant's neck and held tight. "We can play slow so you can keep up. We won't mind, I promise."

Simon's hug inspired the others. Soon Grant had boys' arms around him from every direction possible.

"Hey," a boy in the back of the group spoke up. "I have a friend at school in a wheelchair. Can he come play, too?"

"Sure," Grant answered, his arms full of small, accepting friends. "That would be great."

"...blessing someone out?"

Chapter Twenty-Eight
Thursday Afternoon, February 12

Grant

Grant protested for the third time. "But what if I'm walking in a few months? It would seem such a waste."

Florence wiggled a finger in his direction. "Watch it, young man. You get me riled up enough and I might just bless you out right here in this store."

Doug leaned over to say, "That's old southern church talk for cussing you out without the cussing."

"I'll lay it out straight for you." Florence put her hand on one of the standing wheelchairs for sale. "I'm going to buy one of these contraptions today. Now, if I were to use it, I'd likely fall over and break a hip or two and end up needing the thing. So you might as well use it until you don't need it anymore, and then we can see who God wants us to bless with it next."

Grant held back a smile. "That's a real blessing you're talking about now, not blessing someone out?"

"Are you going to sit there being impertinent, or are you going to help me pick one of these things?"

A salesman with a wide, brimming smile, approached them. "Allow me to help you choose which life-changing technology would best suit your needs." He spoke over Grant's head to Doug. "Standing wheelchairs allow a wheelchair user to transition between sitting and standing without needing separate equipment to hold them upright." He motioned to one of the more expensive-looking models. "This option has an easy access joy-stick, allowing the user to drive the chair even while in the standing position." Next he told Florence, "Our most popular models even include memory foam chairs and adjustable arm lengths."

Grant wondered if the man would ever get around to talking to him. He considered the line of choices and said to Florence, "It's such a huge purchase, I would want to consider all the different factors. Just a minute." He shifted to get his phone out of his pocket and punched in Stewart's number. His brother answered on the third ring, out of breath.

"Hey, Grant." The words were labored.

"You out jogging?"

"Yeah," came the breathless reply. "It's no fun without you. If you hadn't drilled into me how beneficial it was for my health, I'd give this up in a minute."

"Well, I'll give you an excuse to cut it short today."

"Too late. I just got home. Hey, honey."

"What?"

Stewart laughed. "Not you. Brenda came out to the garage."

"Oh. Well, listen, do you have time you could spare? I need your help with something."

"Right now?"

Grant turned his chair so he could better see the gears and levers on the first standing chair in the line. How long would it take to get the hang of using one of these things? He didn't want to go through pros and cons with Mr. Salesperson. "Now, and maybe for a couple hours here and there for the next few weeks as I learn how to use a new piece of equipment."

Stewart's surprise came through the phone. "Did you just ask for help?"

"Yes."

"Brenda, mark it down," his brother said. "I have just experienced the miraculous."

Grant flipped the price tag to see the numbers on it. Florence must have seen because next thing he knew, her bulky handbag was in his lap. She opened it to reveal stacks of bills secured with rubber bands. It looked like enough to buy a car. He let out a low whistle and enjoyed her quick smile. "So have I."

Late Saturday Morning, February 14

Jean

"Turn left here."

Jean glanced in the rear-view mirror. "It feels like I'm driving in circles, Candy. Can't you just tell me where we're going?"

"Nope." Candy grinned like a Cheshire cat. "It's a secret."

"If you're driving us around to drive us crazy," Grant said beside her, "consider yourself a success and let's be done before my legs start to spasm."

Candy laughed and checked her watch. "Okay, go as if you're heading to your place, Jean, and I'll tell you where to turn." She reached up to tap Grant's back, but apologized when he jerked forward and twisted away. "Sorry, forgot you were jumpy about your back being touched. I was just going to ask what was up with all the bottles of green tea back here."

"They help keep away the UTIs," Jean answered while Grant regained his composure. Her own adrenaline was pumping with his reaction. He usually did well; it was only when someone surprised him from behind that the strong response came. "Want one?"

"A urinary tract infection? Definitely not."

"Ha ha." Jean faked a laugh. "A bottle of green tea."

"I don't know." Candy pulled one of the drinks from the bag. "Is it better than coffee?"

"It's an acquired taste, Grant tells me." Jean wrinkled her nose and waved her hand. "But I haven't acquired it. Can't stand the stuff."

Candy opened a bottle and swigged down several gulps. "Not bad. Say, Jean, you'll need to take your ring off. We're going to a Valentine's party and people you know will be there."

"A V-day party?" Grant glanced back. "Isn't that the kind of thing Jean and I should go to alone?"

"Not this year." Candy bounced like a child in the backseat. "You'll like this party. Trust me."

Grant glanced at Jean and winked. "Famous last words."

She smiled at him, then made the turn leading to her subdivision. "This is closer than I've been to my house since we got back. Candy, you were supposed to tell me where to turn."

"Right there." Candy indicated the road to Jean's house. She saw cars filling her driveway and lining the road at least five deep in both directions. "What on earth?"

Candy clapped behind her and Jean thought she looked like Sapphire for a moment. "Florence was going to hire a bunch of guys to do the work, but I knew if the church people heard, they'd want to be part of it. I called everybody and so many people came yesterday and this morning, she had to send the hired guys home. There wasn't anything left for them to do!"

Jean parked at the end of the line of cars. "Candy, what is this about?"

Candy was out of the car pulling Grant's chair from the trunk. "Your dad has been in his heyday, drawing up plans and telling the men what to do. And your mom organized the women and now your freezer is stocked with meals you just have to toss in the oven. That's my kind of cooking. And—"

"Candy, wait," Grant interrupted. "You've lost us."

"No I haven't. I'm just not telling you." She laughed, pushing Grant's chair at breakneck speed toward the house. Jean hurried to keep up. "Look!"

People swarmed through the house, around the porch, and in and out of the garage like ants on a hill, all busy, but all stopping to wave and smile when Candy loudly announced their arrival. Jean's father joined them. "Let me show you around," he said, pride in his voice. "Come on up, Grant. You'll find the house a lot more comfortable than last time you were here."

Jean followed, in awe, as her father took Grant room to room pointing out change. "Rubberized door jams instead of those wooden ones that jar like speed bumps, thirty-six-inch doorway clearance, at least sixty-by-sixty-inch turnaround space in each room around the furniture." He turned to Jean. "Anything we removed got put in the garage. You mother will set up a yard sale for what you want to get rid of, and what you want to keep we can store in the basement. It got cleaned out last night."

Her father led Grant onward through the dining room. "All carpet and rugs are gone and replaced by wood or tile flooring. The lights are voice activated in places where we couldn't move the wiring down below forty-eight inches, and—"

"And here's the best part." Candy rushed ahead and opened the door to the guest bedroom. "They made you a master suite on the ground floor! Now you don't have to get one of those bannister chairs to take you up and down the stairs. Florence and I went to a specialty store to check them out. It was awful. One trip upstairs took even longer than Pastor Stewart takes to decide what kind of muffin he wants at *Jamaica's*."

"I heard that!" a voice yelled from the kitchen. Stewart emerged with a grin, followed by Brenda, who was spooning chocolate pudding out of a bowl topped with what looked like olives. Jean decided not to ask.

"What do you think?" Stewart, Grant, and her father progressed into the bedroom, talking over lowered beds, and a new lowered bar in the closet, and which wall sections still had fresh drywall that would need to be painted later in the week after it dried.

Brenda came close to say quietly, "I hope we didn't overstep, Jean. Originally, we were just going to have a picnic for you two and show our love by offering to help with whatever renovations you wanted, but Florence had the money and your dad had the ideas." She smiled wryly. "And Candy had a cell phone. Next thing you know the yard was full of rugs, and sawdust was flying out the windows."

"I'm...stunned." Jean passed the bedroom and took a peek at what was once a small guest bathroom off to the side. Now it boasted a roll-in shower with bench, grab bars for balance, an open countertop around a lowered sink, and—Jean smiled—walls covered with encouraging Bible verses.

"It was nice of you to keep the colors neutral," Jean said to Candy behind her.

Candy chuckled. "I figured if I used pink and purple, Grant might paint over them and I'd have wasted all that time."

Jean wandered the rest of the downstairs. "This is...amazing."

Florence found them and gave Jean a warm hug. "Lunch is ready. Y'all had better get out there if you want any of Gladys' cauliflower casserole. It always gets snatched up quick."

Candy's voice was skeptical. "People actually want to eat something that has cauliflower in it? This I've got to try."

Jean found Grant and waited while the others went on ahead. When the house had emptied and only they two remained, she looked into the new master bedroom, remembering the days Champagne had stayed in that room, wondering where she was now. Her gaze took in the changes all around her. "It's like a whole new house," she murmured.

"Are you okay?" He touched the curve of her back. "I know you don't like change much. You've had this house the same since you were a little girl."

"Sometimes change is good." She ran fingers through the hair at the base of his neck, where it curled at the edges. "This will be our home now, not just my house. That is good."

He leaned his head against her hip where she stood close to his chair. "I love you, Jean Henderson."

She leaned to drop a kiss on his head. "And I, you, but for today, I'll have to be Jean Jameson again."

He smiled up at her. "But only till the end of the day. Then you're back to being mine again, right?"

"Forever," she said with her own smile. "Now let's get out there, Mr. Henderson. I hear there's a cauliflower casserole waiting."

"Grant isn't my fiancé. He's my husband."

Chapter Twenty-Nine
Late Saturday Morning, February 14

Candy

Candy sneaked to stand just to the left of Jean as Stewart got everyone's attention. "He's not going to preach a sermon, is he?" Jean clamped a hand over her mouth and Candy could tell she was trying not to laugh. "Not that I don't like his sermons," she clarified, "but I just put ice in the drink cups and don't want it all to melt."

If anything, Jean was trying even harder to keep from erupting. Stewart told everyone about how when Grant first woke up from surgery after the shooting, he was pretty out of it and did some funny things. The nurses put mitts on his hands to keep him from removing his feeding tube, but he'd take the mitts off and when the nurses returned to his room, throw the mitts at them. He got to be well-known on his floor for being a good shot.

"But eventually he settled and they all kind of fell in love with him," Stewart said. He smiled over at Jean. "Like Jean did."

Heads turned their way and Jean shrank into herself a little at the stares. Hands fluttering, she did a full pivot turn. When she saw the picnic tables someone had set up across the back yard, she gestured to them. "I'm going to go see if they need help setting up lunch."

Candy knew they didn't; everything had been readied hours ago, but before she could say so, she noticed yet another car joining the line along the road. A familiar one. Melanie and Star exited the car and made their way down the slope to where the workers had congregated.

Stewart was sharing his gratitude for everyone's hard work and willingness to give of their time and abilities to show such love to Jean and Grant. He was laying it on thick, as was right, for their church family had earned the praise.

Grant wheeled to Stewart's side and must have mentioned that he wanted a turn, for Stewart quickly finished and passed the attention to his brother, who gave a similar speech but with much more emotion in it. Candy would have been deeply touched, but Melanie's presence at her side was a fierce distraction. She wanted to just tell Melanie to spit it out already—Billy's plan, and what he was holding over her to force her to be part of it.

I knew you would come, she almost said aloud. *It was the perfect opportunity for Billy to send you to get information about Jean.*

"Nice of you to drop by," she whispered to Melanie. "I'm sure Jean will be happy to see you." Her pat on Melanie's shoulder was deliberate and carefully timed. The tiny recording device on her finger, pulled from her back pocket as soon as she'd seen Melanie arrive, stuck exactly as it should to the side of the collar of Melanie's shirt. Too small to be noticed unless one was looking for it, the device would record everything Melanie said, and also hopefully anyone within two to three feet.

Letting word spread about the workday at Jean's home had been a risk, dangerous, but less so than them waiting for Billy to make a move and them not knowing what it was. By tonight, Lord willing, once Melanie returned to report to Billy, Candy and Jose would know something.

At this point, the smallest clue, even a hint of a clue, would help.

Melanie spotted Jean setting napkins on the tables and moved her way. Grant finished his thank you and Stewart prayed before welcoming them to enjoy the huge dishes of homemade mac n cheese, cole slaw, baked beans, collard greens, and other food considered staples of a Brookside Baptist "dinner on the grounds," as he called it.

Half an hour later, Candy found Jean again. "The women in this church sure can cook. I've decided creamed-corn-cornbread is my new favorite food." Jean looked discombobulated. "There wasn't anything shocking in what I just said, was there? Sometimes I really can't tell."

Jean smiled. "No." She had her fork in hand and once she had put her bite of roast beef into her mouth, used it to gesture across the yard to where her mother chatted on the porch with Florence and Gladys. "My dad just told me he wants to have a family meeting after everyone leaves today. I feel like I've been called to the principal's office." She winced. "I mean, I feel nervous."

"Well, whatever he has to stay, don't stick around here too long, okay? It's still not safe for you to be so easily found."

"I can't stay hidden forever."

"True." Candy scanned the yard. Apparently Melanie and Star had already left. She needed to call Jose to make sure he was recording whatever the bug picked up. "We should know something helpful soon. Hang in there. Besides, if you moved back here, Grant couldn't move in with you yet. I'd say you're much better off having people think you're at Alice's so you can stay with that hunk of yours."

Jean went fuchsia. Candy hugged her. "I'll go before I say anything else. I'm really happy for you." She sent her hand out in a wide arcing sweep. "About the house, and everything."

Grant approached them both. "Jean, you're as red as a beet." He grinned at Candy. "What did you say?"

Candy felt a rare flush spread across her own cheeks. "Never mind. I'm going to hang out with Jose at the precinct now, and do a lot more listening than talking."

He laughed. "Often a wise choice for all of us."

"Some of us even more than others. Congratulations, Grant. The house improvements are great. I'm glad you won't have to wait years to get them done."

He nodded, taking Jean's hand. "Thank you. This really has been an amazing day. I haven't quite taken it in."

"You both are really loved." She started to walk away but turned back to add, "You should tell Jean's dad to keep his family meeting short. It's your first Valentine's together after all. You should get to make it special."

Grant's grin spread wide. He opened the pack of Little Debbie Swiss rolls in his lap and offered one to his wife. "Happy Valentine's Day, my love. Want me to buy you roses on the way home? Or more candles?"

Now that Jean's flaming red face was no longer her fault, Candy could leave in peace. She traveled up the curved driveway to her car, calling Jose the moment she shut the door. "I'm headed your way so we can listen together to what Melanie gets told when she gets back to *Hot Town.* If my guess is correct, we won't have long to wait before we hear something important."

They needed to get Billy soon. Grant and Jean deserved to enjoy being married without the shadow of danger hovering over them. A step forward, knowing the plan, would be a good Valentine's gift for them.

She drove through town and neared the one general store. Should she stop and pick out a card for Jose?

"Don't be ridiculous," she said out loud. All the weddings lately must be getting to her. She was starting to think foolish things. "Get there and get focused," she told herself. "You've got work to do."

Saturday Evening, February 14

Grant

One did not have to be a psychologist to recognize Jean's pacing, clenched hands and tightened features as anxiety. Grant knew she wanted to be anywhere else than in her living room, waiting for her father's arrival.

Grace Jameson clattered pots and pans in the kitchen, cooking away her own nervousness about Charles Jameson's request that they all meet for a talk.

"I'm going to put my wedding dress in the car," Jean announced. "I keep forgetting to take it to the cleaners." She kept a jittered, quick pace up the stairs then down again, dress draped from a hanger held high over her head to keep it from trailing the floor.

She had just kissed his cheek on her way by to the front door when her mother exited the kitchen asking, "Jean, did you move the beaters? I need them to mix—" Her eyes rounded and she stuttered to a halt. "Jean! What on earth happened to your dress?"

Jean turned, her body blocking the middle portion of her dress but unable to hide the dark smudges all along the white satin hem. Grant smiled at the stains, recalling their cause, but felt genuine pity for Jean. She looked like a little girl trying to make up an excuse for missing homework.

"The dog ate it," he muttered with a chuckle.

"Um, just a minute." Jean faked a smile and escaped out the front door, dress flowing behind her like an oversized kite.

"Grant?" Grace asked.

He put hands up. "I plead the fifth."

"You're grinning." Her tone was accusing. "This is a crisis! What if those stains don't come out? Did you have something to do with this?"

He crossed his arms and would have spread his legs into his football stance had he been able to stand. "Yes, ma'am," he said proudly. "I sure did."

"Jean," Grace stated the moment her daughter returned, "this fiancé of yours is being stubborn and not telling me a thing. What have you done?"

Jean looked at him, eyebrows up in question. He shrugged, nodded, and smiled his support.

She faced Grace and said, "I got married, Mother."

Grant would have fallen over had he not already been sitting. Grace, without the benefit of a wheelchair, keeled over onto the loveseat nearby, quite ungracefully, and put both hands to her heart. "Tell me you're joking."

"Not at all." Jean put her hand on his shoulder. He lifted it and kissed her palm. "Grant isn't my fiancé. He's my husband."

"Lord in heaven, help me." Grace waved her manicured nails in front of her face. "What about the reception we've planned for months? The wedding we planned for years? We picked the colors and the dresses and made the invitation list. Hundreds of people are coming."

She stood and flapped her arms once, like an awkward bird. "Oh, Jean, how could you? Your beautiful wedding."

He expected Jean to give the standard apology and was shocked when his wife frowned and said, "No, Mother, *your* wedding. You planned it. You made the decisions. I got informed." She gripped his hand tightly. "Did you ever think to ask if I wanted a huge crowd staring at me? Did you care at all what colors or flowers or cake flavor I might prefer?"

Grace dropped to sit again. "I...I just assumed you..."

Jean left him and knelt before her mom. Her voice was soft. "Maybe you should assume less about me and ask more."

Grace grasped her daughter's hand. "What will we tell them all?"

Grant wanted to shake the woman. Jean had a more gentle response. "We'll still have the big ceremony. Very few people know we got married and we will keep it that way."

Grace blinked three times. He could almost see the gears churning in her mind. "I should have—" She blinked again, then patted Jean's hand. "I'll pay to get the dress cleaned."

Jean sighed. "Thank you, Mother." She stood and turned when a knock sounded at the door. He watched the anxiety mar her beautiful features again. "Daddy's here."

"Let the truth come to the open, so you can all be free of it."

Chapter Thirty
Saturday Evening, February 14

Grant

The table, as plain and unadorned as it was before Grace's arrival, stretched empty on one side, while Jean's mother and father sat across from one another on the other side. Jean and Grant sat close together at the end between them.

"I wanted to bring you all together," Jean's father said, "so I only had to say this once." He put his hands on the table, palms up and out. "I wronged you, Jean. I ran from my responsibilities and..." He put his head in his hands. "I should have been the father you needed. If I had stayed, or not let anyone convince me..." He lifted his head and looked across at Grace. "I want to blame you, but I am to blame as well. I should have done whatever it took to remain in her life. I ask your forgiveness, Jean."

Something had sunk in with Grace since Jean revealed about the wedding and Grace had been faced once again with her wrong assumptions. "I am to blame, Charles." Jean's mother clearly fought tears. She twisted her silver bracelet around her wrist. "I lied and deceived you both. Had I not been so selfish, Jean might not have—" She covered her face with ringed fingers. "It's my fault. Jean, I'm the one who needs to beg forgiveness. From you both. If I'd only—"

Grant watched his wife. The moment they'd begun speaking, Jean had slouched away from the table, shrinking into herself. "It's okay," she said quickly, dismissively, eyes down on the bunched fistfuls of blue skirt clenched in her hands. "You don't need to—"

Grant had intended to stay quiet, a silent support in the background, but he knew Jean needed him more at this moment than possibly ever before. He took her hands, opened them, and placed them on the table within reach of her parents. "They do need to, Jean. It's important that they confess their sins for you to forgive them."

"But I don't need to—"

"Jean, ignoring wrong isn't the same as forgiving it."

He could see her struggle. She hated being addressed so directly, and worse still being the focus of a painful moment of transparency. Given her choice, he knew she would avoid any confrontation, keeping wounds covered, unexposed but untended, avoiding the lancing that would cause pain but also provide healing. He realized he cared as much for the healing of Jean's heart as the healing of his legs. "Please, Jean, let the truth come to the open, so you can all be free of it."

"Freedom," Jean murmured. "You shall know the truth, and the truth shall make you free."

Grace Jameson cried openly. Charles Jameson waited without tears, but his face was lined with sorrow. Jean closed her eyes and lowered her head for long moments. When she lifted it, she said simply, "You...you sinned." He saw the cost of her words in the pain that filled her blue-gray, glistening eyes. She gathered handfuls of the soft material of her skirt again and bit her bottom lip. "You both sinned against me." The tears emerged and ran down her cheeks. She clenched her eyes shut and he put a reassuring hand to her face, running his thumb across her damp cheek, absorbing her pain into his own skin.

She leaned her face into the strength of his hand, and with purpose—and difficulty, he knew—placed her hands back onto the table's polished surface.

"We did." Her father took her right hand in both of his. "I did."

Grace held her left hand. "I did."

Jean forced her head up and looked at each of her parents. "I forgive you."

Charles dropped his forehead down onto their joined hands on the table. Grace stood and rushed off, returning with a box of tissues, which she used liberally. "And you," she said across the table. "Charles, I sinned against you."

"And I against you." He hesitantly patted Grace's hand. "I'm not saying I'd ever want to live with you again, but I would like your forgiveness."

Grant choked down a laugh. He glanced at Jean, who was too absorbed in the previous moments to catch the humor.

Grace blinked several times, looking for all appearances like she was batting her eyes at her former husband. "Do you think we can be friends?"

"Friends." Charles took Grace's hand, and Jean's, and brought them together in the center of the triangle they made. "All of us."

Grant sat back, content to watch as Jean rose and hugged first her father then her mother. He thought of Champagne and prayed that when the day came for him to face her and forgive, he would be able to exercise the same level of grace shown so freely by this woman he loved.

"Well, since that's settled," Grace said, tossing her head a bit and giving her nose one last blow, "let's get back to the wedding plans. We have so much to talk about."

Charles laughed, but Grant noticed he removed his hand from Grace's. "Some things never change." He rose from the table. "I'm headed back to the hotel. Grant, you want to leave and get a late night snack?"

Grant looked at Jean. Her face was pale but shining. He could endure Grace's chatter for the evening. He took his wife's hand in his. "No thanks. I belong with Jean."

Late Monday Afternoon, February 16

Champagne

All was set. Billy had told Melanie to be ready on Friday, February twentieth, ten p.m. at the old train station, but Champagne texted as

Slash and convinced him to move it up to today. She wasn't waiting five more days to finish this.

Billy would update Melanie. By now, the bug Candy had planted on her was in some stack of dirty laundry, so Champagne passed on the plan to Candy and Jose.

Melanie's job is to contact Jean and convince her to come with her to the train station out behind the old mill off Tunnel Road. Star's job is to have her bound and unable to escape by the time they arrive in Billy's hired car.

Candy called immediately. "You need to get him to believe Melanie has Jean and have him meet us early, before he gets any hint we're on to him and makes a run for it. This is all wasted if he gets away."

"Don't I know it." Champagne was sick of cheap hotels and even cheaper beer.

"Jose's going to have unmarked backup teams stationed half a mile away in each direction from the station. You've got to make sure Billy comes himself. He can't send a liaison."

"How am I supposed to do that?"

"He thinks you're Slash, so think like Slash. You'll come up with something."

Champagne heard talking in the background. It sounded like Jose. "Champagne," Candy said, "I have to go. I've got to get in touch with Jean right away to tell her not to go with Melanie, no matter what Melanie tells her. I'm going to call Gladys first to make sure Sapphire is safe with her. We don't want a child hostage situation on our hands and you know Billy would use her if he needed to."

"I know it." Champagne closed the call and tossed Slash's phone onto the bed. She picked up the generic phone with a pre-paid phone card she'd bought earlier that afternoon at a mall on her way into town and punched in a text.

Jean, it's Candy. I dropped my phone in the toilet so had to get a new one. We've heard from Champagne and need your help. She told us her location and is close, but she says you're the only one she trusts enough to talk to.

Champagne sent the long text, then started a second one.

She has evidence against Billy. If we get Billy, we can free Melanie and Star. Meet us at—

She checked out the window, then texted the hotel name and room number.

We're set up in the room next to hers and even have police ready and armed just in case. You'll be totally safe.

Champagne paced the room four times before Jean replied.

I can come right after work.

Champagne checked the clock. Jean didn't get off for another hour. *Come now. Tell your boss it's an emergency.*

I'll be there in fifteen minutes.

Champagne's legs gave way. She dropped to sit on the hotel bed and rubbed her hands over her face. A knock sounded on the door. Slowly, each step a choice, Champagne crossed the room and turned the knob.

Melanie stood waiting. "Well? Is she coming?"

Champagne motioned her inside. "She'll be here in fifteen. Is Star with you?"

"In the car. She says she'll drive if you promise she won't get shot at."

Champagne gathered her things into a pile on the bed. "That's it then. Time to contact Billy and tell him everything's ready just as he wanted it."

‘Billy
has
Jean.”

Chapter Thirty-One
Monday Evening, February 16

Grant

Candy called at thirty minutes after four. "Grant, I can't get Jean on the phone and it's important. I tried calling the bank but they said she left early for some emergency."

"Yeah." Grant set his weights down and pushed his body to a sitting position on the bench. "She called and said she had to meet you and Jose at a hotel."

"What are you talking about? Jose and I are at police headquarters."

Unease twisted his gut. "She said you'd found Champagne. She was at a hotel with evidence, but she wasn't willing to talk to anyone but Jean."

Candy's tone was urgent. "I've been trying to contact Jean for half an hour. Whoever told her to come to a hotel wasn't me."

Grant felt his heart thunder, but it wasn't from the workout. "Could it have been Jose?" He yanked his chair over to his weight bench and pulled a muscle throwing his body into it the fastest way possible.

"Jose's been here with me all afternoon. It wasn't him."

Grant wheeled to the front door. "Come pick me up. We have to go find her."

"How?"

"There aren't that many hotels in the area. We start with the one downtown and work our way out from there."

He could tell Candy was running, or at least walking at a clip. Her breath came in small puffs. "Wouldn't it be faster to call the hotels?"

"Faster, yeah, but they're not going to know anything. Whoever called Jean won't have her check in with a desk manager."

"Good point. What if—wait, I'm getting a text."

Grant waited, his palms dampening around his wheels. His mind raced. Why hadn't he asked which hotel? Why had Jean thought the summons was from Candy?"

The silence lasted too long. "What, Candy? Tell me."

"It's a text from an unknown number." Candy's voice was flat. He'd only heard her talk like that when a friend was beaten black and blue, or something equally terrible happened. "It says Billy has Jean. He wants the passwords now and is ready for the swap early."

Grant had braced himself, but still the words punched deep into the pit of his stomach.

"It could be a ploy of Billy's," Candy said quickly.

He did not respond. Where was his wife?

"We're in the car," Candy said. "We'll get you in five and be at the outskirts of the train station in ten. Jose already has his teams on their way. The car with the tinted windows, where Slash will supposedly be, is less than a mile away." Conviction carried through the phone. "We're going to do everything possible to get Jean out of this safely, Grant."

It was a nice sentiment, but carried no weight at all. They didn't know where Jean was, who had her, or what their plan was. Grant closed his phone and set it onto his legs. "God, You know where she is. Please keep my wife safe. Bring her back to me."

Jose's car pulled into the parking lot and Grant wasted no time getting in. "Leave the chair," he said. Jose raced at the highest speed an unmarked car could go without lights flashing, but it still felt like Grant could have gone faster wheeling himself. A yellow taxi pulled behind them when Jose took the final turn to their spot to wait for the signal from his front line team. Already at the station set to rendezvous, the team in the car reported back narrative on what they observed, but so far there had been no sign of a vehicle or individual. One of the outlying policeman, stationed with binoculars behind the old abandoned mill building, called in an incoming car from the west just as the taxi passed Jose, made a sharp turn, and stopped horizontally across the road, cutting off their progress.

"Something's wrong." Jose's voice held the tension Grant felt. He should have taken the time to stash his chair in the trunk. He was a sitting duck in the backseat, both a target and a liability.

"Get eyes on this taxi, and weapons set on every door."

"The windows are dark," a voice said through the radio. "I think I see two people, but can't verify."

A different voice, lower, came through the static connection. "Vehicle from the west parking at train station point. Passenger in back left seat verified as Billy Bradon. Wait—Bradon just put a phone to his ear—he's giving directions to the driver to continue on—car is headed directly for you, Boss."

Jose opened his door and aimed his glock at the taxi, using the door as cover. "Step out of the vehicle with your hands up!" he shouted.

Candy's phone beeped. She checked it and said, "Jose, shut the door and sit down. Quick!"

He put his gaze on her face, his frown deep.

"Now, Jose!"

He sat and shut the door just as Billy's car came into view. "Talk, Candy," he ordered.

"No time to explain." Candy leaned so far forward her nose nearly flattened against the windshield.

"Billy's checking his phone again," the voice over the radio reported. "He's opening the door."

Grant could not see the lawman but knew his gun was steadied, target in sight ready to pull the trigger at one word from Jose.

Billy stepped out of the car, a smirk overtaking his face.

"He can't see us?" whispered Candy.

"No."

She exhaled loudly. With one last check of her phone, she told Jose, "Send your guy, the one hiding behind the building, out into the open. He's got a bullet proof vest on, right?"

Jose did as directed, frown still in place. Grant leaned as far to the side as he could, searching the tinted windows of the taxi. Was Jean inside? Did someone have her tied up, or threatened? Was she scared?

The policeman walked toward Billy, who stood in open view of them all, making a point of not taking any cover. Grant supposed they were meant to be impressed by his courage, but Grant only saw arrogance. If only Grant had his body in the shape it was before the accident. He could take the man down in thirty seconds.

"Do you have what Slash wants?" the policeman said, voicing words fed to him by Jose through his earpiece. Jose words were fed by Candy, under protest, but she told him she'd explain soon and for now he would have to trust her.

Billy's smile was unconcerned. "Do you have what I want?"

The policeman checked his earpiece. "Slash doesn't like this setting. It's not where we planned. He wants you to ride in the taxi to the station."

Billy glanced at the taxi, then at Jose's car. Even knowing he could not see in, Grant felt himself ducking behind the seat. He noticed Candy slid her body down under the dashboard. Billy agreed and Candy murmured some sort of joyful sound. She grabbed Jose's leg from her perch on the floorboard and shook it. "This is it! Have him tell Billy he has to search him down before he can meet with Slash. When he does, cuff him!"

Would it work? It seemed too simple, but the pride Billy mistook for bravery was his undoing. He submitted without argument to the pat down. The policeman turned Billy's body and began his search just as the door to the backseat of the taxi opened.

Champagne stepped out.

Candy popped her head up and laughed. "Billy's face—look at it! She's not dead, Billy. I'd have given all my shoes and purses to have gotten that on video. Ha!" Candy opened the car door and ignored Jose's warning to stay inside. She shouted at Champagne to do the honors. The policeman already had the struggling Billy in a firm grip, but Champagne sauntered to his side, gave him a hearty slap across the face, then smacked handcuffs around the wrists pulled behind his back.

Others from Jose's backup teams had Billy's accomplices and driver pulled from the vehicle and read their rights. Star exited Champagne's taxi. She had been driving.

"Where is Jean?" Grant asked. Had everyone forgotten her but him? He opened his door to yell the question again, loudly enough for Candy to hear. She spoke with Champagne, then skipped like a kid on summer break to his doorway. "Jean and Melanie are back in Champagne's hotel room. Melanie informed Champagne that Billy had a tail on Jean, so they got her to the hotel to keep her safe out of the way until this was over."

Grant fell back against the seat and closed his eyes. "Tell Champagne thanks," he said to Candy. She ran off, still laughing with joy, spouting prophecies of how fun it was going to be to do this with all twenty of Slash's other dirty connections over the next days and weeks.

"I wish you were here, Susan," she shouted to the skies. "You'd have loved seeing this. We got him!"

Jose blew out a loud breath. "That woman is going to take years off my life." He started the car and did a four-point turn to bypass the taxi and Billy's car, asking over his radio as he maneuvered for directions to Champagne's hotel, and giving Candy permission to remain behind and enjoy the fun of the arrest. "Things are well in hand here," he said to Grant. "Let's go get your fiancé."

My wife, Grant said within. He thanked God, letting his head fall back against the seat, relief flooding every part of him. *Let's go get my wife.*

Early Tuesday Morning, February 17

Candy

Candy stood at the grave, her jacket wrapped tight around her though it was not cold. "So you're Slash's mother. The woman who started it all." The marker was simple, bearing a name, two dates, and a dash between. Just a dash, a small cut into the stone representing such a deep cut into the world. "Champagne says you created the chain that enslaved so many of us women for so many years. You should have loved your son more than alcohol. You should have chosen his need to feel loved over yours." She knelt, not to leave flowers, but to face the name on the marker as if she looked the woman in the eye. "This is my solemn oath. I will break the chain you forged. Champagne has disappeared again, but if I ever find her, I will help her and others heal. Every woman and girl I know who bears the mark of Slash I will take to the throne of God Himself and offer them eternal freedom and total healing from everything they have suffered."

She rose and held her right hand up, no less serious than had she been summoned to a witness stand in court. "Your selfish choices will no longer hurt and destroy. Jesus and I will work to set the captives free. I was the first to be set free." She slapped her hands together in triumph. "But I won't be the last."

Her shout of victory at first felt out of place in such a landscape of death, but then Candy recalled words from the God of life and never had they felt more appropriate. She lifted her hands and her voice to the sky and shouted, "Oh death, where is your sting? Oh grave, where is your victory? Thanks be to God, who gives us the victory through our Lord Jesus Christ!"

Tears filled her eyes. She took one last look at the grave of Slash's mother. Later that day she would go to Slash's. After today, she would never return to either.

"I forgive you," she said, "and I walk away free of you."

With her head held high, her hair blowing behind her, Candy turned and walked out of the graveyard singing *Victory in Jesus*, not once looking back.

Three Months Later...

"Your big day is tomorrow. Are you nervous?"

Chapter Thirty-Two
Friday Night, May 1

Candy

Candy made her way down the church aisle, the peace in the building soaking into her soul. Halfway to the pulpit, she saw she was not alone. "Jean. I'm surprised to find you here."

Jean looked up from her position on the altar steps with the serene smile Candy had come to expect. "Hi, Candy. Come and join me?"

Candy did so, marveling that there wasn't yet a worn spot on the carpet where she so often found herself on her knees there before the Lord. "Giving up more people?"

"Not tonight." Jean looked upward. "I was just thanking God for all He's done for us, for fixing so many broken pieces and making them into something beautiful and whole."

"That's why I'm here, too. I'm amazed at how much peace comes with forgiveness. I always thought if I gave up my bitter hold on people it would leave me open to them controlling me or taking advantage of me again. But it's totally the opposite. It's taken time and I'm not saying I'm done yet, but forgiving Slash, and Billy, and the hundreds of guys who used me and the thousands of people who looked the other way, or condemned me instead of praying for me, has set me free in a way I never thought I could be."

"I know what you mean." Jean's voice held joy. "I don't live my life in Rod's shadow, or my parents' stress, or even my own insecurities anymore. It's a beautiful thing." She turned to Candy. "Have you ever heard from Champagne?"

Candy shook her head. "Jose has kept feelers out for her on the circuit, and we got a tip that she might have come back into town recently, but it's probably just another prankster trying to get reward money."

Jean tucked a strand of hair behind her ear. "I think of her out there, still running, hiding, afraid and ashamed. I wish there was some way to tell her she's forgiven and loved and valued."

"For you to say that, after all that's happened, is more Christ-like than anything I can think of."

"God has created good out of every bad thing," Jean said. "Grant told me a few weeks ago that when he closes his eyes and prays, he doesn't wheel boldly to the throne of grace in his chair. He runs in." She clasped her hands together, as if praying. "I want to have that kind of perspective, where the earthly brokenness falls away and I live by the eternal."

"Like that Kintsugi stuff." Candy sighed. "Sure wish Champagne had left all that paste Florence bought, and the pieces to your pot, too. Can't figure out why she stole your broken pieces, of all things."

"Maybe she needed the message more than I did."

An easy silence fell between them in the sanctuary. Eventually Candy asked, "You heard that Jamaica is coming back?"

Jean smiled. "Yes, with Pansy and her new baby boy. I'm so glad." Her gaze on Candy held a question mark. "Where will you live now that they'll need their place again?" Her smile expanded. "Has Florence recruited you for Alice's day care center?"

Candy pretended to shudder. "That's not for me. Kids aren't my gift. No, I'm..." She hesitated, then shared her news. "I'm moving to Charlotte."

Jean turned with surprise. "You're leaving?"

"It's time." Candy shifted to sit with her back against the steps, using her elbows for support. "I don't want to leave everyone, but I've been asking God to show me what He wants me to do for Him. This week He made it about as clear as it could possibly be, which is good because I can be pretty thick-headed sometimes."

Jean curled her knees up to her chest and slanted her head to the side. "What happened?"

"First, this woman called and said the ladies in her church were volunteering at a safe house in Charlotte, and they wanted to start a strip club ministry but were completely terrified and had no idea how to start." Candy felt the excitement bubble up within her. "So I thought I could go and speak to them on what to do and what not to do, that sort of thing. But then I called the safe house and found out they are terribly short-staffed, and the staff they do have don't have any real experience, and they're having trouble with their girls going back to their pimps. Once I told them my story, they basically offered me a job on the spot—another reason I came to pray tonight."

Candy talked to God in between talking to Jean. When her prayer and her story both ended, she looked across at her friend with a smile to say, "Your big day is tomorrow. Are you nervous?"

Jean wrapped her arms around her knees and rested her chin on her arms. "Petrified. I keep repeating our old verse on fear in my head. I have a feeling I'll be quoting it all the way down the aisle."

Candy chuckled. "It's a good thing you never tried for a job on stage." She sat up straight. "And speaking of, I called the strip club closest to that church to see if the manager would even let a group come. Some will slam the door in your face and I wouldn't want that to happen to a group just getting started. Get this: the manager told me they could come and then told me—no joke, true story—that his wife had started going to church lately and was a lot nicer than she used to be. He said that though he was adamant about not losing any of his girls to competing clubs, if he lost them to Jesus, he was okay with that. Can you believe it?"

"Wow."

"I know! If that's not a big, huge open door, I don't know what is."

"It sounds like you've definitely found your place."

"Yes." Candy sighed. "But it will be hard to go. I used to hate Oakview and wish myself anywhere but here, but now it's home because this is where I found the Lord, and you, and Brenda, and Florence, and everybody."

Jean put a hand on her arm. "We'll miss you very much, Candy. Nothing will be the same here without you."

"Things will be quieter, that's for sure." She chuckled. "But some people won't mind that." She felt her eyes burn and blinked hard. "Promise you'll come visit? I'll give you a tour of the safe house."

"Of course."

She felt lit up from the inside out, like that verse in Psalms that talked about looking on God and being radiant. "Maybe we call Jose to come, too. We could help arrest some losers over a weekend for fun."

With a squeeze where her hand held Candy's arm, Jean said with a smile, "You couldn't keep me away."

Late Friday Night, May 1

Champagne

Champagne pressed the base of her ratty, torn shirt against her mouth so her sobs would not be heard. Candy's tip had not been a prank. Champagne had returned to Oakview two days earlier after reading about Jean's upcoming wedding in the paper. Shame drew her to the church, but anger at her life and herself overtook the shame and led her to a bar instead. She'd spent a day drinking, another day enduring the consequences, and early that morning had found herself sneaking up to the back of Jean's old-fashioned home. The haze of predawn darkness shielded her as she treaded around the side and up the porch steps, noticing with the familiar wash of guilt the wheelchair ramp overrunning half the stairs.

She had to see them. Though they surely hated her and longed for justice to find her, she had to know if they had found any measure of happiness. She couldn't live with the voice inside that said she had destroyed them completely.

No one was home. The house looked abandoned.

Tired, so tired, Champagne had considered stretching across the porch swing and letting sleep pull her into oblivion for a few blissful moments, but fear of capture kept her moving. She crossed the yard and the brook, and felt herself pulled toward the church up the hill, a place of great power, inside which people were made brand new.

Born again, that's what Candy had called it once.

Champagne was surprised to find the door unlocked. Weren't they worried about theft? She had made her way inside and wandered down a side aisle, touching pews and sections within the stained-glass windows. Her legs carried her up into the baptistery to more closely consider the painting on its wall of a lion and a lamb. The lion was huge and majestic, but the lamb was unafraid. What did it mean?

The sound of voices approaching sped Champagne's heart but froze her feet. She considered her exit options, but just as she climbed out of the baptistery into the choir loft area, the double doors to the auditorium opened and a group of people flooded inside.

Champagne ducked behind the organ pipes, the barrier between the choir section and the pulpit stage hiding her from sight. She listened and realized she had no chance of escaping now. The people filling the church with sound were there for Grant and Jean's wedding rehearsal.

She made sure the bag and box she had brought in were safely out of sight behind the organ. Peeking out when it felt safe to do so, she could see people she had once called friends, and once betrayed, laughing, joking, loving, smiling. They were happy, all of them. None looked with pity or sorrow on Grant's chair or on Jean for her loss in him being disabled.

She watched in awe and a great depth of confusion as they prayed and gave thanks for God's goodness to them.

No one mentioned her, not once.

Until now.

Champagne had waited through the rehearsal, planning to leave the moment the auditorium cleared, but then Jean and Grant had remained after, Grant kissing Jean in that long, loving way Champagne had long since envied.

Grant had told Jean his brother was taking him out for dessert and would drive him home later. After another kiss and a soft goodnight, he had wheeled out of the church, but Jean had remained, praying there at the altar steps, listing people she loved. She spoke of her husband—strange that she would call him that already—and spent more time asking God for him to have courage and purpose than to have his legs healed.

She had prayed for Champagne.

And then Candy came in, and Champagne had heard the impossible. Forgiveness. For her. She had not asked for it, though she had longed to—to beg, plead, prostrate herself before these people and their God—but knew she was so far beyond the line of undeserving that any amount of sincerity, any level of humility, any attempt to do enough good to make up for it would fall impossibly, insultingly short.

Yet here was the forgiveness she hungered for desperately, nothing about it contrived. They didn't even know she was there.

Candy and Jean continued talking but Champagne heard no more words. She pulled the worn Bible from her purse, the book full of hope and life she had not dared believe, certain the message within its pages was too good to be true.

Hours passed as she read. Champagne was not aware when darkness fell, or when Candy and Jean stood to leave. She searched the Scriptures with all her soul and the God within them with all her heart. Sometime before sunlight conquered the authority of the night, everlasting love found her. Champagne was born anew.

As dawn arose, she set her precious Bible in the box beside her and reached for a seat cushion someone had left on one of the choir chairs. Using it as a pillow, she curled up behind the organ pipes at Brookside Baptist Church and for the first time in years, slept in peace.

"At least
you'll
go down
well-dressed."

Chapter Thirty-Three
Saturday Morning, May 2

Grant

Today was the day. Finally, the world would know Jean was a married woman, and he a married man.

Grant recalled their private wedding when Jean had wheeled down the aisle, a gift greater and more full of love than any he could have imagined. "I'd rather sit beside you than stand alone," she'd said, flooding his heart with awe.

Today was his turn. Grant adjusted the jacket of his black tuxedo. "Hey, Jimmy," he said, using his brother's childhood nickname. "Can you make sure everything looks good below the chest section of this thing? My pants could be down around my ankles and I wouldn't know it."

Stewart grinned. "You wearing the wedding boxers I gave you?"

Not a chance. They were red silk with hearts and "I Do" printed all over them. "I'll take that to mean my pants are where they should be." He pulled a slip of paper from the inside pocket of his jacket. "Take this back to Jean for me, will you?"

"Want me to send it with someone else so I can pray with you before we go out?"

"Actually I was sending you away to have a minute with God by myself."

Stewart clapped him on the shoulder. "Just tell me if you want me to leave. Don't beat around the bush."

Grant laughed. "I love you, big brother."

"Whoa. I didn't figure I'd hear that from you until we were in nursing homes and about to kick the bucket."

Grant thought of Susan and Ian. *Death can find a person long before old age. Best to say what's important when you can.* "Well, you'll probably be deaf by then, so I thought I'd get to it now."

Stewart pulled him into a hug. "And I couldn't be prouder to call you my little—" He held his hand up to Grant's superior height. "—bigger brother." He chuckled. "I'd offer some reassurance about how great marriage is in case you were having cold feet, but your feet should be plenty warm by now."

"For marriage, yes." Grant pictured the full church auditorium and wiped his damp palms on his jacket sleeves. He couldn't reach his pants over the portion of the standing chair holding up his chest. "For a ceremony with hundreds of people watching, wondering if this chair will tilt and I'll fall flat on my face? Not so much."

"Well, if you do, at least you'll go down well dressed." Stewart opened the door, but shot back, "And we'll have it on video forever."

"Thanks for that thought."

Stewart left the room and Grant imagined him handing Jean his note. It instructed her to walk down the aisle, just in case she had the thought of coming to him in a wheelchair again, and the note ended with, "I'd rather stand beside you than sit alone."

He pushed the lever and his standing chair rolled to the door. "Make me a godly husband, Lord," he prayed. "Help me love Jean like You love her." In the ceremony, Stewart would talk about the strength of a three-fold cord. "May my words and actions today honor You."

He took his place at the front of the aisle. Stewart came to stand at his side, nodding back to the double doors connecting to the foyer. Through a small opening only inches wide, he caught a glimpse of Jean's face peeking through. She caught his gaze, her own taking in his standing position, and she beamed a radiant smile.

How he loved that woman. In just moments she would be at his side promising to love until death, again. He would never deserve the priceless gift of her love, and vowed to never take it for granted.

The soft strains of *Ode to Joy* spread from a CD player throughout the auditorium. The doors opened and his parents made their way together down the aisle. His mother palmed his cheek, then wiped at her eyes before lighting the Henderson side of the unity candle.

After them came Grace Jameson, alone, as solid in her opinion of not wanting to be escorted by her ex-husband as she was that the bridesmaids must wear satin, with absolutely no ruffles of any kind.

Candy was the first bridesmaid to enter, "relieved beyond words," as she'd said at the rehearsal, that Grace had picked lavender as the dress color instead of yellow. She had her arm through Jose's, who pulled at the collar of his shirt twice on the way down the aisle. Next came Florence, snuggled up against her husband's side, looking as happy as she had the day of their own wedding almost four months ago.

Brenda, as maid-of-honor, came last, her belly making a rather grand entrance ahead of her. She held little Sapphire by the hand and helped her drop flower petals as they walked. The crowd gave a collective "Awww" when Sapphire emptied her basket before she reached the front pew and asked for more petals. They'd decided to forgo a ring bearer, giving Stewart the rings instead, and Grant was glad. He was ready for this ceremony to start. He wanted Jean near.

She appeared in the doorway, so lovely, light streaming into the foyer behind her from the surrounding windows, her father at her side. Loved ones stood and faced the back. Grant glanced at the woman at the organ, Susan's mother, who raised her hands to play the loud, majestic strains of the wedding march.

Her fingers plunged onto the keys. The pipes shot out sound.

And someone let out a bloodcurdling scream.

Saturday Morning, May 2

Candy

Along with every other person in the church, Candy's head swiveled from facing Jean at the back in her gorgeous white dress to the organ off to the side of the choir loft. Susan's mother looked frozen at the keys, her eyes huge. Candy craned her neck and gasped when a woman lurched to her feet from behind the choir partition wall.

"Champagne?"

"I'm sorry! I'm so sorry!" Champagne held her hands in front of her body and spit out words as quickly and uncomfortably as Candy had that time her mother caught her making out with Sam Snyder under the bleachers. "I fell asleep back here and by the time I woke up the church was full of people." She looked pleadingly at Jean, who had made her way down the aisle without anyone watching, something she probably appreciated. "I couldn't leave without people seeing me and I didn't want to mess up your wedding, so I decided to just wait back here until everyone left." She gestured a palm toward the organ. "I didn't know the pipes were going to blast like a volcano erupting!" She climbed over the partition, revealing clothes that badly needed to see the inside of a washing machine and flip flops with one strap broken. "I promise I didn't plan to ruin your wedding," she said to Grant, who stared with eyes nearly as wide as the organ player's. "I'm so sorry."

Candy put her head in her hand. What next? Would Star show up to sing karaoke at the reception?

She kept her face hidden, hoping Champagne would just leave before Grant had to kick her out or—wait, would Jose need to arrest her? Did he have handcuffs in his suit?

A giggle interrupted the silence. Candy peered through her fingers at Florence, but her fellow bridesmaid was watching Jean. Beautiful, white-clad Jean put her hand on Grant's arm, threw her head back, and laughed louder and with more abandon than Candy had ever heard from her.

Jean's response was met initially with shock, but the joy in her laughter spread with contagion to Florence, Brenda, Candy, then the congregation.

Everyone smiled but Grant. Candy's stomach clenched as Champagne and Grant faced off, their gazes locked. Champagne's eyes overflowed with regret; Grant's face remained unreadable.

He closed his eyes and Candy wondered if he was trying to constrain his temper or was praying. It must have been prayer because when he opened his eyes, he took Jean's hand, and with his free hand summoned Champagne to them. She started forward, but then stopped and put her palms out again, saying, "Wait a sec." She returned to reach behind the partition and pulled out a familiar turquoise vase.

Jean gasped. "I thought that was gone forever!"

Grant viewed her. "Isn't that the Kintsugi pot I ordered for you?"

She nodded, tears in her eyes. "It's a long story that I'll tell you later. It came in the mail months ago, but I broke it, and I put the pieces here on the altar. They disappeared and I gave up hope of ever seeing my precious vase again." She ascended the stairs and received the vase, turning it side to side to view all angles. "Champagne, did you fix this?"

Champagne dipped her head once, her gaze fixed on Grant. "I wanted a way to show...I guess...that I care, and I'm sorry, and, I don't know, that I'm not lying any longer." Her smile was shy but real. "Jesus has restored me and forgiven me, like this pot." Candy's heart surged with joy at her words. "I don't have to hide anymore."

Jean pulled the vase close to her heart. She looked to her husband, her eyes questioning and unsure.

Grant Henderson's stone countenance cracked into a smile. "Hiding would probably be a good habit to give up."

Her face spoke confusion until he nodded his chin to the organ pipes. She blushed bright red, then her own cheeks ballooned around a huge smile.

She walked to face Grant. Jean joined her just as she said, "I don't ever expect you to for—"

"I forgive you, Champagne." He put his arm around Jean. "And I thank you for keeping Jean safe from Billy." Champagne dropped to sit on the steps and weep, and he turned to his wife. "I told God I wanted to honor Him today. I guess that's why she's here."

Candy could not help but laugh with Jean when she responded, "We could have just sent her an invitation."

"I think it's time to step in," Florence whispered beside Candy. She took Candy's hand and pulled her up the steps, across the platform behind the pulpit, to join Champagne on the stairs. They helped her to her feet and led her to one of the few empty spots on the front pew.

Jean followed. She hugged Champagne and said, loud enough to be heard five rows back, "I am truly glad you're here."

"Oh, here come the waterworks again," Candy muttered. She turned her grin to Florence, then to Brenda, who had kept surprisingly uninvolved from her spot near the unity candle. Her focus seemed fixated on the flickering flame and her brows were together.

Candy had expected Grant's disapproval but was surprised to see such unhappiness on Brenda's face. She would not even look at Champagne. Candy went to her side and touched her shoulder with hesitation. "You okay?"

Brenda seem to wake out of a stupor. Her gaze took in Champagne's weeping, Grace's regular exclamations of disbelief, and Gladys' personal fanning with that paper fan that had probably outlasted its potential centuries ago. She ended her perusal at Sapphire standing level with her knees. "Go find your mommy and sit with her, okay, sweetie?"

"Okay." The little girl skipped down the steps to join her mother.

Candy considered Brenda's problem might not be with Champagne at all. "Brenda?"

Her friend grabbed her arm in a grip that sent pain shooting up Candy's arm. "I'm sorry, Jean," she said. "I'm sorry, Grant, but I think I need to go."

Stewart was at her side in two seconds, an arm around her. "It is the baby? Is it time?"

She nodded, leaning into his embrace. "The contractions started early this morning. I was hoping I could get through the ceremony, but—" She winced and Stewart paled.

"Get going," Grant said. "Both of you."

Stewart looked from his wife to his brother. "But your wedding..."

Grant just pointed at Brenda and said, "More important."

Grace Jameson stood. "But—"

Stewart nodded and rushed his wife down the steps to the aisle. "Do you, Grant, take this woman to be your lawfully wedded wife?" He shot out the vows like a movie on fast forward.

Grant smiled at Jean. "I do."

"Do you, Jean Louise, take this man?"

She moved closer to Grant. "Yes, I do."

They were halfway to the foyer doors. Stewart called out, "By the power invested in me, I now pronounce you man and wife."

Candy had run ahead. She held the door open. "Don't forget the kiss."

Stewart stopped and kissed Brenda's cheek. Brenda laughed breathlessly. "Their kiss, Stew."

"Oh, right." He turned and shouted, "Kiss her, Grant!"

Grant obeyed with enthusiasm and the crowd clapped. Jean, face flushed, turned to the first row and said, "Well, Mother, you wanted the day to be memorable!"

Candy let the doors close behind her. She hurried with Stewart and Brenda to drive them to the hospital and welcome a new life into the world, smiling at the happy laughter she could still hear echoing from inside.

"God has
been
so good
to us."

Chapter Thirty-Four
Saturday Afternoon, May 9

Candy

Streamers bordered the doors to *Jamaica's Place* in bright pinks and blues, the spring breeze waving them in welcome.

"It's a good thing we put tags on these gifts," Stewart commented with a survey of the tables marked for gifts for Pansy's new baby, Brenda's new baby, Florence on her big road trip—for her or for the victims if she found them—and finally a table for Candy and Champagne. "We'd never get them sorted if they weren't labeled."

"At least some of the baby gifts are obvious." Candy collected pink gift bags covered in baby animals or princesses onto Brenda's table, and blue bags with cars or trains or sports equipment onto Pansy's. "I've been wondered something all morning." She rummaged through a yellow bag sporting rubber duckies until she found a nametag, then put it on the table of gifts for Pansy's little boy. "It's nice of you all to make this a goodbye party for Champagne and I along with the baby showers, but is it really to send us off with love, or to celebrate that we're leaving town?"

Brenda laughed, joggling baby Candace in her arms. "Oh, Candy, we'll miss you terribly. Nothing is going to be the same around here without you."

The glass door to *Jamaica's* opened with a cheerful jingle of bells, and guests filed in. By the time everyone got inside, the bell had rung so many times Candy was sure she'd developed a twitch. Florence was one of the last to arrive. Doug parked their camper on the opposite side of the street while Florence rushed to Candy and directed her attention to the window near the back of the massive vehicle. "Look!" she said with a grin half the size of Texas. Candy saw puppy paws scratching against the window and behind them a puppy face barking protest at being left behind. "He got me a dog!"

"That'll make for an interesting rip," Candy mumbled. She hugged Florence. "You always wanted a dog. I'm happy for you, Flo."

"I'm happy for me, too." She hugged Candy back. "But not as happy as I am for you. What adventures you are going to have!"

"No kidding. Did I tell you Jose got Champagne and I connected with a guy in Charlotte who works with the Internet Crimes Against Children? We went in there and he was all sorts of impressed with Champagne's website hacking abilities, but then he was really floored when she showed them a bunch of ways they could improve their sites posing as minors to draw in predators. He asked about a zillion questions, made us promise to come back, and then showed us some videos of when they lure buyers to houses. It was great. These guys would show up expecting to see a fifteen-year-old girl they'd bought online, and instead the door would open to a policemen with handcuffs." She laughed out loud. "I begged him to let me get in on some of those sometime."

"God has great plans for you, Candy." Florence swept her arms to encompass the scores of church family and friends filling the café. "For all of us."

"That's true." Candy got inspired. She scraped a chair across the floor near the coffee counter and stood on it. "Hey, everybody," she shouted. "I have something to say."

A visitor had wandered in from the sidewalk, probably curious about the big crowd. Candy heard the woman ask what was going on, why Candy was giving a speech. She laughed when Gladys responded, "She can't help herself. You should hear her pray." Gladys shook her head and patted Sapphire beside her. "I'm convinced she thinks God is half deaf, and has a flare for the dramatic."

"In case I don't get a chance to say it to each of you personally," Candy said, "I want to thank you for your support and help and encouragement about this new move and new ministry. I spent so many years alone and scared and totally rejected, thinking God hated me, and you—" She swiped at her eyes. "You changed all of that. I'll never forget you."

She looked over the people filling the café, so many of them dear friends now. "And don't you ever forget God's got great plans for you!" She smiled at Florence, then at Jean and Grant, Stewart and Brenda, and even at Gladys. "For all of us."

She stepped down, sparing the group all the other things she wanted to say. "You all look hungry," she announced and looked to Stewart. "Should we get started?"

It was the perfect sendoff. They ate cake, talked, drank coffee—those who liked that sort of thing—and ate some more. Melanie gave her testimony and then sang *His Eye is on the Sparrow.* "I used to sing this because the melody was pretty and the words felt like a fairy tale I wished would be true," she said. "Now I sing it with all my heart because I know it *is* true." She sang the chorus again, and as the words "I sing because I'm happy; I sing because I'm free" floated over them all, Candy had to wipe her eyes dry.

"Did Star come with Melanie?" Florence asked at her side. "I don't see her."

Candy shook her head with a smile. "She went back to school to become a veterinarian. Star is free now from Billy's threats to distribute her photos now that he and all his cronies, plus over twenty other connections of Slash's, are all behind bars."

"I'm glad to hear it. And Jamaica's coming today?"

"Sometime this afternoon."

"I hope it's soon. We're leaving in about an hour."

"She'd said that—"

The bell jingled and Candy turned to see Jamaica enter the café, her daughter Pansy behind her. Pansy's smile was shy and in her hands she carried a sleeping baby boy.

"That poor baby won't be sleeping long with all this noise," Florence commented. She motioned Jamaica over, telling Candy, "Melanie agreed to work at the day care at Alice's, and Brenda is volunteering there, too. She'll watch her own little Candace, but also offered to take care of Pansy's boy during the day so Pansy can finish high school." Florence grinned. "And I've still got so much money left,

I'll be able to supply salaries for workers so we won't have to charge much, if anything, to moms in need. Oh, Candy." She put her hands together and sighed. "God has been so good to us."

Candy looked to where Grant and Jean argued over whether white or chocolate cake tasted better and smiled. Jean had told her that, four days ago, after she rubbed Grant's feet rough and fast to get the blood circulating, she had pinched his big toe hard and he had felt the pressure. "He has indeed."

She met Jamaica with a heartfelt embrace. "It's wonderful to be back," Jamaica said, hugging Florence next. Florence's chuckle blossomed into a full-blown belly laugh when Jamaica innocently asked, "So, did anything interesting happen while we were gone?"

Saturday Afternoon, May 9

Jean

The line of people who hugged Candy and said their goodbyes had stretched so long, and people had said so many nice things, Candy had begun to fidget. Jean stayed by her side as the last of them wished her well. Stewart gave her a brotherly smile on his way by to the coffee counter. "You'll be missed, Candy. You definitely left your mark here."

"Literally. Did you see?" She pointed at the wall running alongside the stairs to the second floor, clearly glad to draw the attention away from herself for a moment. "Champagne turned out to be quite the artist. She painted vines and flowers all around the verses I wrote on the walls and turned them into artwork. I spent half the night writing verses all over the walls around the store so she could work her magic down here, too. The whole place is covered with words straight from God. And she fixed all of Jamaica's mugs that I broke with gold. They're selling like hotcakes. Jamaica wants me to break more!" She shook her head and commented wryly to Jean, "I wish the message I was asked to give was as easy as leaving a message behind on a few walls."

"What do you mean?"

Jean was shocked when Candy put a finger to her mouth and bit her fingernail. "Well, talking about freedom in Christ comes easy to me when I'm in a strip club or in front of a group of bikers, but now God's asking me to give that message to ladies in churches. I feel about as qualified for that job as a broken shoelace."

Behind the counter now, Stewart poured honey from a little bear-shaped container into a cup of peppermint-flavored tea and handed it to his wife. "You'll do great."

Candy's shoulders went up and down self-consciously. "I was reading about Balaam and his donkey the other day, and I figure if God can speak through a donkey, then I guess He can even speak through someone like me!"

Jean threw her arms around Candy's neck. "I'm going to miss you so much."

Candy surprised her by tearing up. "You were scared to even shake hands when I first met you." She put her hands on Jean's shoulders. "Jean, you are the most beautiful women I have ever known. I'm so grateful God sent you into my life, or me into yours, whichever it was. Promise me you'll keep in touch?"

"Absolutely." She smiled over Candy's shoulder at Brenda. "Charlotte isn't that far away. We three can meet halfway for lunch."

"Sure." Brenda carefully handed baby Amelia to Stewart and headed toward them. "You can shock us with your dramatic adventures."

Jean motioned toward where Champagne stood close to the wall leading to the restrooms, in the shadow of a potted palm, for all appearances trying to fade into the décor as much as possible. Jean knew that feeling well. "Champagne, you'll come with her, won't you?"

Brenda detoured to intercept her. "We'd love it if you would."

Champagne hesitated, but when her smile did appear, it was genuine. "Okay."

"We've got to get going." Candy led the way out of *Jamaica's Place* to her waiting car. The men were loading her trunk with gifts and supplies. She opened the backseat door to toss a few final bags into the car and stopped short. "There's a huge box filling up over half the backseat. What's that about?"

Jean grinned. "Just one more gift from all of us. You can open it when you get there."

Grant shut the trunk and turned his standing wheelchair to join Jean, putting his arm around her waist. "What'd you get her?"

She grinned back over her shoulder at Brenda. "A big cooler."

He followed her gaze. "That's way too practical for the look I just saw. What's it filled with? Red high heels and purple feather boas?"

She laughed out loud. "That would have been a fun idea." She put her own arm around his torso above where the chair held him upright. "No, it's filled with cans of whipped cream. Something to remember us by."

He kissed her forehead. "That's real love. You might just make her cry."

The group on the sidewalk waved as Florence and Doug drove by in their camper. "Hey, look!" Pansy pointed at the large back window, covered in white, dripping letters. "We love you, Florence," she read. "At least, I think that's what it says."

"The words seem to be melting." Jamaica crossed her arms and yelled to Candy. "Did you use my whipped cream on their camper? That vehicle is going to be an ant magnet wherever they stop for the night."

Candy was still waving. "Didn't think of that. I was just using the resources available. You didn't have any shaving cream on hand."

Jamaica huffed good-naturedly, said her goodbye, and headed back inside. Jean shifted to peer through the window into the shop. "Jamaica added cheesecake to her dessert options." She tapped one finger to her chin. "I wonder if she has any pickles."

Grant grimaced. "Pickles? With cheesecake?"

"Or salsa."

Candy's dilapidated car sputtered to life and jerked forward when she shifted into gear. When it idled at the stop sign half a block from where they stood, she stuck her head out the window and yelled, "The day you stand on your own, Grant Henderson, call me. We'll throw a big party at *Jamaica's* and invite everybody!"

He lifted a hand and shouted, "Sounds great."

She rounded the curb and waved out the window until her car was out of sight. The rest of the crowd meandered their separate ways, leaving Jean and Grant alone on the sidewalk near two flowering bushes and a fire hydrant. Her husband faced her and pulled her to him, the brace of the standing wheelchair between them a reminder of all he still had to overcome. "Lord willing, and with your help..." He touched his forehead to hers. "I'm going to be standing, and walking, by our first anniversary. Sooner, I hope."

She put her warm, slender hands on the sides of his face. Now was the perfect time to tell him. "Sooner?" she asked. "Maybe by the time you hold our first baby in your arms?"

His eyebrows flew upward and his Adam's apple bobbed as he swallowed. He coughed, tried to speak, and coughed again. "Do you know something I don't?"

Her kiss was full of love. She knew her eyes gleamed with delight and her face radiated joy. "Let's just say, Mr. Henderson, that in a few short months you and I are going to have a lot of explaining to do."

He has made
everything beautiful
in its time.

Ecclesiastes 3:11

So the men answered her (Rahab the harlot), "Our lives for yours, if none of you tell this business of ours. And it shall be, when the Lord has given us the land, that we will deal kindly and truly with you."

Then she let them down by a rope through the window, for her house was on the city wall....

So the men said to her: "We will be blameless of this oath of yours which you have made us swear, unless, when we come into the land, you bind this line of scarlet cord in the window through which you let us down"....

And she bound the scarlet cord in the window.

-Joshua 2:14-15, 17, 21

The book of the genealogy of Jesus Christ, the Son of David....

Salmon begot Boaz by Rahab, Boaz begot Obed by Ruth, Obed begot Jesse, and Jesse begot David the king....And Jacob begot Joseph the husband of Mary, of whom was born Jesus who is called Christ.

- Matthew 1:1, 5-6, 16

ACKNOWLEDGMENTS

Enthusiastic thanks to Betsy Wescott for not only loving this series and volunteering to be a beta reader, but also for introducing me to your wonderful book club. Having Shredded chosen as one of your books was an honor, and getting to get together with you all and talk through Restored was just plain fun. Thanks to Jill Rogers, Amy Walker, Sherry Souther, Jill Beshears, Linda Horton, Jenny Hix, and Mary South for finding typos, giving opinions, and all the encouragement about this whole series. You all are fantastic!

A very special thanks to Bryan Helton for your insights on life in a wheelchair. I'm praying with you that God will get you back on your feet again, but I thank you that you aren't waiting until then to honor God with your life. You didn't ask for paralysis, but you are letting God use it for good. That's my definition of a hero.

Thank you also to Diana Helton for your perspective on not only the practical aspects of paralysis, but the emotional and spiritual struggles as well. I am blessed to call you a friend. We need to get together to paint again sometime!

To Jeannie Stephenson, I feel like a broken record, but it's worth saying again how grateful I am that God put you into my life way back when I was young, idealistic, and pretty clueless. You've been a mentor and friend, and I value knowing you'll give the truth to me straight even when the truth is hard to hear. My books are better and more effective because of you.

To Sue Huey, I think your name is somewhere on or in every novel I've written, so you've gone all over the world with me making a difference. Thanks for being a loyal mainstay (boring word but I couldn't think of a more accurate one) on my team.

To Brian, husband and best friend. Thanks for being my first listener and caring about all those pesky details. I'm not sure how you thought it was encouraging to regularly claim, "They're all going to die. You're going to kill them all," as we made our way through this one, but it was funny, and you're still the first person I want to read to every time.

To all of you who buy my books, give them to others, or share about them, thank you. Stories can't make a difference if they are not told, so please keep passing the word!

Most importantly, as always, thanks to Jesus my Savior and King. I don't want to write just to entertain people. I want to say something that matters. Nothing matters outside of You. With You, we all matter and what we do has eternal value. Like the boy with his little loaves and fishes, I offer my books. Take them wherever You want and use them however You wish. They, like me, are yours.

READER CLUB/DISCUSSION QUESTIONS
PART ONE: Chapters 1-5

1. The prologue reveals that Slash is not just a predator but also a victim. Many victims grow up to become either continued victims or predators. Why do you think that is? Why do you think someone like Slash would choose to become a trafficker as an adult?

2. Did your feelings about him change at all learning what happened to him as a child? How?

3. What's your opinion of Candy sneaking a Bible to Slash? (Heb. 4:12; Isa. 55:11)

4. Do you think sometimes we rely too much on the justice system to bring change that only God can bring? Can any earthly system really transform lives? Hearts? Why or why not? (Psalm 108:12; Rom. 3:20; Psalm 60:11)

5. Would you have worn the yellow bridesmaid dress for Florence? =) (1 Cor. 13:4; Eph. 4:2)

6. Jean notices that men joked about Grant's shooting as a coping mechanism. Can you think of a time of crisis when others responded in a way that didn't make sense to you or even felt wrong? Tell about it. (Eph. 4:32; Rom. 12:10)

7. How do you tend to try to cope with heavy stress (in your natural flesh)?

   Ignore it by shopping, reading, watching TV, etc.

   Attack it by making a plan or decisions.

   Absorb it by internalizing and analyzing it personally.

   Other.

8. How should we deal with crisis and stress?
(Psalm 55:22; 1 Pet. 5:7, Phil. 4:6-7; Psalm 62:8)

9. What do you think about Florence and Doug? Would you find them cute or annoying?

10. Melanie and Star are obviously captive to Billy in some way. Is it surprising to think that in places that seem free, there can still be slavery? What other places might hide trafficking behind a veneer of personal choice?
(Psalm 14:3; Amos 2:6; Isa. 30:12-13; Micah 2:1-3)

11. Do you think Alice's fear and refusal to go against Rod is reasonable? The Bible tells women to submit to their husbands (Eph. 5:22). Do you think this still applies when a husband is being abusive? Why or why not? (Be aware that, if in a group setting, your words might be to a woman is secretly suffering abuse.) What would you advise her had you been Florence?

12. Do you think the home can be a secret place for oppression? If you found out a woman in your church was in a situation like Alice's how would you advise her?

13. Like trafficking victims, many domestic abuse victims feel they have no choice but to remain. People who don't understand might say, "Well, she should just leave him." What are some reasons victims might not leave? Do you think there are emotional bonds that can be stronger than even physical ones?

READER CLUB/DISCUSSION QUESTIONS
PART TWO: Chapters 6-16

1. Grant struggles with anger and bitterness over his paralysis. Do you think this is a spiritual failure or a normal process of grief? If normal for a time, when does it cross over into a spiritual problem?
   (Job 3:3, 10:18; 1 Kings 19; Jonah 4:3; Ruth 1:20; Heb. 12:12-15)

2. How does the Bible instruct us to help the grieving? What are some ways that don't help?
   (Rom. 12:15; Col. 3:14; 1 Pet. 3:8; Heb. 13:3; Job 16:2; Gal. 6:2)

3. Candy tells Grant he should stop looking at what he's lost and focus on what he still has. How much do you think perspective affects our attitude and lives, especially in difficult times?
   (Prov. 17:22, 13:12; Phil. 4:11-13; Col. 3:15; Prov. 23:7)

4. With a watching, needy world all around us, how should believers live differently through trials? Should it make a difference that we have Christ, or is it normal for us to look and act the same as unbelievers when the really hard times come?
   (1 Thess. 4:12-14; 1 Pet. 3:15; Col. 4:5-6; 2 Cor. 1:3-4)

5. Who might be affected by how Jean, Grant, Candy and others responded to Slash's revenge? Do you think our response to evil is being watched? Does it matter what we do? How we speak?
   (1 Cor. 3:13; Matt. 5:43-48; Luke 6:35; Prov. 24:10, 19-20; 2 Cor. 4:8-10)

6. Was it a good idea for Stewart to take Grant to see the wheelchair basketball team? Why or why not?

7. Were you surprised when Jean's father appeared? What about the presents he brought? How would you have felt had you been Jean?

8. Jean's father and mother both made choices that had consequences for their daughter. How much do you think parents should consider their children when making life decisions? Do you think the argument that "children are resilient" is a valid one? Why or why not?

(James 3:16; 1 Tim. 5:8; Mark 9:42; Jer. 17:9; Prov. 24:12; Phil. 2:3)

9. Slash tried healing his pain of being hurt by his mother by making sure he punished every person who ever hurt him again. What are some ways we might try to heal wounds that only make them worse?
   (Prov. 20:22; 1 Pet. 3:9; 1 Thess. 5:15; Heb. 10:30; Deut. 32:35; Prov. 17:14)

10. What do you think Slash was like as a child those first years after he left home? Do you think bad behavior in a kid can be a cover for deep hurt at home? Could anything have changed his path? What would it take?
    (Matt. 19:13-14, 18:5; 1 Cor. 15:58; James 1:19-20)

11. Would you support Brenda's choice to return to *Hot Town* despite the danger? Brenda is a very different woman here than back in *Shredded.* Do you think it really is possible to learn to overcome fears as she did? What does it take for people like Brenda to make significant, lasting change?
    (Heb. 13:6; Isa. 41:10; 1 John 5:4; 2 Cor. 10:5)

READER CLUB/DISCUSSION QUESTIONS
PART THREE: Chapters 17-23

1. Do you think Grant was right to confront Jean's mother with her avoidance of the truth? What might have happened—or not happened—had he not?
   (Matt. 18:15; Matt. 5:9; Eph. 4:15; Rom. 14:19; Luke 17:3-4)

2. Grant thought that women would probably give reassurance where it was wanted. Do you think we women sometimes jump in to make someone feel better, rather than letting the unpleasant truth work its way to the surface to be addressed? Why might we do that? Can our desire to sooth sometimes do more harm than good? How?
   (Isa. 30:10; James 5:20; John 8:32)

3. What did you think of Candy's words that predators like Rod aren't being produced in churches, but rather that abusers are drawn to easy situations? In your own church, can you think of aspects that might appeal to a predator and make things easier for him? (See I Am Safe at www.kimberlyrae.com)

4. Do you think church workers should learn about grooming behaviors of abusers and be on the lookout, or should we expect God to keep our ministries free of bad people?
   (Isa. 1:17; Matt. 10:16; Psalm 10:14)

5. It takes a crisis of fear with Jean at Jamaica's for Grant to fully understand something Jean had tried to get him to see. Have you ever had a major event that changed your perspective on something important? Explain.
   (Psalm 119:71)

6. When Slash heard about the thief on the cross and asked for mercy, did you feel like Champagne, that he should not dare ask for forgiveness after all he'd done? Do we have a line in our minds that if a person crosses it, they are (or should be) beyond saving?
   (Ezek. 18:23; 1 Tim. 1:12-17; 1 Tim. 2:4; Isa. 13:11; Rom. 2:5-6; Rom. 3:23)

7. What does that feeling tell us about ourselves? Do you think wanting justice for oppressors is righteous? Do you think it can cross over into pride? Where is the line for that?
(Psalm 7:11; Psalm 72:4; Matt. 7:1-2; Psalm 99:8; Isa. 13:11; Prov. 6:16-19)

8. Candy giving a Bible to Champagne and Slash made a difference in their lives for eternity, though not immediately. Have you ever given a lost person a Bible? Why or why not?
(Ecc. 11:1, 6; Isa. 55:11; Acts 13:47; Rom. 10:17)

9. Do you really believe God's Word can transform people? If we really did, how would that show in our lives?
(Rom. 1:16; Heb. 4:12; Acts 8:26-40; 2 Kings 22-23)

10. Was Candy's response to Slash's death surprising? Why or why not? Have you ever grieved over what should have been?
(Psalm 73:26)

11. Candy and Jean both leave people at the altar, giving them to God. When you read that, did someone, or several people, come to mind? Are there people you need to give over to God?

12. Do you agree with Jean that forgiveness is not the same as feeling responsible for people, or needing to understanding why they did what they did? How would you define forgiveness?
(Matt. 18:35; Col. 3:13; Luke 17:3-4; Mark 11:25)
The Greek word for forgive is "aphiēmi" which means "to send away," to "depart," or "to yield up."
(http://www.patheos.com/blogs/christiancrier/2014/06/22/top-7-bible-verses-about-forgiveness/)

READER CLUB/DISCUSSION QUESTIONS
PART FOUR: Chapters 24-34

1. Do you think it was good for Jean to express her insecurities? Have you ever done that when you felt vulnerable? How did the person respond?

2. Do you think being open and honest as Grant and Jean try to be will help their marriage or hurt it? Why?
   (Rom. 12:17; Rom. 13:8; Eph. 5:21-33)

3. Florence has a great time spending Alice's money. Do you think she made good choices? What are some other things you would have wanted to spend some of the money on?

4. Would you have been happy to be surprised with house renovations and a big party, or would you have wanted to be asked and informed first? Do you think it's important to know what a person likes and dislikes before we try to minister to them, or should we just do what comes to mind and assume it's direction from the Spirit?
   (Gal. 5:14; Matt. 7:12; 1 Pet. 3:8)

5. What do you think about Grant and Jean keeping secret on being married and then having the big wedding months later? Would you be okay with doing that? Why or why not?

6. Was the forgiveness meeting with Jean's parents concluded satisfactorily, or did it leave more to be desired? Had you been Jean, how would you have felt beforehand? Afterward?

7. What did you think of the strip club owner saying he was okay with losing his girls to Jesus? That truly happened! Do you think God can prepare the way for us in ways we'd never expect? Has He done that for you?
   (Eph. 3:14-21; Isa. 46:10; Isa. 25:1; Job 42:2)

8. How did the verse, "the goodness of God leads men to repentance" play out in Champagne's salvation? If those who wronged us listened in our conversations, would our words draw them toward our Savior or away?
(Rom. 2:4; Prov. 18:21; Matt. 12:36-37; Matt. 5:13-16; Eph. 4:29; Prov. 12:18)

9. What do you think will happen to Candy? Champagne? Do you think Grant will walk again?

10. How did you feel saying goodbye? Did you like the ending?

11. Do you like whipped cream more now at the end of the series or less? =)

KIMBERLY RAE
SHADOW
SOMEONE IS WATCHING

SNEAK PEEK AT
THE SHADOW

Lucias Maddox Moore licked his thin lips and sighed. Meagan Winston was special. Extraordinary, really. She had to be tired from this last eleven-hour flight to Atlanta, as he was, but still she smiled at disembarking passengers near her and even helped an elderly woman with her bags before reaching for her own. Within the next twenty-four hours, her hair would be blond again. She always dyed it back after she returned from India. Lucias knew these things. He knew Meagan better than anyone. Perhaps better than she even knew herself.

"Need help?" Lucias edged around a woman holding a fussy baby, and with his free hand grasped the small red carry-on Meagan had used every trip for the past three years. He pulled it down from the overhead compartment and placed it into her outstretched hands.

"Thanks." Her eyes met his for a brief moment and she smiled.

The baby near him cried, and Meagan turned from him to pick up the pacifier the kid had thrown to the floor. She wiped it clean with her bright red scarf and handed it to the frazzled mother.

Look at me, Meagan. Smile at me again. Lucias clenched his briefcase in both hands, hating it when she gave her smile, the smile he lived for, to the baby instead. She cooed at the kid then pulled her carry-on down the narrow aisle toward the exit door of the plane. He watched from behind as he had all six trips, dreading their parting, scrambling for a way to delay it.

This last trip had been the most successful, his largest sale yet. He'd brought back something special this time, something that would be worth a lot to his connection. All because of Meagan. He had to find a way to thank her, to tell her how much she meant to him.

Lucias quickened his pace the moment he stepped from the tunneled jet bridge onto the carpeted airport terminal floor, but other passengers merged between them. The woman with the baby stopped right in front of him to dig a ratty stuffed animal out of her diaper bag. He moved to the side and ran to catch up. He almost called out Meagan's name.

Instead he came to a sudden halt in the center of the concourse passageway and watched her walk away. Again. Now was not the time, or the place. It had to be when no one else was around. He looked at the crowd rushing around him and felt his breathing quicken. Claustrophobia slid up his spine and clamped tight around his throat. Lucias counted his steps toward the shuttle, grandly named Automated People Mover, that would lead him out of the world's busiest airport. There were too many people, too many strangers, all of them probably judgmental hypocrites like his old co-workers, so quick to claim he had an anger problem.

His co-workers didn't know him at all. He hadn't been angry when he did it, just hurt. Claudia had rejected his love, had been cruel, had laughed at him. The police had never found any evidence, they never even found a body, but he still lost his job. His co-workers were afraid of him, afraid he'd done it, but they didn't need to be. He was good to people as long as they treated him fair.

The shuttle doors closed him in. He tried to calm his heart rate and ignore the heavy, fish-tinged breaths puffing out of the pot-bellied businessman to his right. The shuttle shot to twenty miles an hour within seconds, and fish-breath man grabbed the metal pole with the hand he had just used to wipe sweat from his neck. Lucias positioned his feet in a stabilizing position, both hands clamped around his briefcase handle, safe from the billions of bacteria thriving unseen across the surface of the pole, the walls, the people. "Arriving at B Gates," the robotic voice announced above his head. He liked it better when they called them Concourses. The doors opened, people exited, and he inhaled a lungful of clean air before a new batch of bodies crammed in around him. No, even if he caught up to Meagan, the six million-square-foot Atlanta airport was not the place to tell her his feelings.

"Arriving at A Gates." He jostled his way through the open doors and headed for the escalator that led to baggage claim. If he hurried she might still be there, collecting her two charcoal grey suitcases that he knew bulged with jewelry.

He stepped off the escalator and strained for a glimpse of the baggage area. His foot caught on the wheel of a passing child stroller, and his briefcase flew as he tumbled to the ground.

The woman pushing the stroller stopped. "Are you okay?"

He scrambled to his hands and knees. "Where is it?" He grabbed the edge of the stroller and pushed it out of the way. "Where is it?" he shouted.

The woman saw the briefcase just as he did. She picked it up but he rose to his feet and snatched it from her hands. "It's mine!" He backed a step away and clutched it to his chest. People around them stopped, looked. Some pointed fingers. He forced himself to hold the briefcase in one hand and drop it to his side. *Turn. Walk calmly. Act natural. Think about something pleasant.*

When Meagan was frustrated, she would find a place to sit down, then close her eyes and bow her head. He followed her example and chose a bench far from the staring people near the stroller. He dropped his chin and tried to think. This was not the day to bare his heart. January eighth was a possibility. Meagan's twenty-sixth birthday was circled in red on his pocket calendar, her name in bold. But to wait two weeks would be hard. He'd rather create the perfect moment before then, something special they both could remember forever.

He clenched the briefcase and battled inner fears. What if she laughed at him? Rejected him? He could not bear it.

He lifted his face and gazed across the baggage claim area. Just beyond the fourth carousel, she materialized into view, so beautiful, like a touchable ray of sunshine. She headed for one of the seven possible exit doors, pulling the two grey suitcases, her red carry-on slung over one shoulder. He watched until the crowd hid her from his vision, like clouds blocking the light.

His heart stilled. Meagan wasn't anything like Claudia. If he did everything just right, Meagan would care for him. She had to.

OTHER BOOKS BY KIMBERLY RAE

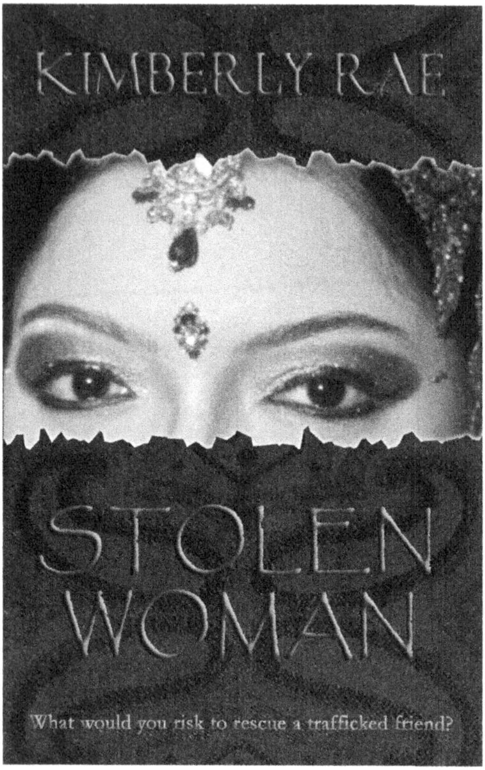

Human Trafficking...Asha knew nothing about it before meeting 16-year-old Rani, stolen from her home and forced into prostitution in Kolkata, India. Asha must help this girl escape, but Mark, a third-generation missionary, keeps warning her away from the red-light district and its workers. Will she ever discover why? And will they ever stop their intense arguments long enough to admit their even more intense feelings for one another?
When Asha sneaks out one last time in a desperate attempt to rescue her friend, someone follows her through the night. Is freedom possible? Or will she, too, become one of the stolen?

KIMBERLY RAE
STOLEN
CHILD
Do you know who you are?

Asha returns to Asia with only one priority higher than reuniting with Mark and beginning a ministry rescuing trafficked women: first she must find her birth family and discover why they gave her up.

The path to answers, however, is shrouded with secrets, superstitions, and lies. Why did her parents never tell anyone about her? Why are the village women so afraid? And what is the terrible curse everyone hints at but no one will explain?

When Asha's safety is threatened, Mark follows to Bangladesh in search of her. Will he find her in time to tell her what is truly on his heart? Or will the dangers continue to separate them until it is too late?

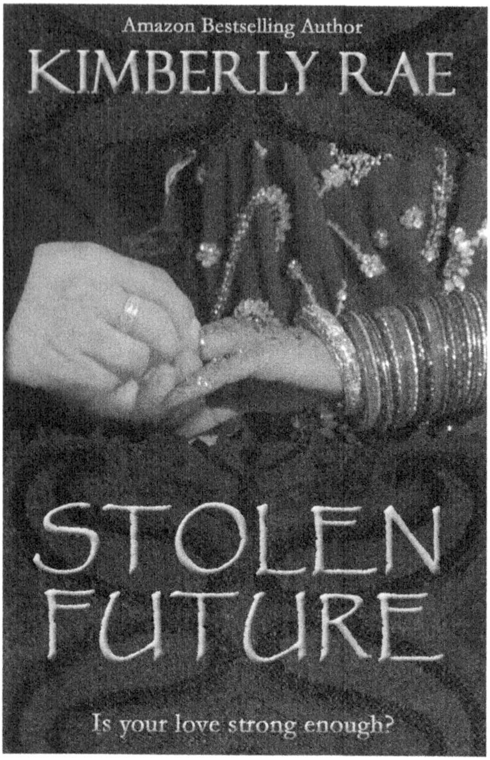

In Ahmad's game of vengeance, can anyone win?

Ahmad has the perfect plan, one that will punish everyone who had a part in exposing him. The ultimate revenge would be to see Asha become a trafficked woman herself. If he succeeds, will Mark sacrifice everything, even his integrity, to get her back? And what will happen to their future together if he finds her broken and abused?

Experience the exciting conclusion of the Amazon Bestselling Stolen Series Trilogy, as Mark and Asha battle human trafficking and their own worst fears.

ABOUT THE AUTHOR

Award-winning author of over 20 books, Kimberly Rae has been published over 200 times and has work in 5 languages.

Rae lived in Bangladesh, Uganda, Kosovo, and Indonesia. She rafted the Nile River, hiked the hills at the base of Mount Everest, and stood on the equator in two continents, but Addison's disease now keeps her in the U.S. She currently writes from her home in Hudson, North Carolina, where she lives with her husband and two children.

Rae's Stolen Series, suspense and romance novels on fighting human trafficking, are all Amazon bestsellers.

Find out more at
www.kimberlyrae.com.

Made in the USA
Columbia, SC
25 September 2021

45509932R00186